island in the sea

also by anita hughes

island in the sea

A MAJORCA LOVE STORY

ANITA HUGHES

St. Martin's Griffin ⚞ New York

ISLAND IN THE SEA. Copyright © 2016 by Anita Hughes. All rights reserved. Printed in the United States of America. For information, address St. Martin's Press, 175 Fifth Avenue, New York, N.Y. 10010.

www.stmartins.com

The Library of Congress Cataloging-in-Publication Data is available upon request.

ISBN 978-1-250-08042-4 (trade paperback)
ISBN 978-1-250-09150-5 (hardcover)
ISBN 978-1-4668-9234-7 (e-book)

Our books may be purchased in bulk for promotional, educational, or business use. Please contact your local bookseller or the Macmillan Corporate and Premium Sales Department at 1-800-221-7945, extension 5442, or by e-mail at MacmillanSpecial Markets@macmillan.com.

First Edition: April 2016

10 9 8 7 6 5 4 3 2 1

To my mother

island in the sea

chapter one

JULIET OPENED THE LOW GATE and climbed the steps to the villa. She gazed at the garden filled with purple daisies and pink bougainvillea and thought she had never seen so much color. The sky was bright blue and the villa was painted pale pink and the silk curtains drifting out the open windows were turquoise and orange and yellow.

She knocked on the red wood door and instinctively tucked her hair behind her ears. She knocked again and turned to look at the view. She had only been in Majorca for two days but already she thought the whole world consisted of narrow streets and bright plazas and views of fishing boats bobbing on the Mediterranean. She saw the Tramuntana Mountains and sweeping green valleys and olive trees clinging to the cliffs.

She opened the door and smelled pine and cigarettes and garlic. She peered into the living room and saw dark wood floors and yellow plaster walls and high mosaic ceilings. The room was scattered with floral sofas and wooden coffee tables and plump striped cushions. There was a grand piano and French doors that led out onto the balcony.

She walked farther and saw a garden with a tennis court and swimming pool. There was a sundial and a stone fountain and a fishpond filled with neon-colored fish. She heard someone groan and saw a man lying on a chaise longue. He wore navy shorts and a yellow silk shirt and had a paperback book covering his face.

"I don't think Keats ever imagined his poems would be used as sunscreen," she said, as she approached the man.

"If you're from the cleaning service I like keeping my clothes in the bathtub." The man kept his eyes closed and his hands around a tall glass filled with ice cubes. "I hate having to walk all the way to the closet after taking a shower. I told the service I don't want another maid. It's difficult to sit around being drunk and depressed if someone is scrubbing the floors and making your underwear smell like potpourri."

"I'm not from the cleaning service," Juliet replied.

"If Paco sent you tell him I'll have his money next week," the man muttered. "Though there is a nice Picasso in the library you could take as a trade. It's only a print but it's worth a pair of Zegna loafers."

"Not from Paco's either." Juliet smiled, enjoying the game. She glanced at the view and saw the monastery of Valldemossa and the stone farmhouses of Deia. She saw high white clouds and the sea shimmering like a sheet of diamonds.

"Well if Manuel sent you tell him I was going to come down today and pay for the fucking cigarettes," the man grumbled. "You'd think a man's credit would stretch to a pack of Marlboros and a king-sized Cadbury Fruit & Nut bar."

"I'm Juliet Lyman, senior executive at Yesterday Records." Juliet moved closer so her shadow blocked the sun. "You must be Lionel Harding."

Lionel removed the book and sat up. He put his drink on the glass side table and smoothed his hair. He studied Juliet's glossy brown bob and blue eyes and tan legs and whistled.

"I knew Gideon would send a henchman sooner or later, but I didn't think she'd be a brunette wearing a J. Crew Theory dress and Dior perfume."

"How do you know my perfume is Dior?" Juliet demanded.

"I write love songs, I have to notice the details." Lionel reached for his drink. "I can describe everything about a woman: her thick dark lashes, her small pink mouth, the heart-shaped mole on her neck." He took a long sip. "Tell Gideon I haven't turned in my expense report in months because I know he doesn't approve of aged scotch and Cuban cigars. Who would have thought the owner of one of the most famous record labels would turn into an old prude? The last time I saw him he was eating stewed prunes and reading *The Economist*. I told him he might as well buy himself a plot at Forest Lawn."

"He did, he had me pick one out for him and his wife, right next to James Stewart and Elizabeth Taylor." Juliet nodded. "I'm not here to count the number of towels in the bathroom or limit your consumption of Courvoisier."

"Then why are you here?" Lionel's eyes traveled over her blue knit dress and white sandals. "If Gideon thought I needed entertainment, I have a stack of Spanish *Playboys*."

Juliet felt her cheeks turn pink. "I'm here because you're six months late with your songs and Gideon said if he doesn't get them by the end of the month you owe him your advance." She opened her red Coach purse and took out her phone. She flicked through the screens and looked at Lionel. "One hundred and sixty-six thousand dollars and sixty three cents plus the nine thousand dollars he sent to your tailor in London and the fifteen hundred dollars he paid for your mother's eightieth birthday present."

"A man can still appreciate a Gieves &Hawkes single-breasted suit when he's depressed," Lionel snorted. "And how often does a woman turn eighty? Mom fell in love with a diamond-and-sapphire Harry Winston necklace when we flew to Barcelona. Airlines deliberately delay their flights so you hang out in the duty free stores," Lionel sighed. "I always end up with an extra bottle of cognac or a carton of Toblerone chocolate."

"They call it an advance because they give it to you before you do the work." Juliet shielded her eyes from the sun. "But if you don't write the songs you have to give it back." She slipped her phone in her purse. "You've had eighteen months to complete twenty-four songs and you sent Gideon a haiku and a limerick."

"I was experimenting with different forms." Lionel pouted. "You don't think the Romantics changed the course of English poetry by copying Robert Burns and Sir Walter Scott? Have you ever listened to Jimi Hendrix? He was called the "warrior poet" because his lyrics touched your soul. Do you know how much time he spent sitting on a beach? Those words didn't come to him overnight." He slipped his sunglasses over his nose. He had dark wavy hair and bright green eyes and a small cleft on his chin. "I might be forty-two but unlike Gideon I still think like a young man, and the young constantly reinvent things. Not all love songs have to sound like Simon and Garfunkel on a constant loop in the elevator."

"Your songs are on the constant loop in the elevator." Juliet followed him into the villa. She saw a wide kitchen with stone floors and a low-beamed ceiling. There was a large silver refrigerator and open cabinets filled with ceramic bowls and white china cups. The counters were littered with half eaten chocolate bars and a basket of tomatoes and a wilted fruit salad. "'Going to Catalina' is the third most recorded song in history, behind 'The Girl from Ipanema.' It won three Grammys when it was released in 1996 and went on to sell two million copies."

Lionel opened the fridge and took out a bottle of Grey Goose. He filled two glasses with ice and added vodka and a squeeze of lime. He handed one to Juliet and raised his glass.

"Well that deserves a toast." He drained his glass and set it on the tile counter. "All this talk about money makes me hungry. Why don't we save the threats until after lunch?"

"If I return to Los Angeles without a check for one hundred sixty-six thousand dollars or an album of new songs I won't have a job," Juliet protested. "They better be on a laptop waiting to press SEND, or in a manila folder ready for me to transport through customs."

"If you're a senior executive at Yesterday Records how come we haven't met?" Lionel opened the breadbox and took out four slices of bread. He spread them with mustard and sliced ham and Gruyère cheese. He added heirloom tomatoes and red onions and handed a plate to Juliet.

"I've only been at the label for ten months." Juliet bit into the sandwich. "I graduated from NYU and spent the last six years at Sony Records in Manhattan."

"Did Gideon lure you to Los Angeles with the promise of a silver convertible and your own miniature palm tree and a table at Wolfgang Puck's next to Tobey Maguire?"

"He convinced me to switch labels so I could work with Anson Smith and Juju Miles and some of the most progressive artists in the music business."

"Instead he sent you to Majorca to babysit an aging songwriter." Lionel dribbled tomato on his chin. "It could be worse, I could have accepted Richard Branson's offer and stayed at his hut on the Galapagos Islands. I heard the fresh sea bass is divine but you have to use an outhouse. At least Sir Bob's villa has a billiard table and a wine cellar stocked with Château Rothschild Burgundy."

"This is Bob Geldof's villa?" Juliet spluttered, wiping her mouth with a checkered napkin.

"I think Bob offered it to me." Lionel rubbed his forehead. "It could have been Phil Collins, we were all skiing in Gstaad and I've never been good at high altitudes. The thin air makes me forget things. Phil does have a lovely place in Montreux; I stayed there years ago. It's a pity his marriage ended, Orienne made the best chocolate fondue."

"I thought you rented this villa," Juliet frowned.

Lionel ate a last bite of his sandwich and laughed. "I couldn't afford the gold faucet in the guest bathroom. I have creditors in four languages: I owe Luis in Lisbon for two boxes of Cuban cigars and Sven in Copenhagen for a sterling silver Georg Jensen lighter and Riccardo in Milan for three pairs of Bruno Magli suede loafers. Not to mention my monthly order from Harrods of five jars of marmite and six packets of caramel toffees. The price of shipping these days is criminal."

"It's so beautiful here." Juliet gazed out the window at window boxes filled with hydrangeas and hibiscus. "I would think Majorca is the perfect place to write love songs."

"Now you're trying to lull me into doing what you want." Lionel took his drink and walked into the living room. He sat on a floral sofa and spread his long legs in front of him. "What if I told you Gideon did something so terrible, that if I wasn't the kind of guy who couldn't pick up a fly swatter, I would sue him for everything he had."

"I wouldn't believe you; he's one of the most philanthropic men I've met." Juliet removed a stack of crumpled newspapers from a red-and-white-striped love seat. "He donates thousands to charity: water to build wells in Africa and purchased computers for an entire village in Peru and gives ten percent of the label's profits to Save the Ocean Foundation."

"I'm sure even Benedict Arnold did a few good deeds and Judas had a whole group of friends." Lionel tapped a cigarette from a gold cigarette case. He lit it slowly and blew a thin trail of smoke. "I'll make a deal, I'll tell you the whole story, and if you think he still deserves one hundred sixty-six thousand dollars, I will find a way to pay him back."

Juliet glanced at the plaster walls lined with Picassos and Manets and Cézannes. She saw the French doors and pink marble fireplace and tall wooden bookshelves. She didn't have time to sit around watching Lionel smoke cigarettes and drink dry martinis, Gideon expected her to return with an album of new songs.

"Gideon doesn't want the money." She shifted on the silk love seat. "He wants you to write music."

"He should have thought of that before he picked up an iron tong and drove it though my heart." Lionel got up and walked to the entry. He stubbed his cigarette on the stone floor and opened the door. "Take the offer or leave it. I've got an appointment with a bottle of vodka and a copy of *The Picture of Dorian Gray*." He turned and glanced at Juliet. "Look, all I've got left to my name is a two-bedroom flat in Chelsea. If you don't agree after you've heard the story, I'll sell it and give Gideon the proceeds."

Juliet stood up and dusted her skirt. She walked to the door and held out her hand. "All right, you have a deal."

"I knew you'd come round." Lionel's face broke into a smile. "No one can resist a juicy story, plus I make an excellent Spanish omelet. We'll start tomorrow, don't come before noon, I need my beauty sleep." He drew another cigarette out of the gold case.

"Oh and tell Gideon to extend your reservation for two weeks, and make sure your room has a private bath. I've stayed in Spanish bed-and-breakfasts and you don't want to listen to your neighbor singing *Carmen* in the shower."

"Two weeks!" Juliet exclaimed. "What did Gideon do?"

Lionel leaned on the door and his whole body sagged. His forehead was suddenly lined and his green eyes dimmed. He looked at Juliet and frowned.

"He rewrote my whole past."

Juliet climbed the steps of the Hotel Salvia and opened the red gate. She loved the three-story stone building with its black shutters and wrought iron balconies and peaked slate roof. She loved the lush gardens filled with green trellises and citrus trees and beds of pink azaleas. And she loved the location perched just above the main square of Sóller so she could browse in the elegant boutiques and eat tapas at the outdoor cafés.

Mostly she loved that everywhere she turned she saw the mountains and deep valleys and the horseshoe-shaped bay of Puerto de Sóller. She gazed at the turquoise swimming pool and tall pine trees and thought she had never been anywhere so beautiful.

She opened the front door of the hotel and entered the drawing room and admired the thick oriental rugs, antique chandeliers, and striped silk sofas. She glanced at the maple sideboard set with a crystal water pitcher and ceramic fruit bowl and felt like she was in a private home.

"Good afternoon Miss Lyman." The concierge looked up from his notes. "Did you find the Casa Rosa?"

"Yes, thank you." Juliet inhaled the sweet smelling air and her shoulders relaxed. "It's not far from here and the scenery was spectacular. I don't know how one gets anywhere in Majorca; I kept having to stop and admire the view."

"The Casa Rosa is one of the finest private estates on this side of the island," the man replied. "Would you like to make dinner reservations tonight? Chef Pedro is making baked saddle of lamb with olive crust and a rosemary sauce. You and your gentleman friend will enjoy your private terrace, the tables are set with silver candelabras and bottles of Mallorcan olive oil."

"I don't have a gentleman friend." Juliet blushed. "I'm here alone."

"But you said you were visiting a gentleman at the Casa Rosa." The concierge frowned.

"Lionel Harding is a business associate," Juliet explained. "I'm too tired to eat out tonight, perhaps I could get a sandwich and a glass of milk in my room."

"Everyone dines outside in Majorca in the summer," the concierge insisted. "Even the fishermen pull up their nets and have a cold beer and a plate of fresh oysters. There's plenty of time to stay inside during winter when the wind is icy and the valley is covered in fog."

"I won't be here that long." Juliet smiled. "Though I'd like to extend my reservation two weeks, I'm afraid my business is going to take longer than I thought."

"All the more reason to enjoy the nightlife." The concierge flicked through his book. "The music is lively and there is always dancing on the square after midnight."

Juliet pictured women wearing oversized sunglasses and bright chiffon dresses and strapless sandals. She saw men in sports coats and linen slacks and suede loafers. She imagined sitting alone at a table while couples held hands and sipped glasses of full-bodied Spanish wine. She imagined soft music and the scent of butter and garlic mixed with French perfume.

"I'm going to take a long bath and climb into bed." She walked toward the staircase. "Perhaps another night."

"Miss Lyman," he called after her. "May I ask what line of business are you in?"

"I'm in the music industry." Juliet turned around. "I'm an executive at a record label."

The concierge studied her smooth brown hair and blue eyes and small pink mouth. He saw her knit dress and long legs and white sandals. "Perhaps you should think about changing careers, a beautiful young woman should not be alone in Majorca on a Saturday night."

Juliet climbed the three flights of stairs and fumbled with her key. Gideon had booked a queen-sized room with her own balcony. Juliet gazed at the orange wool rug and turquoise walls and sloped ceiling. She saw the four-poster bed and mahogany desk and high-backed velvet chair.

She slipped off her sandals and placed her purse on the oak end table. Lionel might be prickly and abrasive but she was glad Gideon insisted she come to Majorca. The countryside was spectacular and the food was delicious and everything seemed to move slowly. She pictured the orange tram that took tourists to Puerto de Sóller and the sailboats with their billowing sails and a warmth spread through her chest.

She walked to the balcony and remembered the concierge thinking she had a boyfriend. She flashed on when she graduated from NYU and got her first interview at Sony. She'd worn a new navy wool suit and beige pumps. She remembered sitting across from Jane Backman and trying to stop her heart from racing.

"You're twenty-two and graduated summa cum laude from NYU." Jane glanced at her résumé. "You could get an entry level position at an investment banking firm with an expense account and a summer timeshare in the Hamptons. If you take this job, you'll be stuck for years with a mid-five-figure salary and a railroad apartment in Bushwick."

"My father is a linguistics professor at Sarah Lawrence and my mother writes for *The New Yorker*. When I was young I wanted to be a poet." Juliet fiddled with her silver necklace. "But when I was twelve I got my first Ipod and realized words were too quiet. Music makes me feel alive and excited."

"Let me tell you about a career in the music industry." Jane leaned back in her chair. She had straight blond hair and brown eyes and a wide mouth. She wore a purple Alice and Olivia dress and platform shoes. "You'll spend your days in recording studios drinking vending machine coffee and eating Chinese fortune cookies. Your skin will never see the sun so no matter how much Lancôme revitalizing cream you lather on, you'll always look like a figure in a Henry James novel or one of those deathly pale models in a Robert Palmer music video.

"While your friends are meeting hedge fund managers at the Monkey Bar after work, you'll be backstage at the Brooklyn Bowl fending off pre-teen girls wearing sparkly sneakers. You'll spend weekends riding on a tour bus surrounded by smelly socks and dirty magazines.

"You'll never meet a guy who can discuss French literature or applied physics because most musicians stop learning in the seventh grade. And you'll turn thirty-five and realize you're eggs are getting stale and the lines on your forehead are deeper and your friends are getting bugaboo strollers for Christmas." She paused and looked at Juliet. "Do you still want to work for a record label?"

Juliet glanced at the platinum records and silver album covers and bookshelves lined with Grammys. She smoothed her hair and smiled.

"There's nothing else I want to do."

"I should make you walk out that door and think about applying to business school or law school. But I know if music flows through your veins there's nothing you can do about it." Jane held out her hand. "Welcome to Sony."

Juliet wrapped her arms around her chest and remembered the last proper date she had, with an entertainment lawyer she met at a Coldplay concert. He had curly blond hair and brown eyes and liked The Foo Fighters and Imagine Dragons. He invited her to go ice-skating at Rockefeller Center and they drank Irish coffees and talked about the music industry's crazy hours and demanding artists.

Juliet listened to the excitement in his voice when he talked about *Billboard* charts and foreign sales and thought Jane was wrong. But then he had to go to Tokyo to babysit a client who took too many Ambien, and by the time he returned, Juliet was on a tour bus to Philadelphia. After three weeks of voice messages and texts they admitted it probably wouldn't work.

That had been almost two years ago and since then Juliet immersed herself in her job. She loved the strange pit in her stomach when she knew a song was going to work. And she loved the buzz of standing backstage at Madison Square Garden and watching fifty thousand fans wave their arms. Music was like discovering an unknown Rembrandt or owning a vintage Valentino dress or eating the finest gourmet chocolate.

She leaned over the balcony and heard the sounds of laughter and music. Majorca was filled with young people from Australia and New Zealand and Scandinavia. She had two weeks and nothing to do but listen to Lionel's story. Maybe she would finally meet a guy who loved homemade soup and the farmer's market and watching Italian movies on Netflix.

Suddenly she didn't want to soak in the porcelain bathtub listening to Spotify on her iPhone. She was going to an outdoor café and eat tomato confit with Mallorcan cheeses. She was going to inhale the sweet night air and watch the streetlamps dancing on the cobblestones.

She walked inside and stood in front of her closet. She selected a floral dress and silver sandals. She rubbed her lips with red lipstick and dusted her cheeks with powder. She grabbed her purse and hurried down the staircase.

Juliet walked along the promenade and gazed at the lights reflecting on the water. She saw ice cream stores with neon signs and souvenir shops with racks of glossy postcards. She felt the evening air settle on her shoulders and suddenly wished she were back in her hotel room, sipping a cup of hot tea with milk and honey.

She had decided to take the tram to Puerto de Sóller and have dinner at one of the harbor-side restaurants. It had been exciting to board the tram with tourists speaking German and French and Italian. It had been lovely to feel the wind in her hair and inhale the scent of citrus and jasmine. And it was wonderful to arrive at the port and see the sparkling Mediterranean.

But now she saw couples holding hands and stopping to study the menus. She saw families with young children, carrying sand buckets and shovels. She glanced in the windows of sleek restaurants and saw tables set with delicate champagne flutes and flickering candles. She inhaled the damp sea air and felt suddenly alone.

She was about to turn back to the tram stop when she saw a tall house with a wide stone porch and lush gardens. It had blue shutters and window boxes filled with peonies and daisies. The front door was open and she heard a violin playing and smelled butter and tomatoes and garlic.

She climbed the stone steps and entered a foyer with lacquered walls and polished wood floors. There was a dining room with high ceilings and gilt picture frames. The tables were set with royal blue china and gleaming silverware.

"Can I help you?" a young woman asked. She wore a navy dress and ivory pumps. Her dark hair was knotted into a low bun and she wore pale pink lip-gloss.

"The concierge at my hotel gave me the address of Casa Isabella, but there's no sign." Juliet frowned. "The front door was open and something smelled delicious."

"That's the grilled suckling pig with lemon confit," the woman replied. "My father doesn't believe in advertising, he likes to imagine our patrons are casual acquaintances invited over for dinner. He prepares one five-course meal and the menu changes daily." She consulted the leather-bound reservation book. "Unfortunately we're booked every weekend from May until October."

"I'll try another night." Juliet sighed, suddenly realizing she was starving. She hadn't eaten anything except half a sandwich with Lionel. She glanced at the marble fireplace and tall bookshelves and wanted desperately to sit at a table and have a glass of Roija Cabernet and a plate of seafood linguini.

"Antonio Banderas reserves the same table every Saturday night and never arrives before nine P.M." The young woman smiled. "If you promise not to linger over the chocolate fondant, I can squeeze you in."

"That would be wonderful," Juliet exclaimed, following her to a table by the window. "What a beautiful room, it's like a private home."

"My grandfather was a wealthy citrus trader." She handed Juliet a menu. "He loved my grandmother so much he hated being away at sea. He built a house on the promenade so he could see her standing on the balcony when he sailed into the harbor."

Juliet nodded. "That's so romantic."

"Unfortunately his ship sunk and he lost all his money. The only way to keep Casa Isabella was to turn the downstairs into a restaurant," she explained. "After my grandparents died, my parents took over. My mother is the maître d' and my brothers catch the fish and my father runs the kitchen. My mother loves flitting around the dining room; she thinks every night is a party. But my father would rather be upstairs in his study reading a book on medieval history."

"Why doesn't he hire another chef?" Juliet asked.

"In Majorca everything is about family." The woman straightened Juliet's silverware. "No one else would care as much that the monkfish is perfectly sautéed or the lettuce is fresh from the garden or the tomatoes are sliced so thinly they melt in your mouth. My father grumbles but he doesn't let anything leave his kitchen unless it would be fit for the prince and princess of Spain."

Juliet ate cold tomato soup and watched the young woman fill breadbaskets and smooth linen napkins. She listened to the violin playing in the garden and suddenly felt warm and happy. She was in one of the most beautiful spots in the world, eating a salad of feta cheese and red peppers and scallions.

She thought about Lionel and wondered how he could be depressed surrounded by so much beauty. She pictured his living room with its grand piano and French doors and floral sofas. She saw the garden filled with birds of paradise and dahlias. She pictured Gideon with his salt-and-pepper hair and patterned shirts and shuddered. He had made it clear that if Juliet didn't return with a packet of Lionel's songs her job was in jeopardy.

Juliet finished the last bite of almond cake and blotted her mouth with a napkin. It had all been delicious: the Sóller prawns cooked in sea salt and olive oil, the salmon in a marsala sauce with baby carrots, the selection of fruits and local cheeses. She glanced around the room, wishing to thank the young woman but she had disappeared and been replaced by an older woman with dark wavy hair and green eyes.

Juliet walked through the foyer to search for a powder room and heard a woman singing. She listened closer and remembered when she was young and discovered her mother's Carly Simon album. She remembered listening to Carly's bright, clear voice and feeling her lungs expand and her heart race.

She gingerly opened a door and saw the young woman standing at a double sink. She wore a white apron over her navy dress and her hands were covered in soap. She glanced up at Juliet and her cheeks flushed.

"I wanted to thank you for a lovely dinner." Juliet hesitated. "The grilled salmon was delicious."

"My father will be pleased." She beamed. "He refuses to serve fish that wasn't caught the same day, he says you should be able to taste the ocean."

"You have a beautiful voice." Juliet entered the kitchen. The counters were stacked with silver trays and square white plates. Brass pots hung from the ceiling and a planter box held round red tomatoes.

She shrugged. "I've always sung, it helps pass the time when you're peeling potatoes or slicing mushrooms. My brothers used to stuff their ears with cotton wool and I'd get back at them by hiding their soccer ball."

"Have you ever considered singing professionally?" Juliet asked.

"When my mother was young she wanted to be a dancer, she spent hours practicing arabesques in the garden." She untied her apron. "She ran off to Paris when she was nineteen and performed at the Moulin Rouge. She lasted eight months and returned to Majorca and married my father."

"I'm sure she would have been a success if she had continued," Juliet murmured.

"Men sent her flowers and perfume and waited outside her dressing room." She wiped her hands. "She had three marriage proposals and a jewelry box full of gold necklaces and earrings. She drank champagne and ate caviar at smoky cafés and realized there was nowhere she'd rather be than Majorca."

"I don't understand." Juliet frowned.

"Why would I want to sing professionally when I have everything I need right here?" she asked. "A beautiful house and a wonderful family and the Mediterranean outside my front door?" She stopped and held out her hand. "My name is Gabriella, please come back another night. You have to try my father's seafood risotto, it's the best on the island."

Juliet opened the door to her room and slipped off her sandals. She unzipped her dress and pulled a cotton robe around her shoulders. She climbed into bed and thought about her meeting tomorrow with Lionel. Whatever Gideon had done, she had to convince Lionel to write some new songs.

She closed her eyes and pictured the Casa Isabella. She remembered the dining room with its round tables and high ceilings and marble fireplace. She saw Gabriella standing at the double sink with an apron tied around her waist. She remembered her high, clear voice and a tingle ran down her spine.

chapter two

LIONEL PRESSED HIS FINGER ON the alarm clock and waited for his head to stop throbbing. He stumbled to the closet and pulled a bottle of scotch from the box of Bruno Magli loafers. He fished a glass from under a pile of Paul Smith silk shirts and filled it to brim. He took a quick gulp and let his shoulders relax.

He thought about last night and tried to remember when he started drinking. It was probably early, right after the new maid insisted he eat a bowl of paella and plate of green asparagus. He would have to tell the service he didn't want the maid preparing his meals, he felt like a small boy at boarding school forced to eat his vegetables.

He remembered sitting on the porch with a glass of Château Rothschild Chardonnay and a copy of *Ivanhoe* and groaned. Not even a fine wine discovered in the villa's vast wine cellar and a poem by one of his favorite poets could stop the weight pressing against his chest. He finally replaced the wine with straight bourbon and Sir Walter Scott with the latest issue of *GQ* and went upstairs to bed.

Now he drank another sip of scotch and glanced at his alarm clock. Juliet would be arriving in an hour and he hadn't shaved or showered. He thought about calling her and telling her he was sick but she would probably arrive with a carton of chicken soup and a box of Kleenex. He pictured her smooth brown hair and blue eyes and thought she wasn't the type to let a summer cold interfere with what she wanted.

He glanced at his phone and thought about calling Gideon and demanding he put Juliet back on a plane to California. But Gideon would probably send someone who didn't have long legs and wear Dior perfume. He could send an e-mail saying he didn't care if he sent Mariah Carey or Beyoncé, he wasn't writing any new songs. But he pictured seeing Gideon's name in his in-box and decided he would handle Juliet himself.

He put the glass on the bedside table and rubbed the stubble on his chin. He couldn't remember eating anything last night except a Cadbury Fruit & Nut bar and suddenly he was starving. He'd have a piece of toast or a bowl of muesli and then come upstairs and get dressed. He glanced in the mirror at his bloodshot eyes and chuckled. If Juliet saw his drawn cheeks and unbrushed hair she might get scared and never come back.

Lionel heard a knock on the door and hurried down the staircase. He inhaled the scent of furniture polish and fresh cut flowers and admitted the daily maid service had its virtues. At least Juliet wouldn't be able to criticize his housekeeping the moment she entered the stone foyer.

"You've cleaned up," Juliet said, gazing at the plumped floral sofas and neat stacks of magazines. The silk curtains were pulled back and light streamed through the tall French doors.

"My mother did teach me to clean my room before I invited a pretty girl over," Lionel said. He fished in his slacks for his gold cigarette case.

"I think you cut yourself shaving," she said. She motioned to his cheek. "You're bleeding."

"We are the only species that purposely uses a dangerous weapon on our face," Lionel said. He touched his cheek and winced. "I've always wondered what would happen if you sneezed while holding a razor. But nothing makes you feel more alive than a close shave. When I was performing I had a barber come to the house every morning before I ate my porridge."

"Gideon told me you were terrible at managing your expense account." Juliet smiled.

"He seemed happy to indulge me in Brioni suits and Santoni shoes when I was lining his walls with gold records." Lionel grimaced. "I once met a psychiatrist who insisted I could blame Gideon for my expensive tastes. Weaning yourself off Turnbull & Asser shirts is harder than giving up Cuban cigars."

"Do you see a psychiatrist?" Juliet asked.

"God, no." Lionel flicked open a pearl lighter. "Psychiatrists have no desire to cure you, then who would pay for their holidays in Ibiza? I met a female psychiatrist at a party who wanted to give me a free session. But the only time I want to recline on a sofa with a woman is when we're nibbling caviar and drinking Möet & Chandon."

"It's a gorgeous day, should we sit outside?" Juliet walked to the balcony. The swimming pool was a sparkling turquoise and the fishpond was filled with orange goldfish. Two lounge chairs were littered with striped cushions and there was an outdoor bar lined with brightly colored bottles.

"The sun is so strong, I never go outside before three P.M." Lionel inhaled slowly. "You think you'll be young forever but one day you'll look in the mirror and see a character in a horror movie. You'll climb into bed thinking it was the fourth martini or the extra slice of pannetone but in the morning you'll shuffle to the mirror and see the same figure.

"By then it will be too late to reverse the damage so you'll say you don't care that your eyes are puffy and your stomach sags, but secretly you'll long for the days when you could roll out of bed and pull on a white T-shirt and a pair of blue jeans." Lionel gazed at Juliet's smooth brown hair and slender cheekbones. He saw her red linen dress and low white pumps. "Youth is the greatest gift and we don't give a fig about it until it's gone.

"I sound like one of those VH1 flashbacks," he groaned, rubbing his brow. "Let's go into the library, I found a very nice sherry hidden behind a copy of T. S. Eliot's *The Wasteland.*"

Lionel walked down a narrow hallway and entered a room with high ceilings and paneled walls. There was a wide ebony desk and leather wingback chairs. Oriental rugs covered a worn oak floor and a carved elephant stood in the corner.

"The villa has a marvelous collection: Melville, Cervantes, Paul Theroux." He ran his fingers over the leather-bound books. "I love a thick novel or a juicy memoir, but poetry is the greatest form of literature. A poem can't rely on plot or dialogue, it has to move you with six lines of iambic pentameter or terza rima."

"My mother writes for *The New Yorker* and hosts a literary salon once a month," Juliet replied. "She insisted I minor in English in college because she said you can learn everything you need to know by reading Shakespeare's sonnets."

"And I thought you were one of those young heathens raised on The Backstreet Boys and NSYNC," he mused. "Did you leave behind a boyfriend in California? Some blond surfer who takes acting classes during the day and parks cars at Château Marmont at night?"

"I don't have a boyfriend in Los Angeles." Juliet shook her head.

"Don't tell me you are in a long distance relationship filled with Skype sessions and endless texts." Lionel sighed. "The fastest way to end the human race is to conduct love affairs through a metallic device that AutoCorrects every original thought."

"I don't have time to date." Juliet studied the patterns on the rug. "I'm either buried under contracts at my desk or backstage at a concert trying to stop the lead singer from sneaking out for a packet of Twizzlers."

"I could never go onstage without eating a mince pie and drinking a can of orange Fresca." Lionel grinned. "But that's ridiculous, love comes before anything. When I met Samantha I had just arrived in London. I was twenty-two and determined to make it as a songwriter; the last thing I needed was to spend my afternoons moping around Hyde Park and wondering if she would see me again." Lionel opened a drawer in the ebony desk and took out a crystal decanter. He filled two shot glasses with dark red liquid and handed one to Juliet.

"My mother was from a wealthy family in Knightsbridge and did the things girls of her class were supposed to do: took ballet lessons at Sadler's Wells and competed in gymkhanas and learned

to ski in the French Alps. She attended boarding school at Wold-
ingham but instead of going to finishing school in Lausanne or
taking a summer cooking course in Provence and meeting some
young investment banker with his own town house in Chelsea, she
fell in love with the son of a local solicitor and stayed in Surrey.

"They got married and lived in a red brick house with a
tennis court and a swimming pool. I had a perfectly nice childhood: two older sisters, cricket matches on the village green,
and monthly visits to London to see exhibits at the Victoria and
Albert Museum.

"My writing teacher insisted I apply to Cambridge and surprisingly I got a place." Lionel paused and ran his fingers over
the shot glass. "I spent the first year studying the great essayists:
Thomas Carlyle and William Hazlitt and Charles Lamb. But I
realized I didn't have deep opinions on important subjects or a
burning desire to share them if I had." He swallowed the sherry.
"I stumbled on the romantic poets and became enraptured by
Byron and Keats and Browning. There were the answers I was
looking for! Not about the fate of humankind or how we could
improve society but why a man would plunge a knife in another
man's chest in the name of love. I grew my hair long and wrote
poetry every moment I got. But no matter how I arranged the
verses I felt something was missing." He stopped and looked at
Juliet. "Poetry has to hit you like an arrow in a bull's-eye; if it
lands just to the left it may as well never have been written."

"One afternoon I was walking along the Cam and saw a couple of girls having a picnic," Lionel mused. "They asked me to
join them and I accepted. We sat on the riverbank and ate shepherd's pie and one of the girls turned on the radio." He rubbed his
chin. "You're going to laugh but when it came to popular music I

was practically a virgin. I sat and listened to Paul McCartney and Bryan Ferry and Elton John and knew without a doubt if I set my poems to music they would achieve what I'd been trying to convey. From that moment I decided to become a songwriter."

"I would have thought someone like you listened to the Beatles and the Rolling Stones since you were a teenager. Didn't your parents play their records on the stereo or didn't you listen to the radio before you went to bed? I don't remember a time that I didn't turn on the Bangles when I started my homework," Juliet mused.

"We weren't allowed to listen to music after school, and my parents seemed to have missed the swinging sixties. The only time my mother wore leather boots was when she was saddling a horse." He sat on a leather armchair. "But the minute I heard Elton John sing 'Someone Saved My Life Tonight,' I packed my suitcase and took the train to London and arrived at the front door of Penelope Graham. She was my mother's oldest friend and lived with her husband and twin boys in a three-story terrace house in Belgravia."

Lionel stretched his long legs in front of him and closed his eyes. He pictured the vast black-and-white marble foyer and heavy crystal chandeliers and walls lined with Holbeins and Turners. He saw Penelope descend the circular staircase in a Chanel suit and ivory pumps. He saw her study his battered suitcase and worn loafers and usher him into the kitchen.

"You want me to let you stay here and not tell your mother?" Penelope opened the steel fridge and took out a carton of orange juice. She filled a glass and handed it to Lionel.

"Only until I find a job and can afford a place to live." Lionel sat on a suede stool. "I'll work as a valet or a waiter and write songs at night. My twenty-second birthday was last week, if I wait any longer I'll be one of those old crooners with receding hairlines and bell-bottom pants."

"Hardly a receding hairline, you could use a good haircut." Penelope glanced at his dark curls. She studied his green eyes and the cleft on his chin. "Marian had pretty girls but she outdid herself with you." She fiddled with her diamond choker. "I'll let you stay if you do something for me."

Lionel blushed and gripped his glass tightly. He stood up and smoothed his shirt.

"Don't be silly, I'm not trying to seduce you." Penelope laughed. "I have a virile husband who runs marathons and competes in bicycle races in France. My neighbor has a nanny, an Irish girl who's never been in London. She spends all her time when she's not working in her room. Georgina is afraid she's homesick and will go back to Galway." Penelope tapped her fingernails on the marble counter. "I want you to ask her out."

Lionel pictured a girl with blotchy skin in a tweed sweater and opaque stockings. He imagined sitting in a noisy pub and eating plates of greasy fish and chips.

"I don't have any money," he stumbled.

Penelope walked to the pantry and unscrewed a glass cookie jar.

"Her name is Samantha." She handed him four twenty-pound notes. "You can have the room over the garage; it has central heating and you'll have your own private bath."

Lionel climbed the stone steps of the white Georgian manor and took a deep breath. He would take Samantha to the brasserie at

Motocomb's and buy her a glass of Chablis and a Caesar salad. They would talk about the new production of *The Winter's Tale* and Princess Diana's good deeds in Bosnia. He would say he had an early job interview and be in his new room with its Frette sheets and Krupp's espresso maker by 10 P.M. He'd still have time to finish the lyrics to a song he scribbled on the train.

He rang the doorbell and clutched a bouquet of purple daisies. The double front doors opened and he saw a young woman with blond hair knotted into a bun. She had blue eyes and alabaster skin. She wore a paisley yellow dress and narrow leather belt.

"I was looking for Samantha," he mumbled, gazing at her full breasts and long legs.

"I'm Samantha," she replied, accepting the flowers. She leaned down to smell them and her hair escaped its bun. Lionel had the sudden impulse to tuck her hair behind her ears. He wanted to stroke her cheek and run his fingers over her pink mouth.

"Would you like to come in?" she asked. "I'm sure wine bars in Belgravia are expensive, I could fix us a tuna sandwich in the kitchen."

"No, thank you," Lionel said, suddenly flustered. "I have a craving for baked pheasant and creamed potatoes. Have you ever had Motocomb's quince? They serve it with pistachio ice cream and it's delicious."

They sat at the oak bar and drank white wine with crème de cassis. Lionel ordered a wilted lettuce salad with mozzarella and avocado and bacon. He watched Samantha drizzle olive oil on heirloom tomatoes and felt a stirring in his slacks. He gripped his wineglass and suddenly longed for a double shot of whiskey.

"We can finish our drinks and say goodnight." She dabbed her mouth with a napkin. "I'll take a stroll around Eaton Square and pretend we stayed for dinner. I'll pay for the appetizer and you'll only be out two glasses of wine and a bunch of daisies."

"I don't know what you mean." Lionel shifted on his stool.

"I overheard Georgina talking on the phone. She was thrilled Penelope found me a date because she thinks I'm lonely." She looked at Lionel and her eyes sparkled. "If she only knew how wonderful it is to have my own bedroom and not have my sisters borrow my bras and underwear."

"Penelope might have suggested I call, but I wanted to come." Lionel loosened his collar. "In fact I think we should move to the restaurant and share a bottle of burgundy and a couple of sirloin steaks."

"Are you sure?" Samantha murmured. "I don't want to take up your time."

"I've never been surer of anything." Lionel signaled the bartender for their check. He took her arm and led her into the restaurant. He gazed at the silk tablecloths set with bone white china and gleaming silverware and gulped.

"Do your sisters really wear your underwear?" he asked, as the maître d' led them to a table by the window.

Samantha turned around and her face broke into a smile. "We're a very close family."

They ate filet mignon in béarnaise sauce and Samantha told him about growing up in a fishing village on the west coast of Ireland.

"When I was little we used to sell seashells to the tourists," she said, tearing apart a baguette. "I had to tape my coins under my pillow so my brothers wouldn't spend them on ice cream."

"When I was a baby, my sisters wrapped me in tissue paper and placed me under the Christmas tree," Lionel said. He sipped a Château Tour Bordeaux. "My mother found me with a red bow glued to my forehead. She was furious because she had to cut off my curls."

"I'm sure you were quite handsome bald," Samantha smiled.

"Marian didn't think so." Lionel cut a thick slice of steak. "She didn't give me another haircut until I was five years old."

"That's what's wonderful about children; they can be mischievous and innocent at the same time. Yesterday I discovered Abigail wearing her mother's Prada suit; she said she was tired of being eight and wanted to get an important job." Samantha nibbled grilled asparagus. "After I made her take it off, she climbed into my lap and watched *The Sound of Music*."

"Is that what you're doing in London?" Lionel leaned back in his chair. "Being a nanny and waiting to meet some young barrister in a children's boutique on King's Road. You'll help him buy the perfect christening gift for his nephew and bond over cashmere baby booties and Tiffany's rattles. He'll take you to meet his parents at their Mayfair club and propose with his grandmother's sapphire ring."

"I took this job to save money to go to university," Samantha replied. "Most children in Cleggan leave school at sixteen and become shopkeepers and fishermen. I want to teach geography and history and literature."

"I spent a year at Cambridge reading one-thousand-page tomes by Leo Tolstoy and Aldous Huxley." Lionel sighed. "Then I discovered the Romantic poets and felt like Alexander Graham

Bell inventing the telephone. All I wanted to do was tinker with blank verse and anapestic meter. To be honest I wasn't good enough so I decided to become a songwriter. I'm going to get a job and earn enough money to rent a recording studio. I'll compose the greatest love songs since Elton John and Bernie Taupin."

"What did your parents say?" Samantha asked.

"They think I'm still in Cambridge attending lectures and watching bumps races." Lionel fiddled with his wineglass.

"You quit university?" Samantha put her fork on her plate.

"They'll be furious of course, but I couldn't wait any longer," Lionel explained. "Mick Jagger and Keith Richards didn't need a degree; they just had a notepad and a bottle of whiskey."

"This has been lovely but I have to go," Samantha said, as she pushed back her chair. She gathered her purse and walked to the door.

"Wait." Lionel rushed after her. "We haven't tried their flourless chocolate cake."

"Dinner was delicious," Samantha said. "I'll send you my half of the bill."

Lionel watched her stride down the leafy street. He threw three twenty-pound notes on the table and ran after her.

"We were having a lovely time." He put his hand on her arm. "I was about to tell you the story about when my sisters pretended I was their new puppy."

"If I work twelve-hour days I might save enough money to go to a third-rate teacher college in Reading." Samantha turned around. "But if I fail I'll go back to my parents' cottage in Cleggan. I'll work in the family shop selling sand buckets and Irish toffees. You attended the most prestigious university in the world and threw it away because you know if you don't succeed you can return to your country estate with its tennis court and swimming pool."

"I am going to succeed," Lionel said hotly. "All I want to do is write songs."

"Good night, I don't want to take up any more of your time." Samantha hurried along the pavement.

Lionel fished in his slacks for a packet of cigarettes and groaned. He forgot he had given up smoking to save money. He could go back inside the restaurant and have a bowl of rum raisin ice cream, but suddenly his stomach was queasy.

He trudged along the sidewalk past men wearing silk slacks and women in tight cocktail dresses. He had done his duty and he'd be home in bed on schedule. He'd tell Penelope they had a lovely time and the creamed potatoes were delicious.

He stopped at a newsagent and bought a packet of Marlboros. He pictured Samantha's blond hair and high breasts and small waist. He inhaled slowly and thought no matter what he had to see her again.

"That's all for today." Lionel tapped a cigarette into his hand. "I need a nap."

"It's two o'clock in the afternoon," Juliet spluttered. "You just woke up."

"I start drinking at five and need to be refreshed." He lit the cigarette with a pearl lighter. "We'll continue tomorrow."

"What will I do all afternoon?" Juliet twisted her silver necklace. She thought of calling Gideon with her report and flinched. Lionel hadn't done more than tell her about a twenty-year-old unrequited love.

"It's Majorca, there's plenty to do," he insisted. "You can hike up to Valldemossa or take the train to Palma and eat rock lobster with muscular Germans with bad suntans."

"I'm not here to see the views or socialize." Juliet felt her cheeks turn pink. "I'm in Majorca to get you to fulfill your contract."

"How old are you?" Lionel asked.

"Twenty-eight, why?" Juliet murmured.

"Twenty-eight and no serious boyfriend." He stubbed his cigarette in the glass ashtray. "Let me guess, you have an old college boyfriend who's still hanging around or a jilted fiancé hoping for another chance."

"That's none of your business." Juliet stood up and smoothed her skirt.

"When I met Gideon he was the smartest person I knew, he was only twenty-six and had already produced five platinum records. He had a sixth sense about people, he knew exactly what made them tick." Lionel walked to the hallway. "I guess we all get dumber as we age and make poor decisions."

"What do you mean?" Juliet followed him to the stone entry.

"He sent someone to convince me to write love songs who doesn't believe in love." He opened the door.

"I told you I don't have time to date," Juliet snapped.

"Have a lovely afternoon and wear a hat." He slipped his hands in his pockets. "You don't want to ruin that youthful complexion."

Lionel stood at the sink and drank a glass of iced water. His head ached but suddenly he didn't feel like his usual hangover remedy of a Bloody Mary and hard-boiled egg with horseradish. He pictured Juliet pursing her lips when he said he was taking a nap and groaned. The last thing he needed was some twenty-something do-gooder trying to improve his habits.

He rustled through the pantry and found a packet of short-bread and a jar of lemon drops. He entered the living room and flicked through the stack of books on the maple side table. He opened Rudyard Kipling's *Just So Stories* and began to read.

chapter three

JULIET STOOD ON THE BALCONY and gazed at the lush gardens of the Hotel Salvia. She saw the turquoise swimming pool and orange birds of paradise and trellises covered with pink and yellow roses. She inhaled the scent of citrus and olives and realized she was starving.

After she left Lionel she strolled through the plaza and browsed in boutiques selling bright cotton dresses and leather sandals. She bought a wide-brimmed hat and a pair of oversized sunglasses. Then she sat in an outdoor café and ordered a salade niçoise and a glass of lemonade.

She drizzled olive oil on artichoke palms and took a small bite. She thought about what Lionel said—that she didn't believe in love—and bristled. Lionel was depressed and didn't know anything about her.

Finally she walked back to the Hotel Salvia and changed into a swimsuit. She swam thirty laps and wrapped herself in a fluffy white towel. Now she leaned over the railing and gazed at the port lined with billowing sailboats. She saw silver yachts and chipped wooden dinghies.

She walked inside and saw her phone buzz. She picked it up and heard a male voice come down the line.

"I extended your reservation but I haven't heard from you or Lionel," Gideon said. When do I get my songs?"

"I'm working with Lionel every moment of the day," Juliet explained. "I promise you'll have them within two weeks."

"I sent you because you are the best senior executive I've had in a long time." Gideon paused. "Make sure Lionel stays on task. He thinks he's a bloody artist but this is a business. I paid him one hundred sixty-six thousand dollars to deliver those songs six months ago."

"I've made him completely aware of his obligations." Juliet smoothed her hair. "I won't let you down."

"Lionel is brilliant at what he does but sometimes he acts like a pampered schoolboy," Gideon grumbled. "If only accountants could write songs."

Juliet pressed END and shuddered. What would Gideon do if she couldn't convince Lionel to fulfill his contract?

Suddenly she remembered her delicious dinner at Casa Isabella with the baked sea bass and local cheeses. She pictured Gabriella's navy dress and ivory pumps. She remembered standing outside the kitchen and hearing her high, clear voice.

She walked to her closet and selected a floral dress and white sandals. She coated her eyelashes with mascara and spritzed her wrists with White Linen. She grabbed her purse and hurried down the staircase.

Juliet opened the gate of the Casa Isabella and saw a young woman standing on the patio. She wore a blue dress and oval sunglasses. She carried a basket filled with a head of lettuce and red peppers and purple asparagus.

"Gabriella!" she called. "It's nice to see you; I don't think I introduced myself. My name is Juliet Lyman."

Gabriella looked at Juliet's brown hair and blue eyes and her face broke into a smile.

"The American! I told my father you enjoyed the sea bass," she replied. "I'm sorry, we're closed on Sundays, you'll have to return another night."

"I wasn't coming for dinner," Juliet said. "I was going to take the train into Palma and visit La Seu Cathedral and Bellver Castle. I don't know anyone else in Majorca and thought you might like to join me. We can ride the roofless sightseeing buses and see the jellyfish at the aquarium."

"You've been reading your guidebook." Gabriella laughed. "I visited La Seu many times on school trips; we always complained how long it took to reach the cathedral, but when we arrived the mosaics were spectacular. I'd love to come but it's my day off and I have to run some errands."

"Of course." Juliet's cheeks turned red and she felt suddenly foolish. "Perhaps another time."

"You can come with me," Gabriella blurted out. "I'm delivering vegetables from our garden to my grandmother's hacienda in Fornalutx. She always insists I stay and eat pumpkin soup and potato empanadas. It's a long walk but the air is crisp and you can see the whole coastline."

"I thought your grandparents were dead." Juliet frowned.

"Lydia is my father's mother." Gabriella grinned, picking up her basket. "She'll ask you a million questions but she bottles her own wine and makes pistachio ice cream."

They took the tram to Sóller and hiked a steep path flanked by pine trees. They passed sheep grazing and women selling baskets of lemons. Juliet looked up and saw a village perched at the foot of the mountain. It had cobblestoned streets and narrow houses with lacquered window boxes.

"It's gorgeous," Juliet breathed, gazing at the lush palm trees. She saw cafés with striped awnings and an outdoor market selling bottles of olive oil. She turned around and saw the wide sweep of bay and emerald ocean.

"Fornalutx was named the most picturesque village in Spain and now it's full of tourists with Nikon cameras," Gabriella explained. "Lydia has lived here for fifty years, since it was nothing but orange groves and olive trees. She grumbles that she can't leave her house without someone asking directions, but she loves the mountain air and the night sky filled with stars."

They climbed a winding alley and Juliet saw a three-story house with a slanted roof.

"Does your grandmother live alone?" Juliet asked, admiring the double wood front doors.

"She owned a farm but it was too difficult to take care of so my father convinced her to sell it and move to the village." Gabriella knocked on the door. "He wanted her to move to Puerto de Sóller but she said she belongs in the mountains. She's sixty-nine and still hikes two miles every day and collects her own eggs."

The door opened and a woman with silvery hair stood in the foyer. She had green eyes and smooth cheekbones. She wore a white cotton shirt and slacks and white loafers.

"Gabriella!" she exclaimed, ushering them into the entry.

"This is my friend Juliet," Gabriella said in English. "We hiked from Sóller and I promised her a plate of potato empanadas."

"It's too hot to eat anything except bread and cheeses," Lydia replied. "I set the table outside, we'll have a green salad and a bottle of sangria."

Juliet gazed around the room and saw a tile floor and wooden bookshelves. There was a red sofa and stone fireplace. Oak tables were covered with picture frames and vases of yellow sunflowers.

"What a beautiful house," Juliet said, admiring the plaster walls and geometric rug.

"I miss the farm, the goats and sheep made better conversation than some of the shopkeepers." Lydia led them into the garden. "But I love being able to walk to the patisserie and buy a frothy cappuccino. Majorcans make the best paella but terrible coffee."

"You speak wonderful English," Juliet commented, sitting at the round table. A wooden bowl was filled with spinach leaves and heirloom tomatoes. Juliet saw a loaf of bread and a platter of cheeses.

"When I was young I had the opportunity to teach Spanish in San Francisco," Lydia said.. She ladled spinach onto ceramic plates. "I went to the library in Palma and checked out Hemingway and Fitzgerald. I read them so many times the pages disintegrated and I couldn't return them."

"That must have been exciting." Juliet smiled, eating a wedge of Gouda.

"It didn't work out, but I still love American books." Lydia's eyes clouded over. "When I sold the farm I bought a ticket to Paris. People thought it was so I could buy a pretty dress or see the Arc de Triomphe, but it was to visit Shakespeare and Company. I came home with a suitcase full of Hawthorne and Steinbeck."

"I love California; I work for a record label in Los Angeles." Juliet dabbed her mouth with a napkin. "I heard Gabriella singing; she has one of the most beautiful voices I've ever heard."

Lydia nodded. "She sang at Sunday school and the priest said he was visited by an angel. I told her she'll have to sing at her own wedding."

"Are you getting married?" Juliet turned to Gabriella.

"Hugo works in his uncle's hotel in Palma." Gabriella flushed. "We've been together for four years but he wants to wait until he can afford a proper diamond."

"He has curly dark hair and blue eyes and they're going to make beautiful babies." Lydia's eyes sparkled. "But I told them they need to have them while I'm still young enough to win three-legged races on Easter."

Lydia went upstairs to get a photo album and Gabriella carried plates into the kitchen. Juliet offered to help, but Gabriella insisted she finish her wine. Juliet ran her fingers over her glass and suddenly stood up and walked inside.

She was about to enter the kitchen when she heard Gabriella's clear voice. She held her breath and listened to the song float through the hallway. Her voice seemed even higher than before, the notes reaching the ceiling. Juliet closed her eyes and felt a shiver run down her spine.

"You can help me carry the fruit salad," Gabriella said, seeing Juliet standing at the door. "The peaches are from Lydia's fruit trees and they're delicious with ice cream."

Juliet sat at the table and watched Lydia fill silver bowls with apricots. She wanted to say Gabriella had to let Gideon hear her sing. She wanted to promise her a recording contract and a world tour and beautiful clothes and jewelry. But she listened to Gabriella talk about the new menu at Casa Isabella and Hugo's plans for his uncle's hotel and knew she couldn't open her mouth. Gabriella was like a child who woke up every day to Christmas morning.

"I must go." Lydia stood up. "Father Garcia doesn't like it if one is late for church, even if I bring him a fruit tart."

"Thank you for having me," Juliet said, as she held out her hand. "Everything was delicious."

Lydia kissed her on the cheek. "You must come back for dinner. I'll open a bottle of rosé and we will sit in the square and watch the dancing. The butcher thinks he is Frank Sinatra and the greengrocer believes he is Fred Astaire."

They hiked down the mountain to Sóller and Juliet watched the sun dip below the horizon. The clouds turned pink and orange and lights twinkled on the harbor. She felt the breeze in her hair and wrapped her arms around her chest.

"Your grandmother has more energy than some of my recording artists," she said as they approached the tram stop.

Gabriella nodded. "She is proud of being able to do everything herself. She can change a tire and milk a goat."

"How long ago did her husband die?" Juliet asked.

Gabriella hopped onto the tram and shook her head. "She was never married."

Juliet crossed the plaza and hurried up the stone steps of the Hotel Salvia. She pictured Gabriella's dark hair and green eyes. She heard her high, clear voice and felt her chest expand.

She pictured Lydia ladling spinach leaves onto ceramic plates. She remembered her saying she was a teacher in San Francisco, but it didn't work out. She pictured her eyes clouding over and her hands twisting her napkin.

Suddenly she felt something lift inside her. She entered the drawing room and approached the concierge's desk.

"Good evening, Miss Lyman." The concierge looked up from his notes. "It's such a beautiful night, would you like me to make you a reservation at Ca'n BoQueta? The chef makes a delicious salmon tartar and all the young people go there."

"Do you have a library where guests can borrow books?" Juliet asked.

"Of course, follow me." The concierge led her into a room with paneled walls and a beamed ceiling. It had a stone fireplace and tall bookshelves.

"Can I keep them if I promise to replace them?" Juliet asked.

"Take whatever you like." The concierge walked to the door and turned around. "Miss Lyman, there are more things to do in Majorca than sit in your room and read. A beautiful young woman should be drinking mojitos at Bar Nicolás or dancing to the DJ at Nikki Beach."

Juliet approached the bookshelf and saw tattered copies of *Moby-Dick* and *The Sun Also Rises*. She saw a selection of John Grisham books and a pile by Danielle Steel. She looked up and her face lit into a smile.

"Don't worry, they're not for me."

chapter four

LIONEL STOOD IN THE PANTRY and selected a jar of marmite and a loaf of whole wheat bread. He carried them into the kitchen and arranged them on the tile counter. He poured a glass of orange juice and took a long gulp. He glanced at his reflection in the silver fridge and groaned.

Juliet would be there in less than an hour and he was still in his silk pajamas. He studied his reflection more closely and knew that even a shower and a shave wouldn't fix the circles under his eyes or give his cheeks some color.

He had stayed awake all night, staring at the mosaic ceiling. He pictured Juliet in her blue knit dress and white leather sandals. He saw her waving her phone and telling him he owed Gideon one hundred sixty-six thousand dollars. Would Gideon really expect him to repay his advance and where on earth would he find the money?

He slipped on his suede John Lobb slippers and padded down the wood staircase. He sat on the floral sofa, grinding cigarettes into the glass ashtray. He thought of all the things he wanted to say to Gideon: how dare he send an account executive who was as old as his favorite Canali tie. Was he really supposed to take orders from someone who was in kindergarten when he received his first Grammy?

He stubbed out the last cigarette and searched the house for an extra packet of Marlboros. He looked in all the places he hid cigarettes on the rare days he wanted to quit: in the piano, behind the Cézanne, wrapped in a plastic bag in the birdbath. Finally he entered the kitchen and opened the fridge. He ate a container of guacamole and an apple. Then he moved to the pantry and found a tin of Harrods's chocolate biscuits. He poured a glass of milk and slumped on the leather stool.

Lionel glanced at the ceramic clock and thought he could run upstairs and splash his face with water. But maybe if Juliet saw the misery she was causing, she'd pack her red Coach purse and go home. He pictured Juliet telling Gideon he was unsalvageable and they should leave him alone.

He heard a knock on the door and flinched.

"Come in, I'm in the kitchen," he called, spreading marmite on bread.

Juliet entered the room and glanced at the counter littered with toffee wrappers and a half-eaten Violet Crumble. She saw a porcelain coffee mug and a sliced orange.

"What are you doing?" she asked.

"I ran out of cigarettes and got hungry," Lionel explained. "First I tried the tostadas the maid left but they were too spicy. Then I thought I'd make a sandwich but rinsing lettuce and slicing tomatoes was exhausting. So I raided the pantry and found a tin of biscuits and a packet of butterscotch creams."

"It looks like the kitchen in Cinderella when she went to the ball." Juliet collected silver spoons and put them in the sink.

"Maybe you could run down to the newsagent and buy a pack of cigarettes," he suggested.

"Have you thought of quitting?" Juliet asked.

"I used to think about it every other Thursday." Lionel ate a bite of his sandwich. "But then I'd get invited to an industry function that served lamb medallions and chocolate torte. Cigarettes might kill you but they'll never make you fat; I'd rather die of lung cancer than get a middle-aged spread."

"You're thin as a rail." Juliet couldn't help but smile.

"Do you really think a diet of scotch and cigarettes will allow me to live to eighty?" Lionel raised his eyebrow. "I do try to keep in shape, I swim thirty laps a day."

He put the plate in the sink and entered the living room. He filled a glass with bourbon and sat on a striped love seat.

"Have you ever wanted something so badly you can't sleep? You lie on Egyptian cotton sheets reciting William Blake and think you'd give anything to close your eyes. When you do manage to drift off, the thing you want is so close you believe life is suddenly glorious and you can achieve your goals." Lionel ran his fingers over the rim. "But then you wake up and the heater is hissing and you realize it was just a dream."

"When I graduated from college my roommate was moving to Florence and selling her Mazda for practically nothing," Juliet mused. "I never had my own car and pictured visiting the farmer's markets on the Hudson. But I couldn't find an apartment in Brooklyn with a parking space so she gave it to her boyfriend."

"I'm not talking about a bloody car, I'm talking about love," Lionel snapped. "When you're standing in the shower or jogging around the park and all you can see is a pair of full breasts and a small waist and long legs."

"I wouldn't know." Juliet blushed.

"I got a job as a valet at Claridge's," Lionel continued. "Six nights a week I carried Louis Vuitton suitcases through the marble lobby and let small dogs in knitted sweaters nip my feet. I opened doors for men in white dinner jackets and women trailing mink coats.

"But I didn't complain because I had all day to write songs." His eyes darkened. "Except I pictured Samantha's blond hair and blue eyes and couldn't write a word."

"What happened after you had dinner with Samantha?" Juliet asked. "Did you see her again?"

"If love was that easy my career would have been over twenty-five years ago." Lionel sighed. "No one would decipher the lyrics of love songs trying to understand why suddenly the juciest steak tasted like cardboard and they couldn't remember their own name."

He took a sip of bourbon and closed his eyes. He saw his room above the garage with its narrow bed and wood desk and Tiffany lamp. He pictured the dormer window and view of Eaton Square. He remembered crumpling up notepaper and tossing it into the garbage.

Lionel stuck his hands in his pockets and crossed the gravel driveway. He saw the main house with its white columns and wrought iron balconies. He inhaled the scent of hibiscus and dahlias and suddenly missed Cambridge with its tall spirals and leafy gardens.

Penelope had offered him room and board in exchange for tutoring the twins in writing. Lionel loved the main house with its vast kitchen and sunny conservatory and indoor swimming pool. He loved the pantry stocked with jars of orange marmalade and lemon curd. Mostly he loved having access to the Grahams' library. He could spend hours flopped on an ottoman reading Oscar Wilde and Rupert Brooke.

Lionel entered the library and approached the walnut bookshelf. He selected *Of Human Bondage* and *A Sentimental Education*. He added *Madame Bovary* and clutched them to his chest.

Ever since he met Samantha he couldn't stop thinking about her. He wrote a note thanking her for dinner and hoping to see her again. He dropped it in the mailbox of the Georgian manor and waited for someone to walk outside. He saw a maid in a black uniform collect the mail and hurried away.

He tried to write lyrics but the words came in the wrong order. He jogged around Eaton Square and swam laps in the indoor pool. Mostly he sat in the library and read books about unrequited love.

He carried the books into the hallway and heard voices in the study. He peered through the door and saw silver candelabras and a gold silk sofa and thick white carpet. A Degas stood over the fireplace and a Waterford vase was filled with yellow orchids.

"Lionel," Penelope called. She wore a navy Dior suit and tan pumps. "Have you met Georgina? Samantha is her children's nanny."

"It's a pleasure to meet you," Lionel said, as he held out his hand.

"You took Samantha out to dinner!" Georgina exclaimed. She had strawberry blond hair and hazel eyes. "It's a pity you have a girlfriend in Cambridge."

"A girlfriend in Cambridge?" Lionel repeated.

"Samantha said you had a lovely time, but you have a girlfriend." Georgina fiddled with a porcelain teacup. "She said it was very nice of you to take her out and she's sure you'll remain friends."

"Do you have her phone number?" Lionel asked. "She gave it to me but I misplaced it."

"She has a private line in her room." Georgina scribbled on a piece of paper and handed it to Lionel.

He slipped it in his pocket and smiled. "I promised to lend her some books, she loves to read and doesn't have a library card."

Lionel ran up the steps above the garage and entered his room. He flung the books on the bed and picked up the phone.

"Why did you tell Georgina I had a girlfriend in Cambridge?" he demanded.

The phone was silent but finally Samantha's voice came down the line. "I didn't want her to ask if we were going out again. She means well but she's too concerned about my happiness."

"How could you lie?" Lionel asked. "I thought nice Irish girls always told the truth."

"I'm sure with your dark curls and public school education you left a string of girls behind," Samantha replied. "I have to go, I'm taking Abigail to her piano lesson."

"You won't go out with me because my parents have a tennis court?"

"I don't have time to date, I have a full-time job and I'm studying for my entrance exams," Samantha explained. "And I really don't think we have anything in common."

Lionel clutched the phone and felt his heart race. He pictured Samantha's smooth blond hair and blue eyes and knew he couldn't let her hang up.

"You have to give me a chance. We'll have dinner in Mayfair and go dancing at Raffles. We'll visit the National History Museum or see *Swan Lake* at Covent Garden," Lionel insisted. "I'll rent a car and we'll drive into the country. We'll have lunch at a pub and row a boat on the Thames."

"You have a lot of free time for someone who is determined to be a songwriter," Samantha murmured.

"You don't know what you've done. I open a book and read the same chapter three times. I make a sandwich and forget the bread." Lionel groaned. "Yesterday I walked to the newsagent in my dressing gown. And I sit at my desk and can't write a word."

"I'm sure it's just writer's block," Samantha soothed.

"I was creating brilliant lyrics until you came along," Lionel exclaimed. "Now I couldn't write a jingle for laundry detergent."

"Maybe you should change professions," Samantha suggested. "You could be a chef or an actor or a ski instructor."

"You think this is funny," Lionel retorted. "I have to write, it's the most important thing in the world. Without writing songs I have absolutely nothing."

"Then I'm sure it will come back to you," Samantha replied. "Try vodka and tomato juice, it's the cure for anything."

Lionel heard the phone click and slumped on the bed. He put his head in his hands and let out a low moan. He heard the phone ring and picked it up.

"All right, I will go out with you."

"I have Thursday night off." Lionel jumped up. "I'll make dinner reservations at the Savoy and then we'll see *Cats*. I have a friend who's the stage manager, he'll get us box seats."

"I'm taking Abigail and her friends to the puppet show at Regent's Park this afternoon," Samantha replied. "You can meet us at the side gate at one o'clock."

"You want me to chaperone a group of eight-year-old girls to a puppet show?" Lionel spluttered.

"Wear something that doesn't stain," Samantha said. "The girls always want someone to hold their ice cream cones when they ride the carousel."

Lionel wiped his brow and slipped his hands in his pockets. He gazed at the throng of boys and girls surrounding the puppet stage and thought he'd give anything for a scotch and a cigarette.

He had spent the last three hours waiting in line for mince pies and fairy floss. He held Abigail's doll when she rode the Ferris wheel and let himself be blindfolded for a game of pin the tail on the donkey. He barely saw Samantha because she was busy making sure the girls didn't fall in the lake or eat too many bread rolls at lunch.

Halfway through the afternoon, he was determined to tell her she could find another babysitter. But then he saw her tying Abigail's shoelace and felt his heart melt. He studied her blue eyes and alabaster skin and wanted to run his finger over her mouth.

He leaned against an oak tree and waited for Lucy to come out of the bathroom.

"Excuse me." He stopped an older woman with silver hair. "Could you see if there's a little girl inside, blond pigtails wearing a blue sailor dress?"

The woman raised her eyebrows and Lionel flushed.

"I'm watching her for a friend and I'm afraid she might be sick."

Lionel waited while the woman went inside.

She appeared at the door. "There's no one in there."

"She has to be." Lionel's pulse raced. "I've been guarding the entrance."

"Well you haven't been doing a very good job," she turned around. "I'm afraid you lost her."

Lionel raced through the park past the cricket field and the netball court. He searched the playground and the souvenir shop. Finally he reached the lake and noticed a paddleboat in the middle of the water. He saw a small blond girl hunched over the steering wheel.

"Lucy!" he called. "What are you doing? Paddle back to shore."

"I can't," she called back.

"Of course you can," Lionel pleaded. "Put your feet on the pedals."

"I won't." Lucy shook her head. "I'm afraid of the water."

Lionel searched the dock for boats, but they were all out on the lake. He undid his leather belt and slipped off his Ferragamo loafers. He took a deep breath and dived into the water.

He paddled Lucy's boat back to shore and carried her on his shoulders to the puppet show. He set her gently on the ground and she flung herself against his legs. Samantha tried to be angry, but she saw his shirt collar sticking to his neck and his pants covered in mud and covered her face with her hands.

They sat in a café eating vanilla custard and blueberry scones with Devonshire cream. Lionel poured Earl Grey tea into a porcelain cup and added cream and sugar.

"There were two entrances to the bathroom," he explained. "Lucy went out one entrance while I was waiting at the other."

"You're a hero, the girls thought you Prince Charming rescuing Rapunzel." Samantha nibbled a cucumber sandwich.

"Lucy should have remembered she was afraid of water before she climbed in the boat," Lionel grumbled. "I ruined a Ralph Lauren shirt."

"At least you took off your loafers," Samantha said. "Water is terrible for Italian leather."

Lionel bristled. "It's not a crime to like nice shoes. If you invited me to spend the afternoon trailing after little girls with freckles and runny noses so I wouldn't want to see you again, it didn't work. I'd gladly jump in the river for you any day of the week."

"It's a man-made lake, not a river," Samantha corrected. "I invited you for two reasons. Even if I don't agree with your goals, there's nothing more important than having a dream. I didn't want to be the person who ruined it."

"What's the other reason?" Lionel asked.

Samantha looked at Lionel and her face lit up in a smile. "You do have lovely curls and nice eyes."

Lionel put his shot glass on the maple side table and stood up. "That's enough for today, I need some lunch."

"Did Samantha go out with you again?" Juliet asked.

"That's the thing about a love story, everyone wants to know how it ends. Songwriters today think they have to talk about racial equality or the energy crisis but all people care about is how a boy meets a girl."

"I'm only interested in you fulfilling your contract or repaying Gideon one hundred sixty-six thousand dollars," Juliet replied.

"You do know how to ruin a perfectly fine afternoon." Lionel flinched. "I'm going to make a Spanish omelet, would you like to join me?"

"I had a late breakfast." Juliet shook her head.

"I use my mother's recipe; she put milk in the frying pan." Lionel walked to the kitchen. "It makes the eggs fluffy."

"It sounds delicious." Juliet followed him down the hallway. "But I have to write a report."

"If I'm here alone I'll finish the whole omelet myself." He opened the fridge and took out a tomato and a wedge of feta cheese and a green onion. "Gideon won't be happy if I have a heart attack from eating too much cholesterol."

Juliet sat on a leather stool and let her shoulders relax. "I'll stay, but you have to go upstairs and change. I'm not eating lunch with someone wearing pajamas."

Lionel placed ceramic plates in the sink and turned on the faucet. He draped a dishtowel over his shoulder and pictured Juliet's yellow knit dress and white sandals.

Lionel had set the table with a white linen tablecloth and crystal water glasses. He served omelets and scones with strawberry jam. They drank fresh squeezed orange juice and talked about the British music scene in the 1990s.

He told her about sharing the stage with Eric Clapton and drinking Manhattans with Robbie Williams. They talked about hip-hop and the Latin invasion and the never-ending new boy bands. Finally Juliet thanked him for a delicious lunch and said she had to run some errands.

Lionel tossed the dishtowel on the tile counter and walked onto the balcony. He could go down to the newsagent and buy a pack of cigarettes. But he'd have to listen to Manuel complain his shop wasn't a library and he couldn't buy everything on credit.

He could open a bottle of Château Petrus Merlot and lie on a chaise longue by the swimming pool. But the sun was too bright and his head still ached from half a bottle of bourbon.

He entered the living room and glanced at the floral sofas and marble fireplace. He saw the oak floors and baby grand piano standing by the window.

He walked to the piano and sat on the bench. The lid was open and he ran his fingers over the keys. He put his head in his hands and wept.

chapter five

JULIET STROLLED ALONG THE PROMENADE of Puerto de Sóller and gazed at the cafés filled with men wearing navy blazers and women in pastel chiffon dresses. She saw waiters carrying platters of fresh scallops and warm baguettes. She inhaled the scent of tomato and garlic and remembered eating lunch in Lionel's garden.

It had been lovely to sit under the trellis and eat fluffy eggs and scones. It had been fun to hear about Elton John's costume ball at his castle in Windsor.

The moment she left Casa Rosa her shoulders tensed. Lionel wasn't any closer to writing new songs and she had nothing to show Gideon. She hurried to her hotel room and changed into a linen dress and leather sling backs. She slipped the pile of books into her Coach bag and took the tram to Puerto de Sóller.

She opened the gate of Casa Isabella and climbed the stone steps. She lingered in the garden, inhaling the scent of hibiscus and roses. It was almost 9 P.M. and she heard a violin playing and glasses clinking and people laughing. She peered in the window and saw tables set with wide white plates and gleaming silverware.

"Juliet." Gabriella appeared on the porch. She wore a green dress and beige pumps. Her hair was wound into a bun and secured with a ceramic chopstick. "I'm afraid it's too late for dinner. Our last seating was an hour ago."

"I brought a present for Lydia." Juliet reached into her bag. "To thank her for lunch."

"How wonderful." Gabriella examined the books. "She loved meeting you. She said Americans have so much energy, they make her feel lazy."

"I want to talk to you about something," Juliet said. "Maybe we could have a cup of coffee after the restaurant closes."

"I would love to but the dishwasher went home early so I have to clean up," Gabriella replied. "My father doesn't believe in automatic dishwashers, he thinks they scratch the china and smudge the wineglasses."

"I spent two years at summer camp in the Catskills making beds and washing dishes." Juliet grinned. "I'll stay and help you."

"I'll get you a glass of rosé and a bowl of tiramisu while you wait." Gabriella ushered her into the dining room.

Juliet sipped a smooth red wine and gazed at the high plaster ceilings and polished wood floors. She saw the turquoise silk drapes and mosaic bar and thought she'd never been anywhere so lovely. She watched Gabriella collect dessert menus and wondered how she was going to convince her. Then she remembered her high clear voice and shivered.

"There's always one guest who wants to stay and tell you how much he loved the quail with figs and caramelized onions," Gabriella said, handing Juliet an apron.

The last diners finally left and Gabriella dimmed the lights in the dining room. She poured two cups of coffee from a silver urn and added cream and sugar. Now they stood in the stone kitchen, loading dishes into the sink.

"I want to say that my feet ache and all I want to do is go upstairs and take a bath. But I can't leave until they finish telling me my father is a brilliant chef and they haven't eaten such tender duck breast since Tour d'Argent in Paris."

"You're wonderful with people." Juliet picked up a dishtowel. "You make it look so easy."

"My mother and I take turns overseeing the dining room. It's like hosting an elegant dinner party," Gabriella mused. "You want people to remember the soft music and flickering candles and sparkling champagne. And you want them to long for another bite of poached salmon and confited artichoke."

"Have you ever thought about doing anything else?" Juliet asked.

"Hugo would love to open our own café in Deia," Gabriella replied. "A space with wood floors and whitewashed walls and huge glass windows. But we have to wait, it's expensive to start a new restaurant."

"I know a way you could make enough money to buy almost any restaurant in Majorca," Juliet said, as she folded her dishtowel. "You could outfit the kitchen with stainless steel appliances and stock the wine cellar with wines from France and Italy. You could serve foie gras and oysters and caviar."

"We don't deal drugs and I don't play the lottery." Gabriella frowned.

"I've heard Mariah Carey sing at Madison Square Garden and Coldplay perform at Wembley Stadium. I stood backstage at the Hollywood Bowl and listened to the crowd cheer for Taylor Swift, but I never felt my heart race like when I heard you singing in the kitchen."

"Anyone can sing when your hands are immersed in bubbles and you think no one is listening." Gabriella laughed.

"We could make a tape and send it to Gideon," Juliet continued. "He'd fly you to Los Angeles and give you a car and an apartment in Santa Monica. I guarantee your first single will be number one on *Billboard* and iTunes."

Gabriella rinsed the plates and piled them on the tile counter.

"I'm flattered, but I could never leave my family. In America young people go to university or get a new job and end up living on the opposite coast. In Majorca the same priest baptizes you and marries you and his son presides over your funeral."

"You wouldn't have to be in Los Angeles forever," Juliet urged. "You could return to Majorca and you and Hugo could do whatever you want."

"Eventually my brothers will take over Casa Isabella and Hugo and I will open our own restaurant." Gabriella sunk her hands into the hot water. "We'll work so late we'll fall into bed with our clothes on, but when people start clamoring for a reservation and say they've never tasted such fragrant Majorcan vegetables, we'll know we did it ourselves."

Juliet heard footsteps and saw a young man standing in the doorway. He looked like a movie star with dark curly hair and blue eyes and a cleft on his chin. He wore jeans and a denim jacket and sneakers.

"Hugo!" Gabriella called. "This is my American friend Juliet. She offered to help me clean up."

"You'll have to forgive us." Hugo kissed Gabriella on the cheek. "We don't usually ask guests to do the dishes."

"I love this kitchen, it reminds me of summer houses in the Hamptons." Juliet smiled. "I attended a party at Billy Joel's estate and his kitchen was as big as my apartment."

"Juliet works for a record label," Gabriella explained. "She knows lots of famous people."

Juliet opened her mouth to say something but she saw Gabriella's eyes sparkle and her cheeks glow. Hugo whispered in Gabriella's ear and Gabriella flushed. She took off her apron and smoothed her skirt.

"Hugo insists we sample a new tapas bar," Gabriella said. "Would you like to join us?"

"I'm going home." Juliet shook her head. "A warm bath and a glass of sangria suddenly sound delicious."

Juliet stepped out of the porcelain bathtub and slipped on a soft cotton robe. She stood on the balcony and inhaled the crisp night air. It was almost midnight and lights twinkled on the plaza. She heard music and people laughing.

She pictured Hugo whispering in Gabriella's ear and Gabriella's cheeks turn pink. She saw Gabriella fix Hugo's collar and kiss him on the mouth. They seemed so in love, like a couple on top of a wedding cake.

She thought about Lionel's story and wondered if he saw Samantha again. How dare he ask if she ever wanted anything so badly, she couldn't eat or sleep?

She walked inside and climbed onto the four-poster bed. The comforter covered her shoulders and the cotton sheets felt smooth against her skin. She closed her eyes and let the tears spill down her cheeks.

chapter six

LIONEL STOOD AT THE KITCHEN counter and sprinkled sugar on fruit salad. He poured muesli into a ceramic bowl and added sliced bananas. He stirred cream into black coffee and sat at the oak kitchen table.

He had woken early and padded down the wood staircase. He collected magazines and newspapers and stuffed them in the garbage. He emptied ashtrays and dusted the glass coffee table. Then he polished the crystal vase and replaced wilted daisies with yellow sunflowers.

Now he ate a large spoonful of muesli and wondered what to do with all his energy. He could go for a swim but he had already shaved and showered. He rubbed his cheeks and felt the sheen of sandalwood shaving cream. He glanced at his reflection in the fridge and admired his patterned Robert Graham shirt.

Finally he picked up his coffee cup and entered the living room. He searched the Regency desk and found a notepad and pencil. He sat on the striped love seat and stretched his long legs in front of him. He opened the first page and began to scribble.

"Your new maid is wonderful." Juliet had appeared at the door. She wore an orange blouse and beige capris and silver sandals. Her brown hair was tucked behind her ears and she wore silver earrings. "This room looks like a spread in *Architectural Digest*."

"Most people knock before they enter someone's house." Lionel started, stuffing the notepad beneath the cushions. "I fired the last maid, she scented my shirts with cologne. I smelled like the Armani counter at Harrods. I woke up early and cleaned the villa myself; manual labor can be therapeutic."

"I can't imagine you lifting more than a shot glass." Juliet smiled, sitting on the floral sofa.

"When I worked at Claridge's, I spent hours polishing shoes and stacking luggage. By the time I finished my shift I had written whole songs in my head." Lionel glanced at Juliet and noticed her cheeks were pale and she had circles under her eyes.

"You look a little bedraggled," he mused, pulling a gold cigarette case out of his slacks. "Let me guess, your room is next to the honeymoon suite and the walls are so thin the couple kept you awake. I told you Gideon is cheap. He'd take me to dinner at the Connaught and order lobster and truffles and Rémy Martin cognac. Then he'd examine the bill and quibble over an extra scoop of ice cream."

"My hotel is lovely," Juliet said, flushing. "I'm probably still jet-lagged, I tossed and turned all night."

"You should go dancing at Barracuda's in Palma. There's no

better sleeping pill than a double martini and an hour on a sweaty dance floor. You'll stumble to your hotel room and fall asleep in your stilettos."

"I don't have time to dance. I have to think about my job," Juliet insisted.

"That's where you're wrong. Being in love is like drinking absinthe, your mind clears and you think you can achieve anything. I remember my first proper date with Samantha, I felt like Clark Kent becoming Superman." He lit the cigarette with a pearl lighter and blew a thin trail of smoke. "God, she was beautiful. All blond hair and creamy skin, like a figure in a Raphael painting."

Lionel climbed the steps of the white Georgian manor and rang the doorbell. He wore a navy polo shirt and pleated slacks. He juggled a paper bag in one hand and a bouquet of flowers in the other.

He had spent an hour in Harrods's food hall, selecting Godiva chocolates and a bunch of calla lilies. But he remembered Samantha's remarks about his public school education and pictured her giving the flowers to Georgina. Finally he went home and picked peonies from Penelope's garden. Then he searched the pantry and found homemade butterscotch biscuits.

"These are for you," he said, when she opened the door. "I wasn't sure what you liked, so I covered all bases."

Samantha wore a green minidress and white leather sandals. Her hair was scooped into a ponytail and tied with a green ribbon. Her eyelashes were coated with mascara and she wore pink lip-gloss.

"They smell wonderful." She glanced at his twill slacks and leather loafers. "I hope we're not going to an elegant restaurant where waiters pour three types of wine, like a game of cups at a child's birthday party. It's a gorgeous day, I'd rather eat a salad sandwich and feed the pigeons in Hyde Park."

Lionel took her arm and propelled her down the stairs. He stopped in front of a blue Mini and opened the passenger door.

"It's a surprise." He hopped into the driver's seat. "But I promise there won't be entrées with French names or wines that cost more than this car."

"Where did you get the car?" Samantha asked.

Lionel turned to her and grinned. "Penelope lent it to me. I hope I remember how to drive."

Lionel drove out of London and saw green fields and tall church spires. He glanced at the passenger seat and saw Samantha fiddle with the edge of her dress. He clutched the steering wheel and sucked in his breath.

They drove for almost two hours and Lionel longed to stop at a pub for a beer and a plate of fish and chips. Finally he pulled into a village with thatched houses and cobblestoned streets. There was a river and lush gardens and wide willow trees.

"Where are we?" Samantha asked.

"Stratford-upon-Avon." Lionel jumped out of the car. "Birthplace of the greatest poet of all time, William Shakespeare."

They stood in the courtyard of Holy Trinity Church and gazed at the stone monuments and stained glass windows. They visited Ann Hathaway's cottage and explored the Swan Theater. They bought vanilla drumsticks on High Street and watched canal boats glide along the Avon River.

Finally they walked to Henley Street and stopped in front of a house with a slanted roof and lacquered window boxes. It had tall hedges and fruit trees and a goldfish pond.

"Shakespeare's father was a successful glover, and they owned the largest house on Henley Street," Lionel said, leading Samantha into the garden. "William had a privileged childhood and attended the local grammar school. He lived here until he was in his early twenties and then he ran off to London. He wrote thirty-seven plays and a hundred and fifty-seven sonnets and is the most popular writer in history.

"I know you think I should do something important like become a doctor or a lawyer. But can you imagine a world without *Romeo and Juliet*? How many schoolchildren can recite Hamlet's soliloquy or know the words to Shakespeare's sonnets? I can never be like Shakespeare but I have to try. If I write one song that makes people want to get up in the morning or lyrics that make their day a little brighter, I'll have achieved my goal."

Samantha walked to the hedge and inhaled the scent of daffodils and tulips. Lionel studied her slender cheekbones and thought he should have stayed in London. He should have taken her to a smart bar in Knightsbridge or a hip café on King's Road.

She turned back to Lionel and adjusted her skirt. She looked at his curly dark hair and green eyes and smiled.

"You will."

"I will what?" Lionel asked.

"You will write songs they'll play on radio stations and in concert halls. Every artist will want to work with you and you'll have your own table at Annabelle's. You'll travel to Argentina and Turkey and fans will beg for your autograph."

Lionel leaned forward and kissed her softly on the lips. He inhaled the scent of her perfume and felt a throbbing in his chest.

"Let's go. He took her hand and led her onto Henley Street. He hurried along the sidewalk and stopped in front of a restaurant with striped awnings and plate glass windows.

"What are we doing?" Samantha frowned.

"We're going to Benson's and having raspberry scones with lemon curd and clotted cream. Because the only thing that will stop me from making love to you in the back of the car is to sit in a stuffy restaurant surrounded by middle-aged women eating lobster rolls and vanilla custard."

They sat at a table by the window and ate Scottish salmon and ham and tomato sandwiches. Lionel brushed her arm with his fingers and wanted to wrap his arms around her. He wanted to kiss her on the mouth and press her against his chest.

"If you're going to be a great songwriter you have to learn discipline." Samantha buttered a slice of tea cake.

"I'm extremely disciplined," Lionel protested. "I get up every morning and swim fifty laps in the pool. I drink a glass of orange juice and eat a slice of whole wheat toast. Then I sit at my desk until it's time to go to work."

"What do you do at your desk?" Samantha asked.

"I read Sir Walter Scott and Rudyard Kipling." Lionel wavered. "Sometimes I pull out a copy of *GQ* or *HELLO!* You never know where you'll get an idea for a song."

"You can't be distracted by glossy photos or celebrity exposés," Samantha insisted. "You have to sit at your desk with nothing but a notebook and a piece of paper. A real writer gets his inspiration from within."

Lionel watched her spread strawberry preserve on a warm scone and felt his heart lift. He searched his pocket for a pen and scribbled on a napkin.

"What are you doing?" Samantha asked.

Lionel looked up and his eyes sparkled. "I'm writing a love song to the most beautiful girl in the world."

Lionel stubbed out his cigarette and glanced at Juliet's pale cheeks and watery eyes. He walked to the mosaic bar and poured a glass of Grey Goose. He added a twist of lime and handed it to Juliet.

"Drink this, vodka is the cure for everything," he insisted. "It goes down as easily as the cough syrup my mother gave me as a child. I always wondered why she allowed me to have chocolate syrup at bedtime."

"I don't drink during the day." Juliet shook her head.

"You do today; I thought American women were so strong they could trek through Nepal with nothing but a backpack or float down the Amazon in a bikini and sunscreen." Lionel paused. "You are as pale as a character in a Henry James novel."

Juliet took a sip and grimaced. "I must have eaten a bad piece of fruit at breakfast, I'm going to the hotel and lie down."

"You can sit by the pool," Lionel suggested. "I'll rustle up a tostada and a bowl of cold tomato soup."

"I might feel better if you tried to write a song," Juliet replied. "I have to e-mail Gideon and tell him my progress. Think about your first date with Samantha, surely you could write some lyrics about the heady rush of meeting someone new."

"I'm not a trained monkey," Lionel snapped. "I can't write songs on cue."

"Then I should go. I have work to catch up on." Juliet stood up. "I'll see you tomorrow."

Lionel stood at the French doors and glanced at the turquoise swimming pool. Why had he invited Juliet to stay when he couldn't wait to get rid of her? He pictured her drawn cheeks and thought he was only trying to make her feel better.

He walked to the bar and poured a shot of Grey Goose. The alcohol made his throat burn and his eyes sting. He put the empty glass back on the bar and sat on the striped love seat.

He dug the notepad from under the cushions and flipped it open. After he covered two pages in tight cursive he leaned against the silk cushions and put his head in his hands.

He jumped up and walked to the Regency desk. He sifted through the papers and found his leather-bound address book. He grabbed his phone and dialed the number.

chapter seven

Juliet sat at the dressing table and dusted her cheeks with powder. She smoothed her hair behind her ears and rubbed her lips with pink lip-gloss. She glanced at the bowl of peaches housekeeping left on the glass coffee table and realized she was starving.

She had come back from Lionel's villa and climbed into the four-poster bed. She pulled the floral comforter around her shoulders and tried to stop shaking. Finally she closed her eyes and woke to the sound of church bells ringing. She glanced at the sun streaming through the white shutters and realized it was early afternoon.

She called Lionel to apologize and he insisted she spend the rest of the day in bed. She had a summer cold and he didn't want Gideon to blame him if it got worse.

She wrapped herself in a cotton robe and sat on a chaise longue in the garden. She gazed at the twinkling Mediterranean and boats bobbing in the harbor and thought how much she loved Majorca. Everywhere she looked there were green inlets and elegant pastel colored villas.

Now it was almost sunset and the sky turned a muted purple. She slipped on gold sandals and gathered her purse. She was meeting Gabriella in Sóller for dinner and didn't want to be late.

She remembered Gabriella's clear voice drifting through the kitchen and wished she could convince her to record a tape. She pictured Hugo's arms wrapped around Gabriella's waist and felt an empty pit in her stomach.

She ran down the wood staircase and heard her phone buzz. She slipped it out of her purse and read the text. She looked up and saw the concierge standing at the marble desk.

"Good evening, Miss Lyman," the concierge called. "I see you made reservations for two at Ca'n Pintxo. You and your date will enjoy the roasted sea bream, it's the best on the island."

"I was meeting a friend but she just texted and canceled." Juliet looked up from her phone. "Her mother twisted her ankle and she has to work."

"I'm sure you'll find another dining companion." The concierge studied her chiffon dress and small diamond earrings. "It's Friday night and the plaza will be full of young people."

"I think I'll just order room service." Juliet sighed. "Perhaps you could send up a plate of tapas and a bowl of soup."

"I'm afraid room service is unavailable," the concierge explained. "We are having a reception for guests on the terrace. Chef Pedro has prepared a luscious spread including beef tartar and Majorcan vegetables."

Juliet peered outside and saw gold tablecloths set with flickering candles and bottles of olive oil. There were platters of sea bass and grilled scallops and veal medallions. She inhaled the scent of butter and garlic and felt her shoulders relax.

"That sounds wonderful." She followed him onto the patio. "I would love a glass of Torres Pinot Noir."

She stood under the trellis and gazed at the lush gardens. It was almost dark and silver lights twinkled above the swimming pool. She watched waiters in white dinner jackets pass trays of lobster ravioli and smiled.

"I haven't seen you before, are you here on business on pleasure?" A man approached her. He had curly blond hair and wore a blue shirt and tan slacks. "Majorca is one of Europe's best kept secrets. Most people think they have to go to the French Riviera for spectacular beaches or the Italian lakes for gourmet cuisine, but Majorca has fabulous views and delicious seafood and swimming and sailing."

"I'm here on business. I only arrived a few days ago but I love everything about it," Juliet replied. "I've never seen so many colors and everyone is friendly."

"Let me guess," the man said. "You're a model preparing for the runway shows in Paris or an international attorney celebrating winning a big case in Madrid."

"You wouldn't make a very good Sherlock Holmes." Juliet laughed. "I'm an executive at a record label in Los Angeles, I'm working with a songwriter."

"Then you're wasting a very good pair of legs." He grinned. "My name is Henry. I'm a tennis player and my coach rents a hacienda in Palma. Every night he hosts a party with smoked salmon and bottles of tequila and dancing. But the music is too loud and everybody smokes. I'd rather watch the sunset and eat black truffle risotto."

"I wanted to stay in my room and order room service but the concierge said it wasn't available." Juliet nodded.

Henry studied her brown hair and blue eyes and small pink mouth. He ate a last bite of risotto and his face lit up in a smile.

"I'm glad you came; my coach doesn't let me eat dessert. Maybe we can share a slice of almond cake."

They sat at a round table and ate lamb skewers. Juliet watched the sun melt into the Mediterranean and felt light and happy.

"I'm from New Zealand," Henry said. "Everyone thinks it's just green valleys and sheep but we have an opera house and a World Cup sailing team. I wish I could go home more often, but it's a fourteen-hour flight from almost anywhere and if I don't have extra legroom I get a crick in my neck."

"I worked with a band from New Zealand," Juliet mused. "They'd never been to America before, they thought everywhere we went was Disneyland. They filled their suitcases with boxes of Honey Nut Cheerios and Cinnamon Toast Crunch because they'd never seen so many kinds of cereal."

"I've played tennis in the mountains of Peru and at an ashram in India and a castle in Scotland. I love seeing new places but sometimes I wish I went to the same office every day like my father. Every night he trades his briefcase for a martini and on Sundays they eat lunch at the club." He sipped his drink. "But I could never sit still, the only place I'm happy is on a tennis court slamming a ball across the net."

"When I'm in the recording studio I live on black coffee and turkey sandwiches with mayonnaise and wilted lettuce. At night I can't sleep because I have music tracks running through my head." Juliet clutched her wineglass. "But when I'm driving on the I-405 and hear that new song on the radio, I feel like my heart is going to explode."

They ate silver bowls of pistachio ice cream with sliced kiwis. Juliet felt the breeze blow down from the mountains and wrapped her arms around her chest.

"This has been lovely." She stood up. "But I'm going upstairs to bed."

"I forgot your name." Henry jumped up.

"I didn't tell you." Juliet frowned.

Henry slipped his hands in his pockets and smiled. "Then, we'll have to fix that."

Juliet walked to the French doors and turned around. She gazed at the night sky full of stars and at the turquoise swimming pool and pink bougainvillea. She saw Henry's blond hair and broad shoulders.

"It's Juliet," she called. "It's a pleasure to meet you."

Juliet slipped off her sandals and stood on the balcony. She felt her cheeks flush and her heart beat a little faster. It had been fun to drink a glass of rosé and talk to Henry. It was lovely to feel young and bright and pretty.

She pictured Lionel saying she didn't believe in love and flinched. She loved everything about her life: Yesterday Records' glass offices in Santa Monica, her studio apartment a block from the beach, and attending concerts and awards shows and night-club openings.

Suddenly her head throbbed and her shoulders tightened. She walked inside and picked up a paperback book. She climbed onto the four-poster bed and began to read.

chapter eight

LIONEL STOOD UP FROM THE piano and walked to the marble bar in the living room. He poured a glass of scotch and gazed at the candy wrappers and crumpled pieces of paper scattered over the wood floor.

He woke at 3 A.M. and couldn't go back to sleep. The house was quiet and he padded downstairs to the library and searched the shelves. He selected leather volumes of Oscar Wilde and Emily Dickinson and Wordsworth. Finally he tossed the books on the mantel and entered the living room.

The piano was open and he leaned down and inhaled the scent of mahogany and lemon polish. He sat on the wood bench and opened his notebook.

Now he carried his shot glass to the Regency desk and flipped the pages of the notebook. He read the verses quickly and felt his heart hammer in his chest. He read it again and let out his breath.

He thought of all the years he wrote love songs: the midnight snacks of sausage rolls and butterscotch pudding, the endless supply of scotch and cigarettes. He pictured his unbrushed hair and cheeks covered in stubble. He remembered the moment he knew he could discard all the scraps of paper because he had written the perfect song.

He gazed at the rumpled cushions and half-eaten Cadbury Fruit & Nut bar. Juliet would be here soon and he was too exhausted to clean up. What would she say if he told her he wrote the first song in twelve months and it was the best thing he'd written in years?

Then he pictured Gideon in his impeccable Brooks Brothers suit and shuddered. If he told Juliet she would insist he write more songs. And even if he could, would he really give them to Gideon? He sunk on the floral sofa and put his head in his hands.

He heard a knock at the door and jumped up. He scooped up the crumpled sheets of paper and tossed them in the garbage. He grabbed his notebook and shoved it in the desk drawer.

"Your day of rest seemed to do wonders." Lionel opened the door. "You look like an ad in a glossy travel magazine."

Juliet flushed and fiddled with her silver necklace. She wore a yellow linen dress and white sandals. Her hair was held back with a ceramic clip and she wore pink lip-gloss.

"It was just a summer cold." Juliet entered the living room. She gazed at the open bottle of vodka and empty shot glass and raised her eyebrow. "You should open a window, it smells like a nightclub in here."

"I couldn't sleep and sleeping pills can be so addictive. At least with vodka you wake up with a hangover; those lovely little pills look so innocent and the next thing you know you end up like Marilyn Monroe or Judy Garland."

"I'll clean up if you want to go upstairs and get dressed." Juliet picked up a stray piece of paper.

"No! We don't want to upset Gloria." He grabbed the piece of paper and stuffed it in his pajama pocket. "The agency sent over a new maid yesterday; she's in her fifties with black hair and a mustache. I tried doing the dishes but she rapped my hands with a dishtowel and sent me out of the kitchen."

"Why don't we go into the study," he continued. "I'll get a pitcher of orange juice and a plate of muffins and we'll get started."

Juliet entered the study and gazed at the turquoise rug and orange plaster walls. Yellow curtains opened onto the garden and a beige sofa was covered with brightly colored cushions. The coffee table held a stack of magazines and an enamel fruit bowl.

"I didn't know you followed tennis," Juliet said, as she picked up a tennis magazine.

"I've played since I was a boy." Lionel carried a silver tray with a crystal pitcher and blueberry muffins and pots of butter. "It's one of the few sports where grown men don't fight over a ball. I attend Wimbledon every year; it's an excellent place to catch up on music gossip. Sting has his own box and Bono never misses a match."

"I met him at the hotel last night." Juliet pointed to the man on the cover. He had blond curly hair and wide shoulders. He wore a green Adidas shirt and white shorts.

"Henry Adler." Lionel glanced at the magazine. "He was the boy wonder from New Zealand until he injured his back. Three grand slams by the age of twenty-five and a sixth-set upset of Federer at Forest Lawn. God I'd hate to be a professional tennis player: one minute you're an invincible god, the next some young pug who just learned to tie his shoelaces sends the ball over your head and makes you look like you need a walker.

"He's been out for two years but he's making a comeback," Lionel continued, buttering a muffin. "I've read he's very unassuming. He's not one of those tennis Casanovas who thinks his racquet is some large appendage."

"We just shared a slice of almond cake and talked about Majorca." Juliet's cheeks turned pink. She picked up the magazine and studied it closely. "I wonder what it's like to have a whole stadium hold their breath waiting for you to serve."

"You don't worry about the crowd when you're standing on center court, all you care about is connecting with the ball." Lionel bristled. "It's like when you write the perfect song. You don't think about radio stations or music videos, you just want to soak up the words."

"I always thought writing a song is like having a new lover: you let the porridge get cold and leave your socks in the dryer because all you can think about is her floral scent." He paused and his eyes dimmed. "Later, you want to shout from the steps of Buckingham Palace that you're in love, but in the beginning you just want to memorize the shape of her neck and the curve of her thigh."

"Speaking of love, how are the new songs coming?" Juliet asked. "Every night I go back to my room to a new e-mail from Gideon asking when you're going to deliver the lyrics. I wrote back you're inspired by the Majorcan sunsets and gorgeous scenery and working feverishly."

"Just thinking about Gideon makes me ill," Lionel said irritably. "I have no desire to make him happy."

"Well I have a strong desire to have you fulfill your contract and keep my job," Juliet retorted. "If I don't tell him something, he'll book me on the next Virgin flight to Los Angeles."

"He won't do that, last minute reservations cost a fortune," Lionel grumbled. "I'm fulfilling my end of the deal, I'm telling you about Samantha."

Lionel strolled down Elizabeth Street and stopped in front of Baker & Spice. He gazed at the trays of hot cross buns and vanilla custards and strawberry tarts. He inhaled the scent of butter and cinnamon and thought he'd never been so happy.

May was usually filled with leaden skies and a constant drizzle. Eventually the news commentators on Channel Two would declare it the wettest spring in recent history. Suddenly it would stop raining and people would have picnics in Regent's Park, grateful the worst was over. Then it would start pouring again and not let up until August.

But for the last few weeks, Lionel had awoke to blue skies and fluffy white clouds. He jogged around Eaton Square and treated himself to poached eggs and hashers at the Ebury Café. He felt the wad of pounds in his pocket from his shift at Claridge's and felt rich and happy.

Next he would change into a shirt and slacks and climb the steps of the white Georgian manor. He and Samantha did everything together: they took Abigail and her friends to Madame Toussauds and to see the gorillas at the London Zoo. They visited the art galleries on Pimlico Street and spent hours browsing in Belgravia Books.

Lionel didn't even mind that they hadn't made love. He didn't want their first time to be on his narrow bed that smelled vaguely of disinfectant and Samantha refused to sneak him up the grand staircase to her room at Georgina's.

There was so much to discover about each other: Samantha grew up reading her brothers' adventure books: *Lord Jim*, by Joseph Conrad, and *Gulliver's Travels*. She dreamed of introducing a classroom of first formers to the joys of Mark Twain and Willkie Collins. Lionel admitted he got scared every time he read Edgar Allan Poe's "The Raven" and could never finish *Anna Karenina* without crying.

They rode the escalator at Harvey Nichol's and ate warm chicken sandwiches at Harrods's Tea Room. Lionel convinced Samantha to put on a silk dress and heels and have dinner at Alain Ducasse at the Dorchester. He ordered a bottle of Château Margaux Cabernet and a plate of escargots and felt drunk with happiness.

After dinner they strolled back to the Georgian manor and lingered on the stone steps. Samantha let him kiss her a little bit longer, her fingers stroking his hair. Lionel inhaled her scent of jasmine perfume and groaned.

Samantha gave him a final kiss and entered the double front doors. Lionel glanced up at the light flicker on in her bedroom and thought he never realized heaven could be so close.

Now he reached into his pocket for a pound note and took out a folded-up piece of paper. He scanned the page and grimaced.

He had finally written the song that would make him famous. He was as certain as he knew Sri Lanka would win the Cricket World Cup and Boris Becker would lose at Wimbledon. Every time he reread the six verses of iambic pentameter his chest expanded and a lump formed in his throat.

He needed to find a woman with a perfect voice and record the song in a studio. Then he could send it to producers in London and New York and Los Angeles. He put an ad in the *Telegraph* and got one response from a twenty-something woman from Newcastle. She weighed two hundred pounds and ate a whole tin of shortbread during their interview. He murmured he didn't think they were a match and tossed her résumé in the garbage.

He stuffed the paper in his pocket and glanced at a flyer in the window. He read it carefully and felt his heart pound. He ran the last three blocks to the white Georgian manor and raced up the stone steps.

"We're not going to see *Rosencrantz and Guildenstern* tonight," he said when Samantha opened the door. She wore a cotton sweater and capris and held a packet of colored pencils.

"That's fine, I have to go to Abigail's sports day this afternoon. Four hours of three-legged races and wheelbarrow races. I'll need a cup of hot tea and a warm bath."

"We're not going because we're going to the grand opening of the Chelsea Karaoke Bar." He showed her the flyer.

"I'm not fond of karaoke bars." Samantha hesitated. "They're noisy and people get so drunk they pass out in their chairs."

"We're going." Lionel spun her around and kissed her on the mouth. "Because we are going to find the ingénue who is going to make 'Rainy Sundays' the most requested song in England."

They sat at a round table near the stage and drank bottles of brown ale. They listened to men in polo shirts and loafers belt out the chorus of "Bohemian Rhapsody" and young women in miniskirts croon "Eternal Flame." Lionel peered through the smoke and wondered which girl with a shiny face and red lipstick would make his song a number one single.

"Your turn to go onstage," a man said to Samantha. He wore a plaid shirt and blue jeans and had an apron tied around his waist.

"No thank you." Samantha shook her head.

"Opening night rules," the man insisted. "All the lovely ladies have to perform."

"Then we'll leave, thank you." Samantha stood up and grabbed her purse.

"We have to stay," Lionel protested. "Somewhere in this room is a woman with the voice of an angel."

"I don't want to go onstage," Samantha frowned. She wore a yellow blouse and white slacks and yellow sandals. Her hair was knotted into a low bun and secured with an enamel chopstick.

"You only have to perform for a few minutes," Lionel begged. "Sing 'I Will Always Love You,' it's everyone's favorite."

Samantha walked onstage and Lionel took out his cigarette case. He dropped his silver lighter on the floor and bent down to pick it up. He heard a voice coming from the stage and froze.

He sat up and saw Samantha clutching the microphone. Her cheeks were pale and her lips quivered, but she had the most glorious voice he ever heard. He glanced around the room and saw men and women transfixed, their cigarettes dangling from their fingers. Even the bartender stopped pouring drinks and stared at the microphone.

She finished the song and the room erupted in applause. She put the microphone on the stool and walked back to their table. Lionel gazed at her wide blue eyes and pink mouth and slender cheekbones. He threw a ten-pound note on the table and grabbed her hand.

"Why didn't you tell me you could sing?" he asked, pacing around his room above the garage.

He was going to take her to the upstairs dining room at Thomas Cubbitt, but he realized they had to be somewhere completely private. Finally he took her arm and led her down Motcomb Street. He opened the door to his room and turned on the bedside lamp. He flung open the curtains and ushered her inside.

"Everyone sang in my family." Samantha shrugged, sitting tentatively on the brown bedspread. "My sister, Daphne, has a much better voice."

Lionel lit a cigarette and walked to the desk. He took out a piece of paper and handed it to Samantha.

"Sing this."

"I don't know which key," she said, wrinkling her forehead.

"Any key," Lionel pleaded. "Just sing it."

He turned to the window and gazed at the cherry blossom tree. He heard Samantha sing the first line and pause. She started again and suddenly her voice lifted and climbed. He stubbed out his cigarette and tried to stop his body from shaking.

He crossed the room and gathered her in his arms. He kissed her slowly, tasting salt and beer. He unfastened her hair and let it fall down her neck. He ran his hands over her breasts and groaned.

"I've wanted to do this for so long," he murmured. "All I want is to make you happy."

Samantha pulled away and her eyes sparkled. "How do I know you're as good in bed as you are on the piano?"

Lionel unbuttoned his shirt and ran his hands through his hair. He traced his fingers over her lips and whispered. "I'm going to show you."

Samantha kissed him gently on the mouth. He watched her unzip her slacks and wanted to admire her smooth thighs forever. But she clasped his firmness and stroked him until he was dizzy. She took his hand and guided it under her cotton panties. He gasped and thought he had never touched anything so exquisite. He felt the sweet wetness and knew he couldn't wait any longer.

He pulled her down on the bed and nudged her legs open. He felt her fingers press into his back and thought everything he knew about himself was wrong. Nothing mattered except the warm, wet space between her thighs and watching her expression change to one of sheer joy.

Lionel sat at the window and turned on his desk lamp. He gazed at Samantha asleep on the bed and saw her creamy skin and luscious breasts. He saw her eyelids flicker and her mouth form a smile.

He opened the drawer and took out a wad of notes. He counted them and leaned back in his chair. He put the notes away and whispered: "Now, it's time to find a bloody recording studio."

"This muffin tastes like paper." Lionel dusted crumbs from his pajama pants. He glanced at the enamel bowl filled with peaches and ripe figs and frowned. "Sometimes all this tropical fruit gives me a stomach ache. What I'd give for a proper English breakfast: fried eggs and sausages and black pudding, with a side of toast and grilled tomatoes."

"Did Samantha record the song?" Juliet asked. "How did Gideon discover you?"

"We have to stop for today." Lionel put his plate on the glass coffee table. "I have an appointment with a barber in Sóller. I used to see a barber in Mayfair who lathered my cheeks with caviar and ground pearls while he cut my hair. I can see why women love going to the spa; there's nothing more luxurious than having skin like a newborn baby."

"But it's only one P.M.," Juliet protested. "We have all afternoon."

"You were sick, you should get some fresh air and exercise." He glanced at her yellow linen dress and white sandals. "Go swimming or play a game of tennis. Tennis is excellent for the cardiovascular system, and I've always thought female tennis players have the best legs. When I was a teenager, I had a poster of Gabriela Sabatini above my bed."

Lionel stood at the window and watched Juliet disappear through the gate. He found a compact disc and inserted it in the CD player. Samantha's high, clear voice filled the living room and he caught his breath.

He pictured his room above the garage with its narrow bed and wood desk. The cherry blossoms bloomed outside the window and the coffee table was littered with paperback books. He poured a shot of bourbon and took a long gulp.

chapter nine

JULIET CLIMBED OUT OF the swimming pool and wrapped herself in a fluffy white towel. She lay on the chaise longue and slipped on oval sunglasses. She glanced at the marble statues and trellises covered with roses and thought again she had never been anywhere so beautiful.

She had left the Casa Rosa and returned to her room. She scanned an e-mail from Gideon asking when he would receive Lionel's songs and felt a lump in her throat. She finally typed a note saying she was confident Lionel would fulfill his contract and pressed SEND. Then she changed into a red one-piece bathing suit and jumped into the pool.

Now she inhaled the scent of jasmine and hibiscus and wondered why Gideon and Lionel had had a falling out. She thought of all the photos she had seen of them together: riding in Gideon's white Bentley to the Grammys, arriving at the Montreux Jazz Festival, dining at Nobu with Chris Martin.

Juliet remembered the articles she'd read about Lionel: Lionel at his Malibu beach house, displaying his framed Julian Schnabel. Lionel in his pied-à-terre in Manhattan, sitting at his

Steinway baby grand piano. Lionel standing in front of his book-shelf in his flat in Chelsea, wearing a Gieves and Hawkes suit. She remembered his quote saying his two great indulgences were a library of signed first editions and a closet of Salvatore Ferragamo loafers.

She pictured Lionel in his rumpled silk pajamas and John Lobb suede slippers. She saw his hair uncombed and his chin covered with stubble. She saw the filled ashtrays and empty shot glasses and brightly colored candy wrappers. She remembered the sudden pain in his eyes when he told his story and shivered.

"You have the right idea," a male voice said. "I spent the day getting heatstroke on the tennis court. My coach is Swedish and doesn't believe in siestas. But he sits on the sidelines with a straw hat and a pitcher of lemonade."

Juliet looked up and saw Henry's blond hair and thick chest. He wore a blue T-shirt and white shorts. He carried his tennis racquet in one hand and a water bottle in the other.

"You have the pool to yourself, I was just drying off." Juliet blushed, instinctively wrapping herself in the towel. "I have to go upstairs and catch up on my e-mails."

"A friend of mine owns a restaurant in Palma," Henry said. "It just was awarded a Michelin star, I wondered if you'd join me for dinner."

"I'd love to but I'm meeting a friend and her boyfriend." Juliet hesitated. "She canceled last night because she had to work."

"Perhaps they could join us," Henry suggested. "He makes a delicious tuna tartar and his passion fruit sorbet is famous."

"That sounds wonderful." Her face lit up in a smile. "I'd love to."

Juliet stood in front of her closet and selected a turquoise chiffon dress. She fastened diamond earrings in her ears and spritzed her wrists with Estée Lauder Lovely.

She glanced at the ceramic fruit bowl on the coffee table and realized she was starving. She hadn't eaten all day except for Lionel's blueberry muffins. She pictured him carrying a tray of orange juice and warm muffins and pots of butter. She wondered what he'd say when she told him she had a date and giggled. Then she grabbed her purse and ran down the wood staircase.

They drove in Henry's yellow Fiat through the tunnel to Palma. Gabriella and Hugo sat in the back, chatting about his uncle's hotel and Casa Isabella. Juliet gripped the dashboard and felt like she was on Space Mountain. When the car emerged into the Plaza Maya she gazed up at La Seu Cathedral and finally exhaled.

Henry parked under an olive tree and they strolled along the Paseo del Borne. Juliet gazed at the wide promenade with its outdoor cafés and stone fountains and thought she was in Paris. She browsed in the windows of Céline and Gucci and felt light and young and happy.

They turned into a narrow cobblestoned street lined with art galleries and florists. She felt Henry's arm brush her elbow and a tingle ran down her spine. She watched Hugo slip his arm around Gabriella's waist and felt like she had joined some secret club.

"My grandmother brought me to Paseo del Borne every Saturday," Gabriella said. She wore a red dress and white sandals. Her brown hair fell over her shoulders and she wore red lipstick. "She spent all morning trying on clothes at Chanel and Dior. She said even though she lived on an island she adored fashion. Afterward we had tea at the Hotel Can Alomar. I ate persimmon and yogurt and thought I was the luckiest girl in the world."

They stopped in front of a restaurant with a striped awning and tinted windows. Henry opened the door and Juliet saw paneled walls and a beamed ceiling.

"Patrick opened the restaurant two years ago. We played on the tennis circuit together," Henry explained. "I lost my luggage at Heathrow Airport and he leant me his lucky shirt. I won my matches 6-0, 6-1, 6-0 and qualified for the semifinals at Wimbledon."

They ate cold pumpkin soup and talked about music and food and tennis. Juliet tasted baby yams and thought it was lovely not having to worry about Lionel's contract or about convincing Gabriella to record a song. It was wonderful to feel the flush of wine and inhale the scent of citrus and olives.

"When I was young all I needed was tennis," Henry mused. "The rush of being on the court was like riding a magic carpet. But I'd go back to my hotel room and watch movies in German and Italian and realize I'd give anything to have someone to talk to."

"I remember the first time I met Gabriella." Hugo tore apart a baguette. "I walked up the steps of Casa Isabella and saw a young woman standing in the foyer. She had dark hair and green eyes and a smile that lit up the room." He touched Gabriella's palm. "I know her grandmother thinks I should hurry and propose. But marriage is serious and I want the resources to make her happy. I want every day to be filled with good food and laughter and the feeling we are building something together."

My parents have been married for thirty-one years." Juliet nibbled scallops and avocado cream. "My father is a linguistics professor and my mother writes a column for *The New Yorker*. They met at a reading at her apartment. He saw her long brown hair and green eyes across the room and knew he was going to marry her before he introduced himself."

"That's the great thing about love." Henry studied her diamond earrings. "You never know when you'll find it, but when you do you feel like you've waited all your life for that moment."

They paid the check and walked onto the street. The sky was dark velvet and stars twinkled like a thousand fireflies. Juliet gazed at stone buildings covered in ivy and window boxes filled with tulips and wanted to keep walking.

They entered Paseo del Boneo and saw lights strung over the plaza. A band played and couples danced on the cobblestones. Juliet heard people clapping and saw children playing hopscotch.

"What's going on?" Juliet asked.

"Every Friday night Palma has a street party," said Gabriella, taking Hugo's hand. "Come, let's dance."

"I'm not allowed to dance during training." Henry stood on the pavement. "My coach is afraid I'll injure my back."

Juliet watched Hugo put his hands on Gabriella's waist and spin her around the fountain. Gabriella and Hugo moved in perfect rhythm, as if they had danced together forever. She inhaled the scent of cigarettes and sweat and thought it must be wonderful to know someone so well you moved like one person.

She remembered Lionel describing his first proper date with Samantha. She remembered him saying he was so excited he couldn't decide between buying flowers or chocolate. She inhaled Henry's musk aftershave and felt something well up deep inside her.

Juliet entered the Hotel Salvia and took a deep breath. It was almost midnight and the living room was empty. She saw flickering candles and a mahogany sideboard set with a silver coffeepot and porcelain cups and a pitcher of cream.

"I had a lovely time." She turned to Henry. "I'm going upstairs to bed."

"You're going to think I'm old-fashioned." He ran his hands through his hair. "I wondered if I could kiss you good night."

"Here?" Juliet raised her eyebrow.

"The concierge has gone to bed and even the maids have gone home." He leaned forward and touched her hair. "I'd ask to see you to your room but I don't trust myself to leave you at the door."

Juliet glanced at the French doors and marble fireplace and brocade sofas. She studied Henry's brown eyes and wide shoulders. She nodded and moved closer.

"I'd like that."

Juliet entered her room and slipped off her sandals. She tossed her purse on the glass end table and walked to the balcony. It had been delicious to feel Henry's mouth on her lips and his hands in his hair. She had wanted him to follow her up the narrow staircase, but deep down she knew it was best to wait.

She walked inside and unzipped her dress. She slipped on a cotton robe and climbed onto the four-poster bed. She leaned against the down pillows and fell asleep, a smile playing on her lips.

chapter ten

THE SUN GLEAMED ON THE tile counter and Lionel stirred a bowl of porridge. He added sliced banana and nutmeg. He found a spoon and carried it to the round table.

He had stayed awake all night playing old CDs. He paced around the Oriental rug listening to Samantha's voice fill the living room. He pressed stop after each song, promising himself he'd go to bed, and then played another.

He took a small bite and knew he should have thrown the CDs out long ago. But they were like an old teddy bear or a favorite pair of slippers; just knowing they were at the bottom of his drawers made him happy.

He heard a knock on the door and walked to the entry.

"The bloody gardeners woke me hours ago," he grumbled. "I never understood gardening. Why do grown men spend half the day mowing the lawn and clipping the bushes when they have to come back and do it tomorrow? Kipling had the right idea, we should all live in a jungle."

"It smells wonderful in here." Juliet entered the kitchen.

"My mother used to make porridge when I was sick." He

filled a bowl and handed it to Juliet. "Something about holding the warm bowl always made me feel better."

"No thank you." She shook her head. "I'm not hungry."

"You have circles under your eyes." He frowned. "I hope you didn't have a relapse."

"I had a date," Juliet replied. "I didn't get home until midnight."

"I knew you'd find a young Spaniard to seduce you," Lionel exclaimed. "Does he have dark curly hair and flashing eyes and play guitar?"

"He's not Spanish and I wasn't seduced. We had a lovely dinner in Palma." She blushed. "After dinner we discovered a street party. There was wonderful music and everyone danced."

"Let me guess, you listened to the throbbing music and thought you never wanted to be anywhere else." He put his spoon in the bowl. "This morning you got up and hummed the same song in the shower. By the time you dried off you realized you were in love.

"Do you know why people can tell you the name of the song they listened to when they fell in love?" he continued. "Because music is more seductive than girlie magazines and X-rated movies.

"Girls hear a song on a jukebox and think they're in love with the boy with a bad haircut sitting opposite them. They get married and play 'their song' at the reception. It's not until their first anniversary when the guy can't get up to turn off the telly and the garbage never gets taken out she realizes she was never in love, she just got swept away by George Michael crooning 'Careless Whisper.' "

"I'm not in love, I just enjoyed his company." Juliet blushed. "And how can you say that about music? You wrote the greatest love songs of the last two decades."

"They started off as mine but they got shaped and molded like a department store mannequin." Lionel sighed.

"I met Gideon in the dining room of Claridge's. He was one of the hottest young record producers in London and every day he came in and ordered a Cobb salad and a gin and tonic." He sat down and stretched his long legs in front of him. I slipped him Samantha's CD with the keys to his Jaguar. A few days later he called and told me to buy a Patek Philippe watch. I didn't realize when I finally heard our song on the radio that my mother wouldn't recognize it. But Gideon was right, of course; he knew exactly what made money."

Lionel stood in front of the mirror and gazed at his Henry Poole white dinner jacket. He knew he should have waited until he received his advance check but he couldn't resist entering the shop on Saville Row with the plaque reading ESTABLISHED 1860 above the door. He stood while the tailor took his measurements and felt like a prizefighter waiting to go in the ring. Now he studied the satin lapel and thought it was the most beautiful piece of clothing he owned.

He smoothed his hair and wished he had convinced Samantha to buy a dress from Givenchy or Dior. But she gave him a cool stare and said she wasn't going to spend an advance they haven't received, and when she did, she would buy a study guide for her entrance exams and send the rest to her parents in Cleggan.

Lionel shrugged and bit his tongue. He knew she was picturing his parents eating eggs Benedict on Royal Doulton china. They didn't need Lionel's checks and he already abandoned his university education. He pictured Samantha's blue eyes and small pink mouth and thought of the little things she did that drove him crazy but made him want her even more.

"I don't understand why we have to meet Gideon for dinner." Samantha strode along Bond Street. "We spent all last week with him in the recording studio."

"He has something to tell us, he probably got maximum rotation on Capital FM." He pulled her close and kissed her on the lips. "Is it so difficult to sit in the dining room of the Connaught and eat Cornish hens and blueberry tart?"

"You're making a scene." Samantha giggled.

"I want to shout from the rooftops." Lionel ran his hand over her breasts. "I'm in love with the most beautiful girl in the world."

Samantha pushed his hand away and smoothed her skirt. "Let's get to dinner without being arrested."

They entered the dining room of the Connaught and Lionel saw marble pillars and thick velvet wallpaper. Crystal chandeliers dangled from the ceiling and silk tablecloths were set with gold inlaid china.

"Here are my two favorite people in the music business." Gideon stood up. "I ordered plum foie gras and a bottle of Pouilly-Fuissé Chardonnay."

Lionel studied Gideon's Dolce and Gabana suit and Prada shoes. He was only twenty-six and had already produced four gold records. He never mentioned his past and Lionel sometimes imagined him emerging from the womb in a Zegna suit and Gucci loafers.

"Samantha, you look ravishing." Gideon admired her ivory crepe dress. "When are you going to convince this boy he's not Mick Jagger and needs a haircut?"

"Yesterday he gave me a list of places where we need to be seen." She pulled a piece of paper out of her purse. "Annabel's and The Groucho and The Arts Club."

"We don't want people to know our songs but not remember our faces," Lionel protested.

Gideon ate rabbit and mustard cauliflower. "You better add the Viper Room and Château Marmont to that list."

"It would be great to break into America." Lionel nibbled grilled Dover sole. "But we're not even on the radio in England."

"Actually, I've been asked to run the Los Angeles office," Gideon explained. "You should see the size of the palm trees, it's like landing on Lilliput."

"You can't go to California," Lionel implored. "We signed a contract."

"I'm taking you both with me." Gideon waved his hand. "We'll rent you a bungalow in the Hollywood Hills and a Cadillac convertible. We'll even throw in driving lessons so you learn to drive on the right side of the road and don't steer straight into the Pacific.

"We'll have to change the lyrics, Americans don't want to listen to a song about dreary British weather." Gideon rubbed his wineglass. "It will be about a girl who goes to Hollywood to become a star. She hooks up with a guy who makes soft porn and runs back to her boyfriend on Catalina Island. But he sailed away with a Greek heiress on her thirty-foot yacht."

"But the song is about a young woman who goes to London to become a nanny," Lionel spluttered. "She misses her family so she returns to her Irish fishing village. When she arrives she discovers her old boyfriend. He went to Argentina to make his fortune but realized he couldn't live without her."

"I've been meaning to talk to you about that. It can't have a happy ending, you're not writing a Disney sound track. And it needs a catchy title, something Americans will love." He tapped his gold Rolex. "We'll call it 'Going to Catalina.'"

"I can't go to California," Samantha interrupted. "I'm still working for Georgina and applying to university. I shouldn't have taken time off to record the song; I missed Abigail's gymkhana."

She had been so quiet; Lionel forgot she was there. Now he gazed across the silk tablecloth and saw her cheeks were pale and her eyes flickered.

"With your voice and Lionel's lyrics, you can buy as many degrees as you like," Gideon replied. "You'll invite Abigail to Los Angeles and take her to Disneyland and Universal Studios. Send her home with Mickey Mouse ears and a signed autograph of Harrison Ford."

"I'm afraid we have to break the contract," Samantha insisted. "My family is in Ireland, I can't move six thousand miles away."

"I'm sure Gideon only means for a year or so," Lionel said quickly. "You can still apply to university and start next fall."

Gideon nodded, sipping his wine. "You'll record an album and do a nationwide tour and some television spots. After that I don't mind if you live in Biarritz or Monaco."

"You see, it will work out perfectly." Lionel picked up the dessert menu and turned to Samantha. "They serve your favorite spiced apple trifle, let's have a piece to celebrate."

———

"How dare you tell Gideon we're moving to Los Angeles?" Samantha demanded.

They had walked back to Belgravia without saying a word. Now Samantha paced around Lionel's room, clicking her heels on the white wool rug.

"You might enjoy it. The sun actually shines in the summer and you can cross the street without getting run over." Lionel hung up his dinner jacket. "We have to do it, it's our dream. And it's even better than I imagined, we'll be like the Rolling Stones after they appeared on Ed Sullivan. We won't be the biggest singing duo in England, we'll be the biggest in the world."

"It's your dream," Samantha replied. "Releasing the song might give me enough money to apply to the University of London or even Oxford, but my dream hasn't changed. I want to be a teacher."

Lionel gazed at her glossy blond hair and high cheekbones and thought she never looked more beautiful.

"I thought . . ."

"You thought what? That I would stand behind you as if we were a modern-day Robert Louis Stevenson and Fanny Osbourne?" Samantha walked to the door. "It's late, I'm going home."

Lionel stood at the window and watched her cross the driveway. He poured a glass of bourbon and drank it one gulp. He sat on the narrow bed and put his head in his hands. "I thought we were in love."

Lionel climbed the steps of the Georgian Manor and rang the doorbell.

"What are you doing here?" Samantha opened the door. She wore a white cotton robe and yellow slippers. "It's one o'clock in the morning."

"I need to speak to you," Lionel insisted.

"Not now, you'll wake the whole house."

"Then let me in or come outside," he pleaded. "This can't wait until morning."

Samantha hesitated and opened the door. She led him up the circular staircase and down a marble hallway. She entered a room with high ceilings and floral wallpaper. It had thick white carpet and a canopied bed.

Lionel gazed at her dress tossed on the quilted bedspread and her silver brush on the dressing table and felt his heart pound. He wanted to wrap his arms around her and kiss her on the mouth.

"Georgina treats you well." He gazed at the Degas on the wall and the crystal vase of tulips on the bedside table. "I have a bloody room above the garage with a hot plate and a space heater."

"She wants me to feel like part of the family," Samantha explained.

"I want to apologize, I was wrong," Lionel began. "I should never have spoken for both of us, and I shouldn't have agreed to move to Los Angeles. There's nothing more important than you, we'll find another record producer." He looked at Samantha. "We found Gideon, it can't be so hard to find someone else."

"You've been working toward this for months." She hesitated. "It's the most important thing in the world."

"I'll write Gideon a letter saying the deal is off." He sat at the maple desk. "We'll send the CD out again tomorrow."

He grabbed a pen and a notepad. He was about to tear off the top page when he saw Samantha's handwriting. He scanned the letter and turned to Samantha.

"What's this?" He waved it in the air.

"It's my letter of resignation to Georgina, I'm moving to California," she said slowly. "Oxford University has survived for five hundred years, it will be here when we return."

Lionel tossed the notepad on the desk and gathered her in his arms. He fumbled with her belt and slid his hands beneath her robe. He brushed her nipple and felt the rush of desire.

He unzipped his slacks and dropped them on the floor. He slipped the robe over her shoulders and studied her creamy skin. He took her hand and drew her onto the bed.

"I love you." Samantha looked up at him. "I know we're going to have a wonderful life."

She opened her thighs and pulled him close. She guided him inside her until he didn't know where he ended and she began. She kissed him on the mouth and he felt like Odysseus or Zeus. She wrapped her arms around his back and urged him to go faster. Her hands stroked his buttocks until they both tipped over the edge. He came with a brutal force and collapsed between her breasts.

"Are you really going to let Gideon change the lyrics?" Samantha asked, tucking herself against his chest.

Lionel pulled her closer and murmured. "As long as I have you, Gideon can do what he wants."

"I hope you don't mind, but I have to go." Juliet glanced at the ceramic clock above the fridge. "You can spend the afternoon writing songs. I promised Gideon I'd call him tomorrow with an update. It's easy writing e-mails saying you're making progress, but I can't lie over the phone."

"It's only three o'clock," Lionel protested. "I thought we'd have a plate of tapas and a pitcher of sangria in the garden."

"Henry and I are going ballooning." Juliet smoothed her hair behind her ears. "The views are spectacular, you can see clear across to Algiers. But we have to start before the wind dies."

"How I miss the first bud of a romance, when you're sure you are going to spend the rest of your life rappelling on the Amalfi coast or motoring through Provence. Then you realize hanging off a cliff is bad for your knees and the butter they use in French restaurants will give you heart disease." Lionel put his bowl in the sink. "One day you suggest ordering Chinese and watch *Notting Hill* on Netflix, and he discovers a six-pack of Marstons pale ale in the fridge and a packet of crisps in the pantry."

"If you tell me what happened after you arrived in Los Angeles and why you are so furious at Gideon, I might be persuaded to stay," Juliet said.

"That can wait. I don't want to put a crimp on young love." Lionel shook his head. "Though I can't understand why anyone wants to launch himself into the air in a woven basket tethered by something that belongs at a child's birthday party." He paused. "Make sure he brings a picnic, none of those prepackaged sandwiches that cost twenty euros. Have the hotel prepare cold veal cutlets and strawberry cheesecake."

"I'm allergic to strawberries," Juliet replied.

Lionel walked to the entry. "You should have thought of that before you accepted the invitation."

After Juliet left, Lionel piled Majorcan ham and cheese on an olive baguette and lay on a chaise longue in the garden. He sipped strawberry lemonade and opened his worn copy of Spenser's *The Faerie Queen*. But the sun was too bright and the sprinklers hissed and he couldn't concentrate.

He put the sandwich in the fridge and entered the library. He poured a glass of scotch and walked to the bookshelf. He selected a copy of Jules Verne's *Around the World in 180 Days* and began to read.

chapter eleven

JULIET SLIPPED ON A FLORAL dress and added a wide leather belt. She smoothed her hair behind her ears and fastened it with a ceramic clip. She grabbed her red Coach purse and hurried down the wood staircase.

She was meeting Henry in the lobby and they were driving to Valldemossa. They were going to visit the monastery where George Sand and Chopin spent a winter, and eat lamb ravioli and Majorcan spinach at Ca'n Mario.

Juliet pictured Henry's wavy blond hair and wide shoulders and felt a jolt of anticipation. Ballooning had been one of the most exciting things she had ever done. She looked down and saw stone gorges and green inlets filled with wooden fishing boats. She gazed at the deep valleys and shimmering ocean and thought she had never felt so free.

Lionel called and said he had to go to Palma so she had the whole weekend to herself. Henry picked her up in the yellow Fiat, and they drove to the Mercat d'Oliver in Palma. They strolled through the stalls, sampling jams and sausages and local cheeses. They filled a shopping bag with ripe pears and figs and bunches of sunflowers.

Juliet listened to Henry talk about competing in Tokyo and Shanghai and Amsterdam. She told him about seeing U2 perform at the Arc de Triomphe and John Legend ring in the New Year in Miami. She gazed at his thick chest and felt a shiver run down her spine.

"Miss Lyman," the concierge called. "It's lovely to see you, I hope you are enjoying the mild weather."

"It's a gorgeous day." Juliet nodded. "We're going to Valldemossa to explore the monastery."

"You must visit the birthplace of Santa Catalina, she is Majorca's patron saint," the concierge said, as he handed her a piece of paper. "You had a phone call; she asked that you call her back."

"A phone call?" Juliet studied the unfamiliar number.

"You can borrow the house phone," the concierge replied. "If I may say, you look very well. Majorca agrees with you."

Juliet dialed the number and waited for it to answer.

"Juliet? This is Lydia, Gabriella's grandmother." A female voice came over the line. "I wanted to thank you for the books, I read them in one day. I don't know why people say Hemingway is a man's writer; there is nothing sexier than crisp prose. And the Danielle Steel novel was delightful, like soaking in a warm bubble bath."

"It's my pleasure," Juliet replied. "I wanted to thank you for lunch."

"That's why I'm calling," Lydia continued. "I made a vegetable casserole with aubergine and roasted potatoes and wanted to know if you'd come to dinner."

"Gabriella is working tonight," Juliet replied. "She doesn't have a day off until Monday."

"I didn't ask Gabriella," Lydia said. "There's something I want to talk about."

"I'm spending the afternoon in Valldemossa." Juliet hesitated. "But I'll be with a male friend."

"That's even better, you have to bring him," Lydia exclaimed. "I always make too much food."

"Juliet!" Lydia opened the door. She wore a patterned dress and gold sandals. Her silvery hair was pulled into a soft chignon and she wore small ruby earrings.

"Henry is parking the car." Juliet entered the tile foyer. "Something smells delicious, like butter and spices."

"You look wonderful, you are brown as a native." Lydia ushered her into the living room. "I hope you don't think I'm silly dressing up, but I don't have many dinner guests. And if I go into the village for tapas wearing Lanvin, the shopkeepers think I'm going senile."

"That's a beautiful dress," Juliet replied. "And your earrings are gorgeous."

"I do love pretty things; when I was a girl I had a collection of dolls in satin ball gowns." Lydia poured two glasses of wine and handed one to Juliet. "How was Valldemossa? I used to think it was so romantic that George Sand and Chopin spent a winter in the monastery. But he almost died from tuberculosis and she couldn't stand the weather. You're lucky you are here in the summer, our winters aren't so welcoming."

"The views are spectacular and the monastery has been left exactly the same." Juliet sat on a red sofa. "It's like being in another century."

"And your male friend?" Lydia asked. "Is he American?"

"He's a tennis player from New Zealand." Juliet's cheeks flushed. "His name is Henry Adler."

"I love tennis players!" Lydia placed a platter of mushroom empanadas on the coffee table. "Years ago Arthur Ashe held a clinic here. He was so handsome with his coffee-colored skin and dark hair. Nothing happened, of course, but we spent a few lovely evenings making potato cakes."

There was a knock at the door and Lydia rose to answer it. Henry entered carrying a box of chocolate truffles and a bunch of purple lilacs.

"We were going to bring you some wine," he said, as he handed the chocolates and flowers to Lydia. "But Juliet told me you make your own."

"It's not good enough to be served at a Michelin star restaurant but I'm quite proud of it." She popped a hazelnut truffle in her mouth. "There's nothing more satisfying than spending the day stomping grapes."

They sat at a round table in the garden and ate asparagus soup and vegetable casserole with mascarpone cheese. Lydia filled their glasses with a smooth pinot noir, and they talked about Sóller's art galleries and outdoor markets. Juliet remembered Henry's kiss in the hotel lobby and a tingle ran down her spine.

"It must be wonderful to travel the world with a tennis racquet and a pair of athletic shoes." Lydia nibbled sweet potato and baby carrots. "One of the best things about selling the farm was getting rid of furniture gathering dust."

"I've always wanted a house with a garden and one of those big dogs who thinks he is a person." Henry smiled. "All the hotel rooms start to look the same and I get tired of eating cereal from single boxes."

Juliet suddenly flashed on her galley kitchen in Santa Monica with the half empty Life cereal box. She pictured coming home from the recording studio and curling up on the floral sofa with a turkey sandwich. She remembered watching *Gilmore Girls* on Netflix because she was too tired to walk to the bedroom.

"I'd love help with dessert." Lydia glanced at Juliet. "I can't decide whether to serve sponge cake with pistachio or raspberry ice cream."

Juliet followed Lydia into the tile kitchen and sat on a round stool.

"Henry is handsome and charming." Lydia smiled. "And he's obviously in love with you."

"We just met." Juliet blushed. "It's nice to have company."

"It can be difficult living alone but one discovers the things one loves," Lydia mused. "I never would have had time to read if I got married, and I wouldn't have learned to hike or fish. Gabriella's father was always wading in streams, and I was always running after him."

"It must have been hard raising him by yourself," Juliet replied.

"In some ways it was wonderful." Lydia poured coffee into porcelain cups. "I could feed him ice cream for dinner and let him stay up until midnight. We are so careful following the rules we forget to have fun. I never regretted having a child but sometimes I wish I didn't give up my dreams."

"Gabriella told me you think she has a beautiful voice," Lydia continued. "She said you could get her a recording contract."

"She made it clear she wasn't interested." Juliet shook her head. "She said her mother went to Paris to be a dancer and returned after eight months."

"Sonja was a just young girl wanting to experience the cafés and boulevards." Lydia shrugged. "Gabriella has the voice of an angel."

"I've never heard anything like it," Juliet agreed. "She could be a huge star with homes all over the world."

"When I was nineteen I answered a newspaper advertisement to teach Spanish in San Francisco." Lydia filled a pitcher with cream. "My boyfriend, Enrico, worked on a yacht and was gone for weeks at a time. We agreed I would teach for a year and when I returned we would get engaged."

I was so excited, I pored over photos of Chinatown and the Golden Gate Bridge. A week before I was supposed to leave I came down with a terrible flu." Lydia paused. "My mother insisted I go to the doctor and of course I wasn't sick, I was three months pregnant with Felipe."

"What happened?" Juliet gasped.

"I spent three days hunched over the toilet wondering what to do," she replied. "Even if I went to San Francisco, how could I teach and take care of a baby? Finally I wrote to Enrico and told him he was going to be a father."

A month later I received a reply saying he got a permanent job on a yacht in Cannes, he would send money when he could but he was too young to have a child." Lydia took a carton of ice cream out of the freezer. "I've had a wonderful life filled with good food and wine and friends. I've even had heady romances with expensive perfumes and boxes of chocolates. But if I had gone to San Francisco and had the baby, who knows where I'd be now." She looked at Juliet. "I don't want Gabriella to miss out on a great adventure because she thinks she is in love."

"But it's not just Hugo; she adores the restaurant and her family and Majorca."

Lydia picked up the silver tray and walked to the door. "Young birds often don't want to leave the nest, that's why they have to be taught to fly."

They ate raspberry tarts and sponge cake and pistachio ice cream. Juliet gazed up at the velvet sky full of stars and thought she'd been transported on a magic carpet. She felt Henry's leg brush her thigh and felt a shiver of excitement.

"I had a wonderful evening. If I was twenty years younger, I'd insist we go dancing." Lydia stood at the entry. "You must come again; Henry can give us tennis lessons."

"We'd love to." Juliet smiled. "The casserole was delicious and I've never tasted such rich ice cream, I'm going to swim twenty laps in the hotel pool to work it off."

"Talk to Gabriella." Lydia kissed Juliet on the cheek. "I want my only granddaughter to be happy."

Juliet and Henry climbed the wood staircase to her room. She fumbled with her purse and extracted the key. She opened the door and led him inside.

"Would you like a glass of sherry?" she asked.

"I can't, I finally convinced my coach it's too hot to play at noon. Now he has me doing sprints at seven A.M." He glanced at his watch. "I should already be in bed but I couldn't resist saying a proper good night, these last few days have been so much fun."

"I agree." Juliet nodded, feeling light-headed from the wine.

"Usually when I'm training I just sit in a sauna and put hot towels on my back." He touched her cheek. "But I can't stop thinking about you. I know this is sudden and it might sound crazy but you're bright and beautiful and I think I'm in love with you."

"We hardly know each other." Juliet faltered.

"You love swimming and hiking and strolling through outdoor markets. You're passionate about your work and know everything about music." He traced her palm. "I want to take you dancing in Palma and explore the caves in Puerto Cristo. But mostly I want to learn about you."

He pulled her close and kissed her on the lips. He fumbled with her dress and slipped his hand under her bra. She felt a pinprick of desire and caught her breath. She kissed him harder and then pulled away.

"If you don't mind, I think we should wait." She smoothed her hair.

"You're probably right, I'd be a wreck tomorrow morning," he groaned. He pressed his thumb on her mouth and whispered. "Are you sure?"

Juliet suddenly flashed on Lionel 's remark about Spanish hotels and giggled. "The walls are so thin, everyone would hear us."

———

Juliet stood on the balcony and felt the breeze drift down from the mountains. It was almost midnight and she heard a violin playing and people laughing. She pulled her robe around her shoulders and pictured Henry's lips on her mouth. She remembered pushing him away and felt a warmth between her legs.

It would have been so easy to pull him down on the bed. But they had only known each other a few days and in two weeks she'd be leaving. Did she really want to fall in love and have it end?

She remembered hiking in Valldemossa and sharing sponge cake and ice cream in Lydia's garden. Suddenly she thought of her discussion with Lydia about Gabriella and shivered.

She walked inside and climbed onto the four-poster bed. She would worry about Henry tomorrow; now she had to figure out how to convince Gabriella to record a tape. She had to make her see that she had the most beautiful voice and she couldn't waste it.

chapter twelve

LIONEL WARMED A SHOT GLASS with hot water and filled it with brandy. He inhaled deeply, feeling the heat hit the back of his throat. He placed it on the tile kitchen counter and let out his breath. Heated brandy had always been the cure for his allergies.

He gazed at the shopping bag filled with eggs and ham and goat cheese and thought he already felt better. He'd make an omelet with the ingredients he bought at the market in Palma. He was about to crack an egg into the frying pan when he felt the next sneeze coming. He put the egg in the carton and took out his silk handkerchief.

He had started sneezing on the train to Palma. At first he thought it was the jasmine perfume the woman opposite him wore. He tried to move to another seat but the train was packed with tourists in straw hats and children with runny noses. Finally he turned to the window and covered his face with a copy of Dante's *Inferno*.

He continued sneezing while he waited at the doctor's for his checkup. He glanced at the red vinyl sofa and smudged magazines and thought no place carried more germs than a physician's waiting room.

He listened to the doctor lecture him on his cholesterol and the importance of daily exercise. Then he buttoned his shirt and hurried into the Plaza Maya. He tried on wool blazers at Hugo Boss and bought a pair of silk socks in Céline. He sat at a wrought iron table at Ca'n Toni and ordered eggs Benedict and smoked salmon. But the minute he sprinkled pepper on grilled tomatoes he started sneezing. He finally threw ten euros on the table and strode back to the train station.

He heard a knock at the door and called "Come in."

"It's my mother's cold remedy," he explained, clasping the shot glass. Juliet wore a red button-down dress and white sandals. Her hair was smoothed behind her ears and she wore a gold necklace.

"You go to the pharmacist and they recommend four different cough medicines. You end up buying all of them because you don't understand the ingredients. Then you read the labels more closely and realize they all contain the same thing: alcohol."

"I didn't know you were sick." Juliet frowned. "You said you went to Palma for your annual checkup."

"I was perfectly healthy until I got on the train," he replied. "I probably sat across from some Canadian who just visited the Roman Forum. Those germs have been around for two thousand years, they're hardly going to be vanquished by a dose of Nyquil."

"Should I come back tomorrow?" Juliet asked.

"I'll be fine as long as I keep a brandy snifter under my nose." Lionel walked into the living room and gazed at the crystal vase filled with yellow sunflowers. "Sometimes I long for England; it was impossible to have allergies when any pollen was drenched by a summer downpour.

"I was a very healthy child; the only times I visited the matron's office at school was when I gave her a Valentine's card. All the other boys had crushes on the music teacher but I longed for Rose with her Scottish accent and tight-fitting nurse's uniform.

"The first time I had allergies was when we arrived in Los Angeles. We exited the airline terminal and everywhere you looked there were tall palm trees and lush foliage. The driver handed Samantha a bouquet of freesias and I sneezed all the way to the Beverly Hills Hotel.

"But God, California was nirvana; the sun shone and the air was balmy." Lionel sat on a striped love seat. "We lay on chaise longues at the hotel pool and I thought I landed in a Gidget movie. All the women had blond ponytails and tan cheeks and upturned noses." He paused and his eyes clouded over. "But Samantha got terrible sunburns and I couldn't stop sneezing and sometimes I would have given anything for a marmite sandwich and a cup of Ovaltine."

Lionel glanced around the hotel suite at the thick ivory carpet and pink silk drapes and framed Andy Warhols on the walls. He saw the marble sideboard set with poached eggs and Belgian waffles and blueberry pancakes. He inhaled the scent of cinnamon and fresh ground coffee and thought he had never been so happy.

They arrived in Los Angeles two weeks before and drove to the Beverly Hills Hotel. Lionel strode through the pink-and-white lobby and was positive he saw Tom Hanks, and then Julia

Roberts. He clasped his gold hotel key and stopped himself from asking for their autographs.

They spent the first week browsing in Fred Hayman and Ralph Lauren. Lionel bought a pinstriped blazer and polo shirts and a selection of sunglasses. He begged Samantha to buy a Donna Karan dress and Manolo Blahnik sandals. She glanced at the price tags and selected white capris and a pair of Keds instead.

They ate pesto ravioli and rhubarb salad at Spago's and lingered over cheeseburgers and vanilla milkshakes at the Polo Lounge. Lionel squeezed Samantha's hand over the pink tablecloth and couldn't believe they were in Beverly Hills.

But the best part was lounging in the master bedroom with its ivory bedspread and cream satin pillows. He gazed at Samantha asleep under the wooden ceiling fan, and pinched himself to make sure he wasn't dreaming.

"We don't have to be at Gideon's office until two P.M." He sat against the padded headboard. "Why don't we stay in bed and order room service for lunch."

"Men in white dinner jackets shouldn't deliver Cobb salads and Bloody Marys in the middle of the day." Samantha sat at the dressing table. "Normal people grab a sandwich and go back to work."

"The music business is different." Lionel picked lint from his silk pajamas. "Music executives go to nightclubs and drinks martinis and listens to new bands. They don't wake up until noon, and the first thing they need is a cure for their hangover."

"We've been here two weeks and only spent three days in the

recording studio." Samantha wound her hair into a bun. "At this rate it will take months to record an album."

"Gideon says it's about creating an image," Lionel replied. "We're going to be a brand and need the right packaging."

"He was perfectly happy with the way we dressed in London." She rubbed her lips with pink lip-gloss. "I'm not suddenly going to wear miniskirts and stilettos."

"I would hate it if you wore miniskirts." Lionel stood up and walked to the dressing table. "I'd much rather you be completely naked."

Samantha giggled and he reached down and kissed her neck. He inhaled the scent of her lavender shampoo and ran his hands over her breasts.

Samantha stood up and pulled him to the bed. She tossed magazines and newspapers off the ivory bedspread and reclined against the silk pillows.

Lionel unzipped his slacks and lay beside her. He tugged off her cotton panties and found the sweet spot between her legs. He pushed his fingers in deeper and felt her tense and shift and shudder. Then he lowered himself into her, burying his mouth in her hair.

"I think the music business keeps excellent hours," he mumbled, when they were both sweaty and spent. "Now, I think we should order T-bone steaks and ice cream sundaes."

"Here are my two favorite people in Los Angeles." Gideon stood at his office window. He wore a pastel-colored suit and soft brown loafers.

"God have you ever seen so much sunshine? Every room in

my house has a skylight; you could get a suntan while you shave." He walked to the sideboard and poured three glasses of sparkling mineral water. "Donovan says vitamin D is the cure for everything. If we had this kind of weather in England, the national health plan would go under because we'd all live to a hundred.

"The most important thing is keeping hydrated, drink eight glasses of water a day and you can party all night." He handed glasses to Lionel and Samantha. "I had four kamikazes at the Troubadour last night and feel like I could hike the Pacific Trail. And you have to learn how to breathe; Donovan says exhaling correctly is like giving birth."

"I think Donovan should stick to market research, I doubt he has much experience giving birth." Lionel opened a bottle of Grey Goose. He poured a shot into his sparkling water and drank it in one gulp. "Samantha is concerned we haven't spent enough time in the recording studio."

"That's what I love about our girl, her British work ethic." Gideon beamed. "Donovan will be here any minute, he had a noon yoga class."

There was a knock at the door and Lionel saw a man with short blond hair and tan cheeks. He wore a blue-collared shirt and pressed jeans and loafers without socks.

"I have results from our focus group." Donovan waved a glossy magazine cover. "We took Samantha and Lionel's photo and pasted it on the cover of *Seventeen*. We circulated it at local high schools to judge their appeal to teenagers."

"I didn't know teenagers were our audience." Lionel frowned.

"Teenage girls are the biggest music market," Donovan replied. "You didn't see thirty-something women ripping off David Cassidy's puka shells. We want them to dream of having Samantha's cheekbones and sleeping with Lionel's picture under their pillow."

"I'm the songwriter," Lionel protested. "No one is going to see my face."

Gideon and Donovan looked at each other and Gideon fiddled with his Rolex watch.

"We decided you're going to be in the background on the music video," Donovan continued. "White T-shirt, blue jeans, and a navy blazer. And don't cut your hair, teenage girls love dark curly hair."

"But the song is about a young woman's lost love," Lionel said.

"You'll hum the chorus, maybe playa harmonica," Donovan mused. "We had some pushback on Samantha's photo; the girls liked her Lacoste dress but the hair was too severe. This isn't Hyannis Port and she's not a Kennedy."

"I supposed I could wear it down," Samantha suggested.

Donovan nodded. "We're thinking a pixie cut with bangs. It would be great if we could make the hair a statement like Jennifer Aniston and you'll need to start working out. Your legs are fabulous but they need to be toned."

Lionel saw Samantha's eyes flicker the way they did when she was angry.

"We got a membership to Gold's Gym," he said quickly. "It has more contraptions that a torture chamber. And we're going to start Rollerblading on the Venice boardwalk."

"We need to work on Samantha's suntan." Donovan ate a handful of Brazil nuts. "That creamy skin is perfect for a soap commercial, but the song is 'Going to Catalina.' We need a California tan, perhaps with a few sun-kissed freckles on her nose."

Samantha put her glass of mineral water on the sideboard and smoothed her skirt.

"Is there anything else?"

"The study showed there are too many syllables in your name," Donovan replied. "Unless you're Madonna we need something shorter, preferably with an 'i' or a 'y' at the end."

Samantha folded cotton sweaters and linen capris into her suitcase. She gathered her lace underwear and bras and stuffed them in her carry-on.

"What are you doing?" Lionel paced around the hotel suite, clutching a brandy snifter. All the way back from Gideon's office, he kept sneezing.

"I'm leaving," she said. "There's a British Airways flight at nine P.M. If I'm lucky, Georgina hasn't hired a replacement nanny and she'll take me back. I can take Abigail to school in the morning."

"You can't leave." Lionel sneezed into a silk handkerchief. "We signed a contract."

"It didn't include changing my name and cutting my hair and reshaping my legs." Samantha fumed.

"You have better legs than Tina Turner." Lionel sighed. "I could write a song about your legs."

"Donovan isn't interested in your lyrics or how I sing them. He wants a Barbie and Ken to stick on the album cover. I knew I shouldn't have come." She zipped up the suitcase. "I wasted two weeks I could have been studying for my entrance exams."

Lionel put his shot glass on the glass coffee table and walked to the closet. He selected a navy dress and handed it to Samantha.

"Put this on," he insisted.

"I never wear a dress on the plane, it gets wrinkled."

"Put it on and come with me." He patted his cheeks with after-shave and slipped his handkerchief in his pocket.

"What are we doing here?" Samantha gazed around the Polo Lounge.

It was early evening and the room was filled with men in wool blazers and women in chiffon dresses. Lionel saw bartenders mixing brightly colored cocktails and waiters delivering platters of smoked salmon and tuna tartare.

"I'm not the slightest bit hungry," she said. "I'll have Yorkshire pudding on the plane."

Lionel walked to the bar and ordered two gin and tonics. He handed one to Samantha and led her to the white baby grand piano.

"What are you doing?" she whispered.

"I'm going to play and you're going to sing." He sat on the wood bench.

"We can't do that," Samantha protested. "They'll throw us out."

"We don't need designer clothes or mod haircuts or new names," he said. "All we need are your voice and my lyrics."

Lionel saw the maître d' stride over to the piano. He took a deep breath and ran his fingers over the keys.

Samantha began to sing and the whole room grew quiet. People sat in leather booths, craning their necks toward the piano. He saw the bartender clutch a martini shaker and the coat check girl hug a mink stole to her chest.

Lionel played the last note and the room burst into applause.

Men whistled and women wiped their eyes and reapplied their lipstick.

The maître d' approached them and whispered in Lionel's ear.

"The Polo Lounge is honored to introduce Britain's most exciting new musical duo," he announced. "Please welcome Miss Samantha Highbridge and Mr. Lionel Harding."

"California has the most delicious seafood." Lionel ate grilled sea bass with spring vegetables. "It's because the fish spend their lives frolicking in the warm Pacific instead of freezing in the North Sea. And the produce is so tender, the chef probably picked the peas from his garden."

The maître d' insisted they sit in a booth and eat gazpacho and lobster salad and corn tortellini. Lionel nibbled asparagus tips and sipped a Napa Valley Chardonnay and couldn't stop smiling.

"And I'm going to miss salmon burgers with avocado and bacon." He wiped his mouth with a napkin. "God, how many days did I sit in my room above the garage, eating soggy salad sandwiches."

"I do love the fresh fruit," Samantha mused. "The apricots are sweet and the persimmons melt in your mouth."

"We could give it a few weeks," Lionel suggested. "Tell Donovan he can take his *Seventeen* magazine covers and toss them in the garbage."

"I guess we could." Samantha ate chanterelle mushrooms. "I would miss the down pillows and the lavender bath salts are heavenly."

"We better go." Lionel put his fork on his plate.

"We can't leave," Samantha protested. "The chef is preparing strawberry pavlova for dessert."

"It's ten P.M., we should go to bed," he urged. "I need to study your legs if I'm going to write a song about them."

"You know my legs very well." Samantha giggled.

"I have a short memory." He kissed her softly on the mouth. "You'll have to show me what I learned all over again."

"It's getting late." Juliet glanced at the ceramic clock. "Henry and I are having dinner at Casa Isabella."

"Summer love is wonderful," Lionel mused. "You think life will always be about dining on a terrace with a warm breeze and the scent of hyacinths and freesias."

"I'm not in love," Juliet protested. "We hardly know each other and I'm leaving in less than two weeks."

Lionel walked to the marble bar and refilled his brandy snifter. He put it under his nose and inhaled. "Love is like an old Beatles' song; you don't know why the lyrics resonate but you can't get them out of your head. You think it was written just for you and every time you hear it you could burst with happiness." He looked at Juliet. "Don't question it, it's the best feeling in the world."

"I'll see you tomorrow." Juliet walked to the door. "I can't wait to hear about the release of 'Going to Catalina.'"

"Juliet, wait," Lionel called. She turned around and he studied her blue eyes and small pink mouth. "Wear your diamond earrings. And order the roast suckling pig with Majorcan vegetables, it's a local specialty."

Lionel walked to the French doors and gazed at the green trellises and tall birds of paradise. He inhaled the scent of lilacs and roses and suddenly pictured the Beverly Hills Hotel. He remembered lush palm trees and the swimming pool with its pink and white striped cabanas.

He poured another shot of brandy and sat on the striped love seat. He inhaled the brandy and suddenly thought he hated bloody sunshine. He tossed the notebook on the glass coffee table and leaned back against the silk cushions

chapter thirteen

JULIET STOOD ON THE BALCONY and watched the sun dip below the horizon. It was early evening and the sky was pink and orange and yellow. She saw the rugged cliffs and shimmering Mediterranean and thought that if only Lionel delivered his songs she would be so happy.

She walked inside and stood in front of her closet. It felt wonderful to put on a silk dress and strapless sandals. And she loved sitting across from Henry at a café and eating almond cake and vanilla ice cream.

Her phone rang and she picked it up.

"Juliet, it's Gideon." A male voice came over the line. "I get tired of corresponding by e-mail. Young people put a smiley face or a few exclamation marks after a sentence and think everything is all right. I want to know when Lionel is going to deliver the songs."

Juliet gulped, thinking she would never put a smiley face in a business e-mail.

"We're meeting every day," she said evasively. "He is getting very close to fulfilling his contract."

"He's six months late. He's not Chopin and he's not writing a bloody opera," Gideon snapped. "I sent you on a mission and I expect it to be successfully completed."

"I'm sure I've gotten through to him." Juliet fiddled with her earrings. "I just need more time."

"I gave you two weeks," Gideon replied. "If you want to keep your office with its view of the Hollywood sign and your own parking space, that better be enough."

"You have my word," Juliet said. "Lionel will fulfill his contract."

She pressed END and sat at the dressing table. She had to convince Lionel to write the songs, she didn't have a choice. She remembered Lydia asking her to talk to Gabriella and wondered how she could interfere when Gabriella was in love.

She rubbed her lips with pink lip-gloss and thought she wasn't going to worry about Gideon or Gabriella. She suddenly remembered Lionel telling her to wear her diamond earrings, slipped them in her ears, and hurried down the wood staircase.

"Juliet, how wonderful to see you." Gabriella beamed. She wore a navy dress and beige pumps. "I saved you a table next to the window, and my father prepared white truffle foie gras."

"We're glad to be here." Juliet gazed at the crystal chandelier and mosaic ceiling. "I told Henry he has to try the linguini with Sóller prawns."

"My father spent all afternoon stuffing quail and sautéing vegetables." Gabriella smiled. "When he was a boy he wanted to be a tennis player, he's more excited than when we served Prince Albert of Monaco."

"Hitting a ball across a net hardly compares to running a principality." Henry grinned. "But I'll do my best to eat everything on the plate."

They sat at a round table and ate butter lettuce with figs and shaved Parmesan cheese. Juliet drizzled olive oil on pearl tomatoes and took a small bite

"Gabriella's grandparents started Casa Isabella and now her father is the chef and she and her mother run the dining room," Juliet explained. "Gabriella is wonderful with people, she makes you feel like a guest at an intimate dinner party."

"My father owns an accounting firm in Auckland," Henry replied. "When I was fifteen I spent a summer pouring coffee and making photocopies and filing documents. But I forgot to turn off the coffeepot and I never remembered to refill the ink cartridge and sometimes I placed the documents in the wrong order."

"I can't imagine you cooped up in an office." Juliet smiled.

"One day my father called me into his office and fired me. He said it didn't matter what I did as long as I was passionate about it," Henry continued. "I spent the rest of the summer hitting tennis balls, and in the fall a tennis scout gave me a Nike jersey and invited me to join the circuit.

"My parents are very supportive, my mother sends me care packages of thick white socks and tubes of suntan lotion. I buy her Belgian chocolate in Brussels and keep my father stocked with Nike running shoes."

"My parents hoped I would be a language professor or go into publishing," Juliet mused. "I love words but they have to have a rhythm behind them. When I listen to music, I'm like a kitten with a bowl of warm milk."

"Have you ever thought of giving it up?" Henry asked.

"Giving it up?"

"Sometimes I wish I came home to a boiling pot of spaghetti on the stove and a pile of shirts in the laundry, instead of living in hotels with fitted sheets and baskets of fruit and cheeses." He fiddled with his napkin. "It's hard to start a family when your passport has more stamps than a child's coloring book."

"I hadn't really thought about it." Juliet felt a lump in her throat.

"I didn't use to." Henry looked at Juliet and a smile lit up his face. "But lately it's all I think about."

Gabriella's father appeared and insisted they open a bottle of Ferrer Merlot. He and Henry sipped the full-bodied red wine and discussed the French Open and Forest Lawn. Juliet saw Gabriella disappear into the kitchen and strode quickly down the hallway.

"It was a delicious meal." Juliet entered the kitchen. "The rack of lamb with plum confit was superb."

"I hope my father didn't interrupt dessert." Gabriella laughed. "I had to convince him not to ask Henry to sign a napkin."

"Henry loves discussing tennis." Juliet smiled. "He can tell you who won Wimbledon for the last thirty years."

"He's very handsome." Gabriella loaded dishes into the sink. "And he's in love with you."

"Your grandmother said the same thing." Juliet blushed. "We had dinner with her last night."

"She told me she invited you." Gabriella nodded. "I think she misses working all day on the farm. She said the best moment of the day was at sunset, when she slipped on a cashmere sweater and soft leather loafers and fixed herself a martini."

"She thinks you should record a tape and send it to Gideon," Juliet said slowly. "She doesn't want you to miss out on having beautiful clothes and fabulous jewels and owning homes all over the world."

"When I was a girl, Lydia took me to see American movies with Spanish subtitles because she said it was a good way to learn English. But the real reason we went was because she imagined herself living on a grand estate like Grace Kelly in *High Society*.

"She read *American Vogue* and *Town & Country* and owned a black cocktail dress and pearls like Audrey Hepburn in *Breakfast at Tiffany's*. Sometimes she'd have parties and everyone would drink old-fashioneds and listen to Frank Sinatra and Bing Crosby.

"But for me there is nothing more exciting than seeing Hugo walk through the door. He's more handsome than an American movie star, and when we're together, I never want to be anywhere else."

"You have the most beautiful voice," Juliet urged. "People should hear it."

"I sing when I fold the laundry and do the dishes and fix my hair." Gabriella shrugged. "I don't need to perform on a stage."

"Lydia only wants you to be happy. She's afraid you'll regret missing a great adventure."

"My great adventure is marrying the man I love and opening our restaurant and starting a family." Gabriella stacked the dishes on the tile counter. "I'd never forgive myself if I missed that."

"I hope I didn't miss anything." Juliet appeared at the table. "Gabriella let me sample the caramel flan and dark chocolate and sea salt ice cream."

Henry studied Juliet's turquoise chiffon dress and gold sandals. He saw her slender neck and small waist and long legs. "I was telling Felipe how much I love Majorca. The temperature is balmy and the food is delicious and the local scenery is gorgeous."

Juliet blushed and picked up her wineglass.

She nodded. "I agree. I love everything about it."

They sat on the tram back to Sóller and Juliet gazed at the twinkling lights of the harbor. She saw stone farmhouses and the distant outline of Cap Gros lighthouse. She remembered standing in Casa Isabella's kitchen and let her shoulders relax.

She didn't want to worry about going home in two weeks. She wanted to go wine tasting in Binisalem and visit four-hundred-year-old dairies in Porreres. She longed to sit on the back of a scooter with her arms around Henry's waist. She wanted to feel the wind in her hair and inhale the scent of oranges and never want to be anywhere else.

She wondered if her cheeks flushed and her eyes lit up when she looked at Henry the way Gabriella's did when Hugo entered a room. She remembered Lionel saying one couldn't fight love; it was the best feeling in the world. She felt Henry's hand brush her thigh and sucked in her breath.

"I had a wonderful time," Juliet said, standing at the top of the staircase.

They had gotten off the tram and strolled through the plaza. They sat at a wrought iron table and drank aperitifs and nibbled pistachios. Juliet listened to soft jazz and felt warm and light and happy.

Now she gazed at his navy shirt and beige slacks and felt suddenly nervous. Was she ready to go to bed with him?

"I did too." Henry slipped his hands in his pockets. "The prawns were succulent and the duck was tender and the lobster aubergine was perfect."

"Would you like to come inside?" Juliet asked. "The maid always leaves a tray of hazelnut truffles and milky cappuccinos. I can't imagine drinking coffee at midnight but the concierge says a little caffeine with warm milk gives you pleasant dreams."

"I can't. Some journalists are coming to watch me play a practice match tomorrow morning." Henry shook his head. "Sometimes I think they want me to fail so they can write a story that I'm washed up and introduce the new, hot young thing."

"I read an article in *Tennis Today* that your opponents are so afraid of your serve, they wish they could wear a shield like the knights in the Middle Ages."

He reached into his pocket and drew out a black-velvet jewelry case.

"When I told Felipe I loved the scenery in Majorca, I wasn't talking about the green hills and white beaches and limestone caves," he began. "I was picturing your blue eyes and the way your face lights up when you smile."

He opened the box and drew out a string of pearls with an antique clasp.

"Majorcan pearls are unique. They are man-made, but more breathtaking than anything you'll find in the ocean. I saw these at a jeweler in Palma and had to buy them." He fastened them around Juliet's neck. "I never thought I'd come to Majorca to fall in love, but all I want to do is sit across from you at a café and share platters of oysters and bottles of rosé."

He pulled her close and kissed her softly on the lips. He tucked her hair behind her ear and ran his thumb over her mouth.

"Can I take a rain check?" he whispered.

Juliet put the key in the door and smiled.

"I can't think of anything I'd like better."

Juliet gazed in the mirror at her flushed cheeks and smudged lipgloss and ivory necklace. She studied the necklace more closely, admiring the luscious pearls and ruby and gold clasp. She took a deep breath and felt strangely unsettled, as if she were perched on top of a Ferris wheel.

She walked to the closet and unzipped her dress, slipped on a cotton robe, and climbed onto the four-poster bed. She unfastened the necklace and placed it in the black velvet jewelry case. She let out her breath and fell asleep.

chapter fourteen

LIONEL OPENED THE FRIDGE AND took out a loaf of whole wheat bread. He spread it thickly with marmite and sat at the round kitchen table. He took a large bite and grimaced.

He stirred Ovaltine into a tall glass and glanced at the folder of glossy photos. He had dug them out of the closet to show Juliet his publicity shots. But now he couldn't look at the young man with curly dark hair and smooth cheeks without his stomach turning and the feeling that something was pressing on his chest.

He picked one up and frowned. He looked so arrogant, like a scratch golfer who expected to make every putt. He glanced at his reflection in the fridge and thought he hadn't really changed: his hair was still dark and his stomach was flat and he only had a few lines on his forehead.

But the expectation that his good looks and education would provide him every luxury had fizzled like dud firecrackers on Guy Fawkes Day. He turned the photograph over and wondered if every twenty-something young man with long eyelashes and a knowledge of Descartes expected the world to shower him with riches.

He ate another bite of his sandwich and thought it wasn't riches he missed. He had the Alfa Romeo sports car and Malibu beach house and pied-à-terre in on the Upper West Side. What he missed was the youthful ambition, the need to slip on leather loafers and grab a croissant and go out to make your mark on the world.

He heard a knock at the door and called: "Come in."

"I'd ask if you'd like a sandwich but unless you start eating marmite in nursery school, you couldn't swallow a bite," Lionel said.

He glanced at Juliet's floral dress and strapless sandals and thought she never looked so young and pretty.

"The things we learn to love as children last us the rest of our lives. My mother used to pack marmite on white bread and an apple in my lunch box." He dusted crumbs from his slacks. "Even when I was at Cambridge I kept a jar of marmite in my room. I'm glad I never had children, I would hate to subject a new generation to soggy white bread and those little packets of raisins."

"What are these?" Juliet glanced at the photos.

"Gideon insisted we take publicity shots." Lionel handed one to Juliet. "God, have you ever seen such arrogance? I have the strong desire to smack those perfectly shaven cheeks."

"Your shirt isn't as tight and your hair doesn't touch your collar but you look the same," Juliet mused.

"I don't care about the hair, and if I had to walk around with my stomach sucked in, I'd rather be fed by an intravenous tube." Lionel shuddered. "It's the feeling of being important I miss. When you're twenty-three you're certain everyone you meet: the waitress offering you sunny side eggs, the drycleaner who presses your Turnbull & Asser shirts, the kid you hire to keep your sports car waxed, are put on this earth to please you.

"Then you turn forty and realize they didn't give a shit if you liked your eggs over easy or starch in your collars or lemon scent on your upholstery. They were just doing their job and they'll find some other young punk with too much money to work for."

"You're still one of the greatest songwriters of the twenty-first century," Juliet protested.

"Even if I did write another song I've lost that youthful arrogance." Lionel shrugged. "You have to believe you're the best at what you do or you'd never get out of bed. Do you think Ben Franklin would have run outside in a storm if he thought someone else could discover electricity? Would Madame Curie have carried radium around in her pocket if she trusted her husband to discover radiation? The young labor under the assumption they are the only ones who can achieve what they do."

He ate another bite of his sandwich and washed it down with Ovaltine. He stretched his long legs in front of him and his eyes clouded over.

"If only I had realized someone else could write pretty verses, I would have hightailed it back to England while I still had the only thing that mattered."

"What did Gideon do to you?" Juliet asked. "You couldn't return to England if you had a contract. 'Going to Catalina' was poised to be a success, why would you want to leave?"

"I'm getting to that part of the story," Lionel grumbled.

"You better get there quickly." Juliet smoothed her hair. "Gideon doesn't consider patience a virtue. He said I wouldn't have an office to come back to if you don't deliver the songs on time."

Lionel stretched his long legs in front of him and looked at Juliet. "Gideon still has a lot to learn."

"Why does Gideon want to see you alone?" Samantha asked.

Lionel stood in front of the closet and glanced around the hotel suite. It was almost 10 A.M., and room service had delivered poached eggs and sausages and blueberry pancakes. There was a pitcher of maple syrup and pots of orange marmalade.

He gazed at Samantha's ivory silk robe and thought he was glad Gideon hadn't found them an apartment. He enjoyed having *The Observer* delivered with his pineapple juice and his shirts wrapped in tissue paper. Mostly he loved seeing Samantha step out of the marble bathtub, her skin glistening with expensive lotions.

"He wants to discuss the music video." Lionel smoothed his collar. "Donovan probably wants to show me how to hold the harmonica. Yesterday we did twenty takes; I wanted to shove it down his throat. I feel like a street performer in occupied France; these days no one plays a bloody harmonica."

"It suits you." Samantha stood behind him. "You could buy a beret and smoke gaulioses and drink absinthe."

"You're trying to seduce me." Lionel turned around and kissed her softly on the mouth. He slipped his hand under her robe and brushed her nipples. "I'll be back soon and we can have club sandwiches and gin and tonics by the pool."

"I can't." Samantha shook her head. "I have a noon history class at UCLA."

"You're taking a class at UCLA?"

Samantha pulled on a pair of capris and a yellow cotton sweater. She wound her hair into a bun and secured it with a ceramic chopstick.

"I'm not going to sit here reading movie magazines while Gideon decides what color lipstick I should wear in the music video," she said. "If I want to apply to university, I have to keep up with my studies. I'm taking a course on Elizabethan England."

"That's a bloody waste of time," Lionel grumbled. "How can a UCLA professor discuss the plague and London's squalid living conditions when everyone in Los Angeles is healthy as a horse and he can see the Pacific Ocean from his classroom?"

"Why did you fire another director?" Lionel asked.

He sat in Gideon's office, nursing a glass of sparkling mineral water. He gazed at the sun streaking through the floor-to-ceiling windows and wished he hadn't left his sunglasses in the car.

"I didn't fire Igor; he quit." Gideon walked to the sideboard and selected a peach from a pewter fruit bowl.

"How hard is it to direct a music video? It's not bloody *Hamlet*," Lionel scoffed. "These directors think they're vying for Oscars when they're selling a song. It's one step up from a Volkswagen commercial."

"The first director, Jeffrey, quit too. I didn't say anything because I didn't want to upset Samantha." Gideon rubbed the peach on his shirt. "They didn't think she was right for the part."

"What do you mean?" Lionel asked.

"You and I know she's beautiful, but she belongs at the Royal Opera House swathed in diamonds." He ate a bite of the peach. "We need someone with bouncing breasts and a golden tan."

"How do you know if Samantha's breasts bounce?"

"Donovan and I studied the footage." Gideon fiddled with his Rolex watch. "He had a suggestion."

"What kind of suggestion?" Lionel raised his eyebrow.

"That we hire an actress to lip-sync on the video," he replied. "Samantha would record the song in the studio, and she could have final approval on who we choose for the part."

Lionel glanced at Gideon to see if he was joking. He walked to the sideboard and opened a bottle of vodka. He added it to his sparkling mineral water and drank it in one gulp.

"You want to hire an actress to play Samantha?"

"It's done all the time." Gideon shrugged. "Do you think all male rock stars have golden manes and washboard abs? Most of the time you put a line of pretty girls in front of them so no one notices their receding hairlines, but sometimes it's best to use a stand-in."

"Samantha is a stunning blonde with legs up to her shoulders and eyes like amethysts," Lionel spluttered.

"But she's wrong for the video, we need a girl you'd find behind the counter in a soda shop," Gideon said slowly. "We can record the album without a video, but these days radio stations are reluctant to take it."

Lionel gazed out the window at the tall skyscrapers and lush palm trees. He put his glass on the sideboard and suddenly longed for London's narrow alleys and dull gray skies.

"I'm going to sit in a dark bar and drink straight bourbon." He walked to the door. "All this bloody sunshine and sparkling water make my stomach queasy."

Lionel sat on a sagging vinyl sofa in Book Soup and flipped through *Don Quixote*. Ever since he discovered the book by Cervantes when he was in third form he took comfort in his mad adventures. He turned the page and rested his head against the cushions. He thought about his conversation with Gideon and his stomach heaved.

He had left Gideon's office and debated going to Spago's for a chopped salad and dry martini. But he didn't want to watch valets in gold uniforms park Bentleys and Aston Martins. He didn't want to listen to music executives talk about *Billboard* charts and wild parties in Laurel Canyon.

He strolled down Sunset Boulevard and entered Book Soup. He gazed at the bookshelves crammed with Penguin classics and felt his shoulders relax. He selected Dickens and D. H. Lawrence and walked to the back of the store.

He pictured Samantha's slender cheekbones and small pink mouth and thought he couldn't possibly say Gideon thought she was wrong for the music video. He would tell her the deal was off and they were going back to England. He would make up an excuse: his great-grandmother in Scotland had mortal influenza and he had to be with her.

He opened *Little Dorrit* and thought maybe it had all been a waste of time and he should go back to university. He pictured the leafy lanes of Cambridge and thought it would be lovely to spend the summer rowing on the Cam. He imagined eating bread-and-butter sandwiches with Samantha and taking her to King's College Chapel.

Then he thought of his room above Penelope's garage and his long shifts at Claridge's. He remembered the hissing space heater and nights stacking Louis Vuitton suitcases. Could he really give it up when he worked so hard?

He glanced at the orange spines and thought what if Nabokov had abandoned *Lolita* and gone back to teaching university?

What if Shakespeare decided not to risk the plague and stayed home in Stratford-Upon-Avon? What if Oscar Wilde was too afraid of being outed as a homosexual and became a Parliament member?

He had to make Samantha see that the music video was like the silvery wrapping paper you crumpled and tossed in the garbage. It was the lyrics that got under your skin and made your heart beat faster. It was Samantha's high, clear voice that made you feel like you were on top of a roller coaster.

He looked up and saw the clerk frowning at his pile of books. He gathered *A Tale of Two Cities* and *Lady Chatterley's Lover* and took them to the counter. He handed him a twenty-dollar bill and walked into the sunshine.

"You were gone a long time." Samantha looked up from her textbook. She wore a red dress and white sandals and her hair was wound into a low chignon. "I've been studying all afternoon; I thought we could get dinner at Cantor's Deli."

"I brought you a present." Lionel presented her with a green velvet jewelry case. "I passed Harry Winston's and fell in love with the piece in the window."

Samantha snapped open the box and drew out a diamond tennis bracelet. She turned it over and admired the platinum clasp.

"I realized I haven't gotten you a proper gift since I gave you peonies from Penelope's garden and home-baked butterscotch biscuits." Lionel fastened it around her wrist.

"It's gorgeous, but I thought you spent the afternoon with

Donovan, practicing your harmonica," Samantha replied, admiring the sparkling diamonds.

"Actually Donovan wasn't at the office." Lionel walked to the bar and poured a shot of Absolut. He added a twist of lime and drank it in one gulp. "Gideon did say Donovan suggested a small change in the music video."

"I'm not going to wear a pink bikini." Samantha picked up a yellow Hi-Liter. "And I refuse to jump out of a convertible. What if teenagers tried that at home?"

"The convertible wasn't moving." Lionel looked at Samantha and took a deep breath. "Donovan thought you'd be happier if you weren't in as many shots."

"I'd be thrilled, but I'm the one singing."

"He thought they could hire an actress to play your part," Lionel said quickly. "Apparently that young actress who was up for an Oscar was interested, the one who made the socially responsible film about women in Ecuador."

"Penelope Cruz wants to play me in a music video?"

"I'm not sure if it was her, but someone like that." Lionel shrugged. "Donovan thinks your look might not be what they're going for."

"They want a petite actress with dark hair and tan skin and huge breasts?"

"They're not sure what they want," Lionel admitted. His shoulders sagged and his forehead knotted. "But they think you come across as too reserved.

"I told him if you weren't in the video we're breaking the contract and going back to England," he continued. "I booked two business class seats on the morning flight to Heathrow. I even ordered you the vegetarian meal, it's always better than the chicken and mashed potatoes."

"I think it's a wonderful idea," Samantha mused. "I'll have more time to study, the professor assigned the complete works of John Donne and Philip Sidney."

"You do?" Lionel gulped.

"I can't think of anything worse than spending the day standing in front of a wind machine in a miniskirt and stilettos," Samantha said, drawing wide lines in her textbook.

"You never cease to amaze me," Lionel whispered.

He strode across the room and slipped his hand beneath her dress. He felt the delicate silk of her panties and his whole body stiffened.

He took her hand and led her into the bedroom. He unzipped her dress and let it slide to the floor. He studied her lacy cleavage and long legs and thought she was a Roman goddess.

Samantha unsnapped her bra and stepped out of her panties. She unbuttoned Lionel's shirt and ran her hands over his chest. She lay down on the pink-and-white comforter and pulled him on top of her.

"You do know how much I love you." He touched her cheek.

"I do." She nodded. "I love you too."

Lionel drew her arms above her head and plunged inside her. He felt the exquisite sensation of disappearing into endless warmth and thought he was going to explode. He moved faster until her back arched and her body quivered and she wrapped her arms around him. He felt the final blast like a rocket launching and cradled her against his chest.

He drew her close and glanced at the pile of textbooks on the bedside table. He imagined some UCLA professor with blond hair and blue eyes discussing John Donne's sonnets and felt a sudden chill. He draped the smooth cotton sheet around their shoulders and sucked in his breath.

"That's a beautiful necklace." Lionel placed the glass of Ovaltine in the sink. He closed the jar of marmite and put the loaf of bread in the fridge.

"Henry gave it to me, they are Majorcan pearls." Juliet touched her neck.

"He has good taste." Lionel took his cigarette case out of his pocket and tapped a cigarette onto the tile counter. "What was the occasion?"

"He just saw them in a jeweler in Palma." Juliet shrugged, smoothing her hair behind her ears. "The pearls are man-made, I've never seen anything like them."

"If you want to give a woman a gift you buy a silk scarf or a box of chocolates." Lionel lit the cigarette with a pearl lighter and blew a thin smoke ring. "Jewelry always has an agenda: you had to cancel a weekend getaway to Paris or you forgot your anniversary and promise to never do it again."

"You told me I didn't believe in love." Juliet's cheeks flushed. "Maybe you were wrong, maybe I just hadn't met the right man."

"That's the beauty of being young, you still think people change. It's only when you look at the same face in the mirror for decades you realize you'll always have the cleft on your chin." He walked to the entry. "I'm going to the post office, the mailman won't deliver my Harrods's buttercreams until I pay the duty tax. Would you like to join me? We can stop at Ca'n Pintxo and share a plate of tapas."

"I can't." Juliet shook her head. "I have a Skype call with Gideon at three P.M."

"He was always the most punctual person in the music business," Lionel mused. "He was always early for his lunch reservation at Spago's and the first to arrive at the Grammys."

Lionel watched Juliet disappear through the low gate. He searched his pocket for his cigarettes and realized he left them on the kitchen counter. He walked into the living room and picked up the phone.

He dialed the number and waited for it to ring. Suddenly he pressed END and put the phone back on the desk. He entered the kitchen and grabbed his gold cigarette case. He rubbed the engraved letters and slipped it in his pocket.

chapter fifteen

JULIET GAZED AROUND THE HOTEL suite at the orange wool rug and turquoise walls and sloped ceiling. She admired the ceramic vase filled with purple daisies and sideboard set with a pitcher of sparkling water. She grabbed a handful of macadamia nuts from a silver bowl and walked onto the balcony.

She remembered her Skype call with Gideon and her stomach tightened. She couldn't tell him Lionel spent the week reliving his early career. She blithely smiled into the camera and said they were working together to deliver the new songs.

She had hung up and stepped into the white porcelain bathtub. She opened a copy of *Mansfield Park* she found in the hotel's library but couldn't concentrate.

She remembered what Lionel said about people not changing and flinched. He was wrong; people changed all the time. She wasn't the girl who graduated from NYU and expected to sit in the front row of the Grammys. She didn't picture attending music festivals in Montreux and Positano and sipping mojitos with Beyoncé and Gwen Stefani.

She knew working in the music industry was about long

hours in the recording studio and riding on tour buses through the back roads of North Carolina. It was about convincing great artists they still had talent when they thought their latest songs were worthless.

She thought of the last two years when she thought she'd never meet the right guy. She pictured the last few days with Henry: strolling along the promenade in Puerto de Sóller and visiting the monastery in Valldemossa.

She stepped out of the bath and lathered her skin with Aqua de Palma lotion. She walked to the closet and selected a Nina Ricci dress and silver sandals.

She called Henry and left a message inviting him to dinner in her suite. She imagined nibbling salmon seviche and watching the sun set over the Mediterranean. She pictured his thick chest and smooth hands and shivered.

Now she walked inside and saw her phone on the glass coffee table. She listened to the message and heard Henry's voice saying his coach insisted he have dinner with the *Sports Illustrated* reporter. He would sneak out when he could and they could share brandy tiramisu in the plaza.

She gazed at her reflection in the mirror and felt her shoulder deflate. She saw her phone buzz and picked it up.

"Juliet." Lydia's voice came over the line. "I hope I'm not disturbing you, you're probably going to dinner and dancing with Henry."

"Actually I was about to order a room service spinach salad and curl up with Jane Austen." Juliet smiled.

"It's a gorgeous night," Lydia replied. "I was hoping I could tempt you to join me for grilled foie gras with aubergine ravioli in the garden."

"That sounds lovely but I'm quite tired." Juliet faltered. "I don't think I can hike to Fornalutx."

"Good, because I made reservations at the Gran Hotel Sóller," Lydia said. "The chef makes the most delicious apple tartin but he's an old flame and I don't want him to get the wrong impression if I dine alone."

Juliet pictured platters of fresh fish and Majorcan vegetables and realized she was starving. She fastened the pearl necklace around her neck and smoothed her hair.

"I would love to." She smiled. "I'll meet you in the plaza in twenty minutes."

"What a gorgeous hotel," Juliet said, gazing at the tall French windows and marble columns.

They sat at a square table in the courtyard, sipping a smooth Chardonnay. Juliet glanced at the lights strung over the cobblestones and plaster walls covered with ivy and thought she had never eaten anywhere so beautiful.

"The Gran Hotel Sóller was built in the nineteenth century as a private palace and it's the crown jewel of Sóller," Lydia explained, tearing apart a baguette. "I used to bring Gabriella for dinner when she was a little girl, she would order cold tomato soup and a Shirley Temple."

"I'm glad I came." Juliet looked up at the black sky studded with stars. "It's such a beautiful night, it's a shame to stay inside."

"When I lived on the farm, I stopped working at six P.M. and took a hot bath," Lydia began. "Then I put on a pretty dress and a pair of pumps. I fixed myself a martini and watched the sun slide behind the mountains and thought I was quite lucky.

"People think you should only dress up if they live in a city or dine at elegant restaurants, but there's nothing better than Italian silk against your skin. I didn't care if no one saw me except the cows and Felipe, beautiful clothes always made me happy."

"Your dress is exquisite," Juliet said, admiring the teal tunic with gold buttons.

"I had to go to the dentist in Palma and visited my favorite boutique," Lydia replied. "It's tucked in an alley off the Avenidade Jaime III and filled with dresses by Carolina Herrera and Saint Laurent. Every time I enter, I'm afraid I'm too old to wear a new cut or color but the salesgirl assures me I look perfect." She sipped her wine. "One of the pleasures of getting old is your eyesight fades and you are more forgiving with your own reflection.

"I spent the afternoon at La Seu Cathedral," she continued, eating Iberian pig and white truffles. "It has the most fascinating history. The first stone was laid in 1230 by Jaume I to thank God for sparing his ship in a storm and delivering him back to Majorca. But it took almost four hundred years to build and wasn't completed until 1601.

"The spires are as tall as Notre Dame Cathedral and there are over a thousand stained glass windows."

She paused. "I always imagine Gabriella gilding down the aisle in an Oscar de la Renta gown. She would be such a beautiful bride with her long dark hair and green eyes."

"I'm sure she and Hugo will have a lovely wedding," Juliet agreed.

"After I visited the cathedral I went to a little café in La Llonja," she continued. "Cars aren't allowed and the streets are full of florists and fruit stalls. I walked inside and saw a couple sitting in the back. The woman had curly black hair and looked like she'd been crying. The man stroked her hand and tried to comfort her."

"He turned in my direction and I realized it was Hugo. I watched the girl jump up and run outside." Lydia stopped and looked at Juliet. "She wore a cotton dress and sandals and was at least three months pregnant."

"She could have been a friend," Juliet stammered. "It may have nothing to do with Hugo."

"I saw her face when she raced out the door and remembered when I received the letter from Enrico saying he was too young to be a father." Lydia paused. "She looked like a young doe who was lost in the forest."

"Did you approach Hugo?" Juliet asked.

"If Hugo told me the truth, I would have to tell Gabriella, and I couldn't bear to hurt my granddaughter." She shook her head. "I told the maître d' I had a terrible headache and took the train back to Fornalutx."

"I don't believe it," Juliet protested. "He treats her like a precious jewel and when he enters the room she's like a girl on Christmas morning."

"I went home and worked in the garden but my back ached and my knees hurt," Lydia continued. "I made a plate of tapas and poured a glass of wine but I wasn't hungry and I had a headache. Finally I called Hugo's phone and a woman answered. When I asked where he was she said she didn't know." Lydia paused. "She hung up before I could leave a message."

"That's impossible," Juliet exclaimed. "Why would he let another woman have his phone?"

"Perhaps he didn't even know, pregnant women are quite volatile," Lydia mused. "Maybe he wouldn't tell Gabriella so she decided she would do it for him."

"But Hugo and Gabriella seem so in love," Juliet said.

"Every couple who are in love think the word was invented for them," Lydia mused. "But love is like a fishing boat in a storm, it's easy to be thrown off course by a shapely pair of legs.

"I remember the first time I met Hugo, Gabriella brought him to dinner," she continued. "I never saw her look so beautiful, she was like a model in a fashion magazine. Her hair was glossy and her skin glowed and her eyes were like emeralds. After dinner she insisted on helping me with the dishes. She stood at the sink with her arms covered in soap and asked whether I approved." Lydia dabbed her mouth with a napkin. "I said what do you mean and she laughed and said she met the man she was going to marry.

"Young lovers are the most impatient people on earth. They would gladly move the hands of the clock to be together faster. Perhaps Hugo isn't waiting to afford the perfect diamond or buy a restaurant, perhaps he's waiting to make sure he hasn't made a mistake."

Juliet gazed at the aubergine ravioli and foie gras and realized she wasn't hungry.

"You have to tell Gabriella, she must talk to Hugo."

"I've attended Mass every Sunday for fifty years," Lydia said. "God and I don't see eye to eye on many things but we have interesting discussions. The one thing we agree on is you do anything to protect the people you love. If I tell Gabriella it will break her heart."

"What will you do?" Juliet asked.

Lydia took a silver cell phone from her purse and handed it to Juliet.

"I never understood old people who don't embrace modern inventions. If we don't move forward, we'd still be riding donkeys and wearing clothes sewn by the village seamstress.

"I visited Gabriella at Casa Isabella this morning. It's such a wonderful time of day, the sun streams though the windows and the kitchen smells of butter and cinnamon. I brought croissants and we talked about concerts in the Parc de la Mer." She paused. "Then I went to see Felipe and left my cell phone in the kitchen."

Lydia pressed a button on the phone and Juliet heard Gabriella's high, clear voice fill the air.

"You recorded Gabriella singing?" she gasped. "She said she's not interested in a recording contract. I can't send this to Gideon without her permission."

"If she goes to America the romance will die a natural death," Lydia replied. "I can't bear to see her heart broken and I don't know what else to do."

"But you'd be lying and going behind her back," Juliet protested.

Lydia's face broke into a watery smile. "That's why they invented confession."

Juliet stood on her balcony and gazed at the lights twinkling in the plaza. It was almost midnight and a thick fog settled on the mountains. She heard an accordion playing and people laughing.

She had been so upset she didn't remember eating the almond cake with fig ice cream. She kissed Lydia on the cheek and hurried back to the Hotel Salvia.

Now she pictured standing in Casa Isabella's kitchen listening to Gabriella talk about the new restaurant and Hugo's plans for the future. She remembered watching them dance in the Plaza Maya and thinking they were like Amal Alamuddin and George Clooney.

She often had to do difficult things for her work. She remembered an artist begging her to deliver a Dear Jane letter to his girlfriend because he was too afraid she would break down in tears. She pictured the girl unsnapping her heart-shaped locket and saying the artist could keep it, she never wanted to see him again.

But Gabriella was a friend, she didn't want to do anything to hurt her. She couldn't tell Gabriella about Hugo, but how could she do what Lydia asked? If she sent Gideon the recording without her consent, Gabriella would be furious.

She walked inside and unzipped her dress. She slipped on a cotton robe and sat on the floral sofa. She poured a glass of sherry and tried to stop the queasy feeling in her stomach.

chapter sixteen

LIONEL STOOD IN FRONT OF his closet and gazed at the row of Paul Smith blazers. He saw Tom Ford shirts and soft Armani leather jackets. He stroked a Saint Laurent cashmere sweater and thought it had been a long time since he felt like dressing for dinner with a woman.

He picked up a pair of Bally Loafers and remembered the joy of buying a new pair of shoes. He pictured standing in Battaglia on Rodeo Drive and admiring the selection of Prada loafers. He remembered waving his hand and saying he'd take them all and disappearing into the dressing room because he had a giant hard-on. He remembered seeing the shoe boxes stacked on the chrome counter and being afraid he was going to come.

He pictured scooping up silk ties at Lanvin in Paris and Canali suits in Milan. He remembered seeing his reflection in the revolving glass doors of the Hôtel de Crillon and thinking he looked like a million dollars.

He selected a yellow Ralph Lauren shirt and twill slacks. He paired it with a Thom Browne blazer and a pair of Gucci loafers. He fastened Montblanc cuff links around his wrists and glanced in the mirror. He smoothed his hair and hurried down the wood staircase.

Lionel stood at the marble bar in the living room and stirred a dry martini. He heard a knock on the door and called: "Come in."

"You're all dressed up," Juliet said. "Are you going out?"

"Sometimes I enjoy putting on a dress shirt and a pair of slacks," Lionel mused. "Fine clothes are more expensive and addictive than heroin. I once spent five thousand dollars on a Zegna blazer at Barneys because my personal shopper insisted I couldn't eat at Per Se without it. God, you should have seen it on the hanger with its silk lapel and ivory buttons. It was more enticing than a new sports car or a beautiful redhead.

"I walked into the restaurant and the maître d' offered to take my coat, but I held onto it like gold bullion. The porterhouse steak was juicier and the Rothschild cabernet was smoother and the crème brûlé was the best thing I ever tasted." He sipped his martini. "But when I got home and hung the blazer in my closet, it was just a swath of fabric with some nice stitching."

"I thought you said you wanted to meet this evening." Juliet hesitated. "I can come back if you have dinner plans."

"Gloria left a roasted chicken and baby potatoes in the oven. I thought we could open a bottle of rosé and eat on the terrace." He stopped and looked at Juliet. "Unless you are meeting Henry."

"He has to train for a match tomorrow." Juliet shook her head.

"You think love is so resilient you don't have to spend all your time together. But it needs to be nurtured with long walks and candlelit dinners." He sat on the striped silk love seat. "When Samantha and I arrived in Beverly Hills we were inseparable.

Then she started taking classes at UCLA and I worked on the music video and we could barely finish a room service omelet before falling asleep.

"And of course, when 'Going to Catalina' rose to the top of the charts, I thought I was Mick Jagger. We received invitations to club openings and private parties, we were even invited to Prince's wedding." He paused. "I didn't realize the only person I needed to be with was the one whose toothbrush shared a cup in the pink marble bathroom.

"Gideon wanted me to show him your lyrics on my Skype call," Juliet cut in. "He asked me to take a picture of them and send it to him. You have to tell me what happened, you and Samantha seemed to have everything."

He looked and Juliet and his eyes flickered. "I'm about to."

Lionel sat at the Regency desk and ran his fingers over gold card-stock. He flipped through invitations to attend the opening of a new wing at The Getty and meet the chef at Spago's. He glanced at the marble bar lined with brightly colored bottles and longed to relax with a copy of *Catcher in the Rye* and an aged cognac.

He thought of all the events he attended in the last few weeks: a pre-Grammy party at Château Marmont and a private screening of Jerry Maguire. He pictured walking into glass mansions in Laurel Canyon and seeing the lights of the city far below. He remembered sipping Möet & Chandon and nibbling salmon tartare and thinking he was walking on air.

But Samantha signed up for a night class on eighteenth-century pastoral literature so he had to navigate the Hollywood Hills alone. He could never put his Fiat Spider in the correct gear and didn't understand why there weren't any streetlamps. A few times he had to wait for a speeding Aston Martin or chauffeur-driven Bentley to pass before he could navigate a steep gravel driveway.

Gideon insisted he socialize so he dutifully bought Calvin Klein blazers and Hugo Boss shirts. He got daily shaves at the hotel barber and left his patent leather shoes in the hallway. Each time the valet knocked on his door with a pair of gleaming Balmain Loafers he felt a small thrill.

Now he glanced at Samantha's side of the bed with its notebooks and array of pencils and felt something pressing on his chest. She started each day with twenty laps in the pool and a bowl of porridge at the Polo Lounge. Then she slipped on a pair of Keds and walked ten blocks to UCLA. She returned in the early evening with a double latte and pages of new reading.

Sometimes when he entered the suite after midnight he wished he told Gideon he couldn't attend the reception for the king of Denmark. He fingered her copy of *Cranford* and thought he would give anything to share a raspberry cheesecake and discuss Elizabeth Gaskell.

But then he heard" Going to Catalina" on the radio and felt his heart race. The video was on maximum rotation on MTV and the song soared up the charts. He suddenly pictured Amber Harper with her auburn hair and full breasts and chuckled. Donovan might drive him crazy with his research studies and pressed jeans but he knew his audience.

The minute Amber arrived at the audition humming a Beach Boys song Donovan knew she was perfect for the part. Lionel glanced over her résumé at her two years as a drum major at USC and her appearances on *The Young and the Restless* and reluctantly agreed.

He called Samantha to get her opinion, but she said she was too busy with midterms to come to the studio and trusted Lionel and Gideon. Lionel hung up and told Amber the good news, and she hugged everyone on the set. The next morning she arrived wearing a pink miniskirt and carrying a plate of chocolate chip cookies.

Lionel glanced at the invitation to a private showing of Dolce & Gabanna's fall collection. Suddenly he tore it in half and tossed it in the garbage. He called the concierge and then he grabbed his keys and strode out the door.

"I thought you had a cocktail party to attend." Samantha entered the suite. She wore a yellow blouse and white capris and sneakers. She juggled a coffee cup in one hand and a stack of textbooks in the other.

"It's a fashion show." Lionel fiddled with his gold cuff links. "And if I sit on one more hardbacked chair drinking warm champagne and looking at dresses I wouldn't let my daughter wear, I'd never let her leave the house. At least in London you have to wear a coat and stockings to keep warm, here girls think nothing of wearing dresses the size of Band-Aids."

"You don't have a daughter." Samantha giggled, putting her coffee cup on the glass coffee table.

"That's your fault entirely, we could make one right now."

Lionel kissed her on the mouth. "A little girl with blond hair and blue eyes and your gorgeous legs."

"It will have to wait." Samantha pushed him away. "I had a tutorial during lunch and I'm starving. I'm going to order a club sandwich and tackle Thackeray's *Vanity Fair*."

"Actually I made dinner reservations at The Ivy," Lionel said, fixing his tie.

"No one eats at The Ivy except Meryl Streep and Robert Redford," Samantha protested. "I don't have anything to wear and I'll be late with my assignment."

"I'll write your professor a note." He took her hand and led her into the bedroom. "And I already picked out your outfit."

Samantha gazed at the king-size bed and saw a stack of silver boxes tied with gold ribbons.

"What did you do?" she gasped.

"We live one block from Rodeo Drive." Lionel handed her a box. "I went shopping."

They sat at an outdoor table and talked about the new James Bond movie and a gallery opening in Santa Monica. Lionel sipped a Bloody Mary and felt his shoulders relax. Los Angeles was full of things to do and Samantha was perfectly happy. He gazed at her blond hair knotted in a low twist and her mouth coated with pink lipstick and thought she never looked so beautiful.

"If we ate outside in London during the summer, it would probably rain during our entrée." Lionel nibbled penne with tomato sauce and buffalo mozzarella. "And have you ever tasted such delicious tomatoes? They're sweeter than a Violet Crumble.

We should dine out more often, there's a new sushi place on Sunset and a pizzeria in Brentwood."

"We can't eat at restaurants every meal, I have to write two papers and study for my entrance exams." Samantha tucked a stray hair behind her ear.

"You don't have to study. We could stay and buy a house in the Hollywood Hills," Lionel said slowly. "I know you miss London, but we could stock the pantry with quince and lemon curd and install an Aga cooker in the kitchen. When you walk outside, you'd see birds of paradise and the ocean." He took a deep breath. "It's so much easier living in California, there are leafy streets where you can park your car without being afraid it will be sideswiped by a double-decker bus."

"I like having seasons," Samantha replied. "When spring comes you actually enjoy the sun on your face and grass between your toes. Here people complain if they have to wear a long-sleeved shirt and a pair of closed toe shoes. And I don't want my vegetables to taste like candy, I like eating soggy brussels sprouts so I can enjoy a slice of vanilla custard."

"No one likes brussels sprouts." Lionel stabbed a shiitake mushroom with his fork. "And I haven't met anyone in Los Angeles who complains. They all have white smiles and tell you to have a nice day."

"That's the point." Samantha's eyes flashed. "I don't want to be surrounded by strangers with permanent tans and American accents. I want to sit in my mother's kitchen with a cup of tea and a plate of cauliflower cheese. I want to moan that the girls in my first form history class are more interested in the color of their nail polish than the Battle of Hastings."

"But you left Ireland because it didn't have opportunities," Lionel protested. "That's why you live in London."

"But we're still in the same time zone and she understands when I comment about the tube or Prince Harry's red hair." She stopped and looked at Lionel. "You're the one who mentioned children. How could we start a family without grandparents nearby to feed them creamed corn and read *Paddington Bear*?"

"It's the end of the twentieth century. You could fly from Heathrow to LAX faster than you can drive on the M-16 on a holiday weekend." He reached for her hand. "Why would we want to go back to constant rain and snarled traffic when we can eat under fruit trees in the middle of the city?"

"Because life isn't about owning a convertible or eating a perfectly poached artichoke. It's about sharing your accomplishments with the people you love and keeping your promises." She suddenly jumped up. "We said we'd be here for a year and that's what I intend to do. I have to go. You can finish my mesquite swordfish with steamed broccollini."

Lionel drank a long gulp of his Bloody Mary and thought he never loved Samantha more. He wanted to spend every night with her pressed against his chest. He wanted to have an army of blond children with grubby fists and knobby knees.

He glanced at a couple stepping into a cream Jaguar and thought why did it have to be so difficult? They could have houses in Los Angeles and London and Paris. They could take their children to Walt Disney World and sailing in the Bahamas.

He put his fork on his plate and signaled the waiter.

"Chef Lars wanted to tell you dinner is complimentary." The

waiter approached him. "He made his special triple-layer choco-late cake, he is a big fan of your song."

Lionel gazed at dark chocolate surrounded by raspberries and whipped cream. He put his napkin on his plate and stood up.

"Tell Lars thank you," he mumbled. "But I don't want any bloody dessert."

Lionel took off his cuff links and dropped them on the Regency desk. He heard the bedroom door open and saw Samantha wear-ing a pink cotton robe and slippers.

"I'll sleep in the living room." He looked up. "Don't worry, I have my own pillow."

"My mother called," Samantha said. "You invited her and my father to the Grammys. You sent them plane tickets and booked a suite at the Beverly Hills Hotel."

"It was supposed to be a surprise." Lionel poured a glass of scotch from the crystal decanter.

"My mother has lived in the same fishing village for fifty years." Samantha smiled. "She's terrible at keeping secrets."

"How often do we get invited to the Grammys? I thought they would like to attend." Lionel shrugged. "I invited my mother too. They can go shopping on Rodeo Drive and play bingo in the Polo Lounge."

"I was wrong when I said life was about sharing your ac-complishments with the ones you love." Samantha approached him. "It's also about compromise. We don't have to make deci-sions about the future now. Why don't we just try to enjoy our-selves."

"What did you have in mind?" Lionel raised his eyebrow.

"I did a little shopping of my own." She slipped off the robe and revealed a red push-up bra and lace panties.

"Where did you get those?" Lionel gasped, loosening his tie.

"I stopped in La Perla on the way home." She took his hand and led him to the sofa. "I couldn't decide between a black camisole and this push-up bra and lace panties."

"You definitely made the right decision," he whispered, kissing her softly on the mouth.

She stepped out of the panties and let them fall to the floor. He inhaled her scent of floral perfume and lavender bubble bath and never wanted to let her go.

She sat on his lap and unbuttoned his shirt. She put her hand underneath his slacks and felt his hardness. She unzipped his slacks and positioned her body above his.

He unsnapped the bra and let it fall from her shoulders. He laid back against the silk cushions and felt like Paul Newman or Robert Redford.

"I think we'd be more comfortable on the bed," he murmured.

"We better hurry," she whispered. "I can't wait another minute."

He lifted her up and carried her into the bedroom. She pulled him down on the bed and opened her legs. She wrapped her arms around him and drew him inside her. He felt the soft curve of her stomach and silky stretch of her thigh and creamy perfection of her breasts. He gathered her in his arms and heard her gasp. Then he came so violently he thought he would never stop.

He tucked her against his chest and pulled the crisp white sheet around their shoulders. He saw the open copy of *Vanity Fair* and yellow Hi-Liter. He let out his breath and murmured:

"You seduced me so I could help you with your paper on Thackeray."

Then he closed his eyes and wondered if you could die from being so happy.

"I bought these cuff links for my first Grammys," Lionel mused, gazing at his gold cuff links. "Montblanc twenty-four carat gold, handmade in Switzerland. Whoever said clothes don't make the man never wore a custom Armani tuxedo and alligator Ferragamos. I entered the Shrine Auditorium and felt like Cary Grant. I convinced Samantha to wear a red Valentino gown, she looked like Lana Turner." Lionel finished his martini. "I'm going to take the chicken out of the oven. You probably would rather join a friend for some tapas."

"I'm starving and getting a little tired of tapas," Juliet admitted. "I'd love to stay for dinner."

"Why don't you go onto the terrace." Lionel walked to the kitchen. "I'll take the wine out of the fridge and rustle up a salad."

Lionel stood at the kitchen counter and gazed out the window. He saw Juliet sitting under the trellis, rubbing her lips with pink lip-gloss. He saw her smooth brown hair and long legs and felt something tighten in his chest. He selected a Didier Pouilly-Fumé and walked into the garden.

chapter seventeen

JULIET STOOD ON THE BALCONY and inhaled the scent of jasmine and azaleas. It was Saturday morning and the plaza was filled with men wearing linen shorts and suede loafers. Women wore wide straw hats and oversized sunglasses and soft leather sandals.

She walked inside and stood in front of her closet. She was meeting Gabriella, and they were going to visit the outdoor markets. She pictured stalls of pink radishes and colored sea salts. She imagined roasted pig and sausage and realized she was starving.

She remembered dinner with Lionel on the terrace and smiled. It had been surprisingly pleasant to sit at the round table and eat potato soup and warm baguettes. It was lovely to sip a smooth cabernet and listen to his stories about performing for President Clinton and having afternoon tea with Prince Charles.

It was only when they were nibbling Gloria's macaroons and she asked if he was writing new songs that she saw his shoulders tighten. She remembered him downing a double shot of cognac and grinding his cigarette into the silver ashtray.

She glanced at Lydia's cell phone on the desk and flinched.

She had stayed awake all night wondering what to do. It would be so easy to send the recording to Gideon. She pictured him listening to Gabriella's high, clear voice and knew her job would be secure.

She selected a lavender dress and felt her stomach rise to her throat. Gabriella was kind and generous; she couldn't possibly betray her friend. Then she pictured Hugo sitting in the restaurant with a dark-haired girl and shivered. She would do anything to stop her from getting her heart broken.

Gabriella and Hugo had been together for four years, surely Gabriella would sense if he were seeing another woman. She would spend the morning with Gabriella and see if there was something she wasn't telling her. Then she would decide if she should send the clip to Gideon.

She walked down the wood staircase and entered the hotel lobby.

"Miss Lyman," the concierge called. "It's lovely to see you. I hope you are going to visit our Saturday markets. The plaza is filled with stalls selling fresh seafood and ripe fruits and local chutney."

"I'm meeting a friend there." Juliet nodded. "I'm afraid I'll buy too much, everything sounds delicious."

"You have a delivery." He pointed to a ceramic vase filled with tulips and roses. "Should I send them to your room?"

"These are for me?" Juliet gasped, approaching the desk.

"I've never seen such a large bouquet." The concierge nodded. "Here is the card."

Juliet slipped the ivory card in her purse and ran down the hotel steps. She was about to pull it out when she heard her phone buzz.

"I hope you like the flowers. I'm sorry I missed dinner last night." Henry's voice came over the line. "The reporter wanted to discuss the history of tennis upsets since Björn Borg defeated Jimmy Connors at Wimbledon. I was desperate to leave but my coach kicked me under the table and whispered they would give me the cover."

"They're spectacular. The concierge was worried how he would get them up the staircase." Juliet giggled.

"I am playing an exhibition match at Los Monteros in Marbella on Monday. I'll be challenging the fifth-ranked player in the world and really I'd like you to be there.

"Málaga is an hour's flight and a private car would take us to Marbella," he continued. "Los Monteros is one of the most exclusive resorts in the world with a one-star Michelin restaurant and private beach club. The suites have roof decks and you can see the Rock of Gibraltar."

"I don't know if I can take the time," Juliet stammered.

"It would only be one night." He paused. "I'd play better if you were watching and after we could eat tiger prawns at El Corzo and listen to the piano at Bar Azul."

"Can I let you know tonight?" Juliet asked.

"Take your time." Henry's voice was suddenly soft. "And Juliet, I don't mind if you want separate rooms."

Juliet entered the plaza and saw stalls filled with purple cauliflower and red peppers. She inhaled the scent of fresh baked bread and her shoulders relaxed

"There you are." Gabriella approached her. She wore a wide

straw hat and carried a wicker shopping basket. "I was afraid I was going to have to eat the basket of peaches by myself."

"I've never seen so many kinds of fruits and vegetables," Juliet mused.

"Farmers come from all over the Tramuntana Valley and the fishermen haul the fish up from Puerto de Sóller," Gabriella explained. "Hugo and I used to come every Saturday."

Juliet gazed at a bunch of yellow sunflowers and suddenly pictured the ceramic vase filled with tulips and roses. She remembered the ivory card and Henry's invitation to go to Marbella.

"You look a little pale." Gabriella frowned. "Let's sit at an outdoor café and drink a bottle of lemonade."

"Henry called and asked me to go to Marbella," Juliet said, sipping the fizzy drink. "He's playing an exhibition match at Los Monteros. He said I could have my own room and we'd go to dinner and dancing."

"My grandmother took me there when I was little." Gabriella ate a sliced peach. "The lobby was gold and white marble and the pool was made of mosaic tiles. The rooms were decorated in all white and my cheeseburger was served on a porcelain plate." She sighed. "I would do anything to go there on our honeymoon."

"Henry and I haven't known each other long, and I'll be going back to America soon." Juliet hesitated.

"You said Henry told you he loved you."

"But he travels all over the world and I live in Los Angeles," Juliet said. "Even if we were in the same place, I spend all day in the recording studio and nights at smoky nightclubs. I wouldn't have time to Rollerblade on Venice beach or dine at trendy restaurants in Brentwood."

"When Hugo and I had been dating six months my father called us into his study," Gabriella began. "We entered the room and he was wearing a navy blazer and collared shirt and tie. His hair was slicked back and he wore tan slacks and leather loafers.

"I was nervous because he usually wears a shirt with the sleeves rolled up and white chinos. He poured us each a glass of brandy and said nothing was more important than his daughter's happiness. Then he asked Hugo what were his plans for the future.

"I glanced at Hugo and my stomach rose to my throat. He was twenty-two with barely enough money to buy me a scoop of tiramisu or a bunch of daisies. He put his glass on the coffee table and told my father one day he would have his own restaurant. He would buy a beautiful villa and spend every day making me happy.

"I felt his hand graze my palm and knew that everything we faced we would do together. Love doesn't disappear in the face of obstacles; it grows stronger. If you and Henry love each other you'll find a way to see him play in London and Melbourne and he'll send you flowers and chocolates while he's away." She stopped and her cheeks flushed. "And when you are together you'll feel so complete, you'll forget you were apart."

"You make it sound simple." Juliet sipped her lemonade.

Gabriella finished the peach and her face broke into a smile. "At least you'll drink daiquiris in a beachside cabana and mingle with royalty. Los Monteros is the favorite resort of the prince and princess of Spain."

They strolled through the stalls and bought jars of jam and bottles of vinegar and olive oil. They tried on pearl necklaces and leather espadrilles. Gabriella took off her hat and tied a silk scarf around her hair.

"Do you like it?" she asked.

Juliet gazed at the patterned fabric and noticed Gabriella's ruby earrings.

"Your earrings are gorgeous," she said, fingering a silver bracelet.

"Hugo gave them to me yesterday," Gabriella replied. She heard the cathedral bells ring and started.

"I'm late, I promised I'd meet Hugo at the tram stop at two P.M." She kissed Juliet on the cheek. "I had a lovely time. If you go to Marbella, bring me a chocolate praline truffle. The maids leave them on the pillow at night and they're delicious."

Juliet spent the afternoon exploring winding alleys and quaint boutiques. She bought a packet of postcards in the gift shop and a gold bangle in a jewelry store. She admired the elegant mansions on Gran Via Avenue and spent hours studying the Picassos and Miros in the Ca'n Prunera.

She sat on the steps of the cathedral and thought again how much she loved Sóller: she loved the narrow buildings with their lacquered window boxes filled with peonies and lilacs. She loved the outdoor cafés with their striped awnings and round iron tables. Mostly she loved that everywhere you looked you saw green valleys and tall mountains and the deep blue of the Mediterranean.

She thought about the places she usually visited for work: tiny towns in New Hampshire or Virginia. She pictured eating at Denny's after a concert or joining the band at IHOP for breakfast before the bus pulled back onto the freeway. She had always loved the feeling of camaraderie, like she was part of a team.

Maybe there was more to life than being the person with a clipboard and bottles of sparkling water. She thought about the places Henry mentioned: playing the Swedish Open in Stockholm and the Rolex Masters in Shanghai. Attending the Australian Open in February and the weather being so warm, he could swim in the Pacific Ocean.

She heard the cathedral bells ring and walked back to the Hotel Salvia. She entered her suite and saw the crystal vase filled with roses and tulips. She sat on the floral love seat and felt her heart race.

How could she admit to Gabriella she wasn't sure how she felt about Henry because she'd never been in love? Then she flashed on Lionel saying people didn't change. Of course she believed in love, she just never met the right guy.

She fingered Henry's ivory card and pictured watching him play his match. She imagined sipping a bottle of Syrah and nibbling steamed mussels and poached sea bass.

She saw his blond hair and the way his eyes lit up when he talked about tennis. Of course she was falling in love with him, she just had to give herself the chance.

She picked up her phone and dialed his number.

"Hi," she said when his voice came over the line. "I'd love to go to Marbella."

"I'm glad," Henry replied. "I won't have to wear my lucky socks, and after the match we'll go sailing."

"I can't wait." She took a deep breath. "And you don't have to reserve separate rooms."

Juliet stood up and paced around the suite. She felt a little off balance, as if she stepped off an airplane. She fiddled with her gold bangle and suddenly remembered Gabriella's ruby earrings.

She thought about what Lionel said that you only give jewelry if you need to apologize. Why would Hugo splurge on ruby earrings when he was saving up for an engagement ring?

She pressed PLAY on Lydia's cell phone and listened to Gabriella's high, clear voice. If Gideon offered Gabriella a contract she didn't have to accept it. But at least she would have the option if Hugo were seeing another woman.

She took out her laptop and typed a quick note to Gideon. She tapped his e-mail address into Lydia's phone and pressed SEND. Then she walked to the balcony and let the air leave her lungs.

She gazed at the ribbons of pink and orange clouds and thought she had done two things that could change her life. She was going to Marbella with Henry and she had sent Gabriella's song to Gideon.

She poured a cup of coffee from the silver coffeepot and added cream and sugar. She glanced at the bouquet of roses and tulips and Lydia's cell phone and thought she didn't know which frightened her more.

chapter eighteen

LIONEL PUT DOWN THE COPY of *Huckleberry Finn* and rubbed his eyes. He scooped up a handful of pistachio nuts and washed them down with a gin and tonic. He took out his gold cigarette case and tapped a cigarette onto the Regency desk. He inhaled slowly and thought he really should go up to bed.

He pictured his dinner with Juliet and remembered why people spent hundreds of dollars at fine restaurants. It had been lovely to sit under the green trellis and eat Gloria's roasted chicken and baby potatoes. It had been delightful to savor a vintage French wine and talk about books and music. He had glanced at the turquoise swimming pool and pink hibiscus and thought even Casa Rosa had its merits.

But then Juliet mentioned Gideon's name and he felt a cool chill. He swallowed a double shot of Rémy Martin and lit a cigarette. He ground it into the glass ashtray and lit another.

Now he stood up and opened the crystal decanter. He refreshed his glass and hesitated. He couldn't keep dousing his liver in gin and soda water. Then he pictured Gideon's immaculate Dolce & Gabana sports jacket and platinum Patek Philippe watch and downed it in one gulp.

He ran his fingers over the stubble on his chin and remembered the year "Going to Catalina" was released. He and Gideon and Samantha did everything together like a modern-day Three Musketeers. He pictured parties at Gideon's impossibly large Beverly Hills mansion with its signed Andy Warhols and Jackson Pollocks and one perfect Van Gogh. Gideon hired Michael S. Smith and every room had lush white carpet and geometric sofas and crystal chandeliers.

He remembered smoking cigars in Gideon's study with its Bang and Olufsen stereo system. He pictured lying beside the pool and gazing at Samantha in her red swimsuit and vowing they were never going to grow old.

He heard a knock on the door and called. "Come in, I'm in the library."

"It's dark in here," Juliet said, entering the room.

She wore a navy knit dress and beige slingbacks. Her hair was held back with a ceramic clip and she wore a gold bangle.

"When I was at Cambridge, I'd get a touch of insomnia and sit in Magdalene College library," Lionel mused. "Just staring at the bookshelves filled with centuries-old leather bindings was better than warm milk with brandy. I'd select the *Canterbury Tales* or *The Decameron* and curl up in a stuffed armchair. I'd inhale the faded ink and fall asleep before I turned the first page."

He walked to the bookshelf and selected a thin volume. He ran his fingers over the spine and looked at Juliet.

"The first time I read *Tom Sawyer*, I was thirteen. It was my second year at boarding school and I was surrounded by wankers in public school ties and Bermuda shorts. I stayed up all night reading how Tom and Huck faced Injun Joe and dreamed of having a best friend I would do anything to defend.

"I attended Cambridge and my schoolmates were too busy making out with girls to do more than share a pack of cigarettes." He stopped and smiled. "One couldn't blame them, most of them had never been within fifty feet of a female except for their nannies.

"Then we met Gideon and arrived in Los Angeles and everything changed." He sat on a leather armchair. "Here was someone who appreciated a cashmere overcoat and a bottle of Martell Cognac. Someone I could play checkers with and argue whether Mick Jagger was a better songwriter than Keith Richards.

" 'Going to Catalina' stayed at number one on the charts and the album flew out of the stores. Samantha and I stayed in the bungalow at the Beverly Hills Hotel because she still desperately wanted to return to England. But she was at the top of her medieval literature class at UCLA and her legs became golden brown.

"We spent weekends driving up the coast to Santa Barbara and Big Sur. I glanced at her in the passenger seat with her oval sunglasses and silk scarf and felt like Dustin Hoffman and Katherine Ross in *The Graduate*.

"Then Gideon called me into his office and poured two shots of Stolichnaya. He handed one to me and presented me with a dilemma worse than in *Sophie's Choice*." His eyes clouded over and he stretched his long legs in front of him. "And of course, I made the wrong decision."

"I spent the afternoon at Harry Winston's on Rodeo Drive." Lionel slipped on his sunglasses. No matter how much time he spent in Gideon's office, he couldn't get used to the blinding sun streaming through the windows.

"That's why I don't have a serious girlfriend." Gideon took a green apple from the pewter fruit bowl. "Donovan keeps a safe full of sapphires earrings and diamond pendants. He says the best way to stay in a girlfriend's good graces is to give her a ruby ring or emerald necklace before she tells him what he did wrong."

"Donovan is as likely to have a girlfriend as my mother is to go on *Star Search*," Lionel replied. "He's as gay as they come. Have you seen the way he holds a teacup? He may as well have gone to finishing school in Switzerland."

Lionel fished in his pocket and took a blue velvet box. He opened it and displayed an emerald cut diamond on a platinum band.

"I'm going to ask Samantha to marry me," he continued. "We'll have the wedding at St. James followed by a luncheon at the Savoy. We'll hold the evening reception at Claridge's with a five-course sit-down dinner and a twelve-piece orchestra. I'm going to ask Elton John to perform 'Candle in the Wind,' it's Samantha's favorite song."

"You can't get married, you're America's sweetheart," Gideon protested. "Do you think your female fans will throw their bras at you if you have a wedding ring on your finger?"

"My fans aren't old enough to have bloody training bras." Lionel took a gold cigarette case out of his slacks. "And I don't care what they think. Samantha and I are getting married and moving back to London. We'll rent a flat on Belgravia Square with a dalmatian and a key to the garden. I'll write songs all day and she can attend university."

"'Going to Catalina' is still on top of the charts and you're about to release your second album," Gideon protested. "You can't stop now, you'll become one of those *Jeopardy!* questions no one can answer."

"I can write songs anywhere and I promised Samantha we would only be here for a year." Lionel lit a cigarette with a pearl lighter. "The Beverly Hills Hotel is lovely but Samantha doesn't like having her underwear delivered with a satin bow and I'm going to gain weight from the chocolate truffles on the pillow."

"Think about the legends of rock 'n' roll: Eric Clapton and Bryan Ferry and Paul McCartney. They couldn't retire to their country house after a year and still expect to be a success. You have to keep your face in front of your fans or they'll replace you with the next guy with dark curly hair who looks good in jeans and a T-shirt."

Gideon finished the apple and tossed it in the silver garbage can.

"Go on tour with Amber for three months and then you can do whatever you like."

"You're mad," Lionel spluttered. "We can't go on tour. Amber doesn't sing a note."

"Even real artists lip-sync. Do you think Madonna belts out 'Like a Prayer' when she's been up all night drinking tequila?" Gideon shrugged. "The public loves Amber, the video is the longest playing clip on MTV and VHI. We need teenage girls in Atlanta to want to be her best friend and boys in Buffalo to paste her pinup over their beds." He paused. "Can you picture Amber with her bronze skin and honey blond hair bringing a little California to Wisconsin? The new album will fly off the charts."

"It's like hanging a forgery of the *Mona Lisa* at the Louvre. I can't stand onstage and watch her move her mouth."

"The song is fantastic but you're hardly Leonardo da Vinci." Gideon raised his eyebrow. "Music is a business. If you want to stay on Prada's preferred mailing list and keep sending Chanel No. 5 to Samantha's mother, you have to do some promotion."

"How did you know I send Samantha's mother gifts?" Lionel asked.

"My secretary pays the bills," Gideon replied. "You'd be on the road for three months, this is your chance to see Yellowstone National Park and the Grand Canyon."

"I'm perfectly happy seeing the inside of The Polo Lounge," Lionel grumbled. "Samantha will hate it, she gets carsick in a taxi."

"She'd be bored sitting in the back of drafty concert halls, and she'd get sunstroke at outdoor stadiums." Gideon fiddled with his platinum watch. "Why don't you sign her up for a French cooking course and get her tickets to *Swan Lake*. When you return you can propose and I'll throw you an engagement party at Château Marmont."

Lionel poured another shot of vodka and drank it in one gulp. He felt the alcohol hit his stomach and wanted to throw up. "We've never been apart, and I promised we'd return to England."

"She'll understand," Gideon mused. "Sometimes you have to wait for the best things in life and when you get them, they are even sweeter."

"Samantha doesn't like sugar," Lionel grumbled. "She thinks it is bad for you."

Lionel entered the hotel suite and gazed at the ivory sofas and pink silk curtains. He saw the plush white carpet and marble bar lined with brightly colored bottles. He inhaled the scent of lilacs and roses and still couldn't believe they were in Los Angeles.

The last year had been more enjoyable than he could have imagined. He loved having front row seats to the Lakers and a standing reservation at the Ivy. He loved walking into Fred Hayman's and the salesgirl knowing his shirt size. But mostly he loved curling up with Samantha at night and discussing music and poetry.

How would he survive on the road for three months without her? And what would she say when he told her they would have to delay moving to London?

"There you are." Samantha appeared at the door. She wore a white robe and pink slippers. Her hair was tied in a low ponytail and tied with a satin ribbon. "I was about to step in the bath. I have to finish a paper on English gardens and read a poem for my course on romantic lyricism. I thought we could order a Cobb salad and you can recite John Donne."

Lionel gazed at her creamy skin and the outline of her breasts and longed to wrap his arms around her.

"Gideon called me into his office; he's concerned about the new album. A sophomore album can sink faster than Virginia Woolf with a pocket full of stones." He took a deep breath and looked at Samantha. "He wants me and Amber to go on tour."

"Gideon wants you and Amber to go on tour alone?"

"We'd hardly be alone. There'd be dozens of sound technicians and the craft service people with their sugary doughnuts and Styrofoam cups of coffee." He sipped his drink. "Gideon says if we don't go, we'll disappear off the charts. I don't want to stand onstage in front of a bunch of girls barely out of Mickey Mouse ears but we've come so far. If we stop now, it will have all been for nothing. I have to be a songwriter or I won't be able to breathe."

He pulled her close and kissed her softly on the mouth. He inhaled her jasmine scent and wanted to tell her she was right: Gideon was mad and he couldn't possibly go on tour.

But he thought of the great writers and knew nothing would hold them back. Shakespeare performed his plays at the Globe Theater for an illiterate audience who could barely afford the penny ticket, and Dickens printed his stories in a weekly newspaper that most people used to wrap fish. A true artist did anything to support his work. What mattered was that he wrote songs and people heard them.

"Is it wrong to want to achieve great things?" Lionel whispered.

"We said we'd give it a year and then go back to London," Samantha said slowly. "I promised Abigail I'd take her to the zoo on her birthday. I want to visit my sister's new baby and celebrate my parents' thirty-year anniversary."

"We'll send your sister a miniature baseball uniform and a Dodgers cap." Lionel ran his fingers over her nipples. "We'll book your parents a suite at the Connaught and tickets to *Phantom of the Opera*. We'll take Abigail and her friends to the zoo when we get back and buy them peanuts to feed the elephants."

"My parents do love the Connaught," Samantha mused. "My mother and I had afternoon tea there and they serve the most delicious lemon scones with Devonshire cream."

Lionel slipped off her robe and drank in the curve of her

breasts. He gazed at the silky smoothness of her thighs and felt like Michelangelo sculpting the Pietà.

"There's something very important we have to do first." He took her hand and led her into the bedroom.

"What?" Samantha asked.

"I have to memorize every curve of your body so when I lie on some lumpy mattress in a Motel Six in Toledo, I can picture your ripe breasts and golden hair and the tiny mole on the inside of your thigh."

"That sounds like very extensive research," Samantha murmured, stepping out of her panties.

"I know." Lionel unzipped his slacks and drew her onto the bed. "But if we get started now, I think we can cover it."

Lionel plunged inside her and felt as if he was being engulfed by a fire. He pulled her arms over her head and came so quickly he couldn't catch his breath.

Then he rolled off and ran his hands over her stomach. He slipped his fingers between her legs and found the wet spot deep inside her. He pushed in deeper, feeling like he found an enchanted forest. He watched her grip his shoulders and bite her lip. He heard her small gasps and saw the slick sheen on her skin and knew she was everything he desired.

Lionel padded into the living room and filled a glass with scotch. He thought of his room above Penelope's garage with its hot plate and packets of digestive biscuits. He pictured nights scribbling at his desk and smoking endless cigarettes. He remembered crumpling paper into the garbage and the heady sensation when he finally wrote a hit song.

He added a twist of lime and thought once Ford perfected the motorcar, no one rode in horse-drawn buggies. Hardly anyone spent three weeks on an ocean liner when they could fly from London to New York in seven hours.

Human beings had to move forward; it was as natural as turning twenty-one or losing one's virginity. Once you had sex you couldn't spend your nights with a *Playboy* and a towel, you craved a woman with firm breasts and sleek thighs.

He didn't want to write just one good song, he wanted a whole library of hits. He wanted a wall of platinum records and a garage filled with E-type Jaguars.

Three months would go by in an instant and he would return and propose. They'd drive to Montecito and book a suite at the Biltmore. He pictured sitting on the balcony and eating eggs Benedict and blueberry pancakes. He imagined poring over honeymoon brochures of Positano and Ravello.

He slipped the jewelry box in the hotel safe. He put the key in the desk and downed his scotch. He walked back into the bedroom and lay down beside Samantha on the ivory silk bedspread.

"Some people think life is laid out in a preordained path and all we have to do is follow it." Lionel scooped up a handful of pistachio nuts. "But God has better things to do than plot the future of seven billion people like a *Choose Your Own Adventure*. He gave us a better-developed brain than any other species and more than two thousand years of written history to guide us." He paused. "And we still manage to bloody mess everything up."

"Did you and Amber go on tour?" Juliet asked.

"I need a shower and shave." Lionel rubbed his chin. "Let's continue tomorrow."

"I'd rather continue now. Henry asked me to go to Marbella, he's playing an exposition match at Los Monteros." Juliet fiddled with her gold bangle. "I'll only be gone one night, but we really have to finish."

"I spent a weekend at Los Monteros," Lionel replied. "The swordfish is excellent and the wine selection is superb and when you lie on a white chaise longue at La Cabane you feel like King Herod in *Jesus Christ Superstar.*"

"He said he'd play better if I'm there." Juliet hesitated. "Gideon is getting impatient, I can't keep him waiting."

"Take a day off and don't worry about Gideon." Lionel finished his drink. "You are a young American in Spain, you can't pass up a chance to nibble foie gras and rub shoulders with Andy Murray and Roger Federer. I promise when you return, I'll wrap up my story."

Juliet smoothed her hair and walked to the door. She turned around and smiled. "I'll bring you a signed tennis ball."

Lionel stood in front of the mirror in the marble bathroom and rubbed his cheeks. He had showered and shaved but his head still pounded and he had circles under his eyes.

He slipped on his pajamas and poured a glass of sherry. He pictured Juliet in white slacks and a brightly colored sweater. He saw her standing courtside at the tennis match wearing soft leather loafers. He swallowed his sherry and felt something uncomfortable shift inside him.

chapter nineteen

JULIET ADJUSTED HER SUNGLASSES AND fiddled with her gold necklace. She glanced at the turquoise Mediterranean and whitewashed buildings and the distant outline of Africa. She saw waiters in white dinner jackets and inhaled the scent of hibiscus and felt like Grace Kelly in *To Catch a Thief.*

She had sat on the airplane with Henry's hand grazing her thigh and felt a lump in her throat. They hardly knew each other and she was going away with him. What if she forgot her toothbrush or ran out of things to say?

She closed her eyes and thought of the times in her life she had been terrified: her first day at Sony when she bumped into Mariah Carey in the elevator, moving to Los Angeles and learning to drive on the I-405, coaxing a lead singer whose girlfriend just left him onto the stage.

Then the plane landed at Málaga airport and the green mountains and shimmering coastline were laid out like a photo spread in a travel magazine. The skyscrapers of Torremolinos and elegant villas in Marbella sped past the window of the Bentley. The sultry breeze hit her cheeks and she inhaled the scent of the ocean and her shoulders relaxed.

Now she strolled through the grounds of Los Monteros and thought she had never been anywhere so elegant. Women wore Courrèges slacks and silver Prada sandals. Men wore silk blazers and paste-colored shirts. She saw pink flamingos and marble fountains and ponds filled with neon-colored fish.

"There you are." Henry appeared in the garden. He wore a striped shirt and white shorts and long socks. "I wanted to introduce you to my coach, the match starts in thirty minutes."

"I didn't want to get in the way." Juliet hesitated.

"You couldn't get in the way." Henry grinned. "You're the best thing about being here."

Juliet sat on the sidelines and watched Henry lob the ball over the net. She felt the hot sun on her cheeks and suddenly wished she had a glass of lemonade.

"You must be Juliet." A man approached her. He was in his mid-fifties with salt-and-pepper hair and leathery skin. He wore a polo shirt and slacks and leather loafers. "I'm Stefan, Henry's coach. It's a pleasure to meet you."

"Thank you for inviting me," Juliet replied. "The resort is spectacular, I feel like a movie star."

"Henry insisted you be here, it's an important match." Stefan sat beside her. "Henry has the strength of Boris Becker and a stroke like John McEnroe, but once you've been out it's hard to get back on top. You think of all the matches your opponent won while you were away and lose your nerve. Nothing is more important in tennis than believing you are the only one who can hit a ninety-mile-an-hour serve."

Juliet nodded. "Henry is an incredible player."

"A few more months of practice and he could win a Grand Slam," Stefan mused. "It's strange after all this work he's thinking of retiring."

"He is?" Juliet asked.

"All he talks about is hanging up his racquet and starting a family," Stefan replied. "He asked me about opening a tennis school."

Juliet stood up and suddenly felt dizzy. She opened her mouth to say something but her throat was dry and the ground tilted. She grabbed her purse and ran across the courtyard.

Juliet sat at the granite bar and sipped a glass of sparkling water. She ate a handful of macadamia nuts and felt her heart race.

She hated leaving the court but she was afraid she would faint. Hearing Stefan talk about Henry wanting to retire made her stomach turn over.

She took another sip of water and thought she had been overheated and forgot to have lunch. All she needed was a sandwich or a piece of fruit and she'd be fine.

She suddenly remembered Lionel saying human beings had to move forward, it was the most natural thing in the world. She couldn't just go dancing with Henry or visit art galleries. She had to see if she wanted to wake up beside him and share egg-white omelets.

She remembered Gabriella saying the cheeseburgers at Los

Monteros came on porcelain plates and smiled. She was at one of the most beautiful resorts in the world with a handsome tennis player. She would go into the bathroom and splash her face with water. Then she would go back on the court and watch Henry win his match.

She ate another handful of macadamia nuts and jumped off the stool. She took a deep breath and thought she was ready to fall in love.

Juliet smoothed her hair and glanced around the restaurant. The walls were covered in red velvet wallpaper and the tables were set with gold plates and gleaming silverware. She gazed out the sliding glass doors at the pink and yellow lights flickering on the swimming pool and caught her breath.

After Henry won his match they spent the afternoon at La Cabane. They sipped margaritas and talked about Stefan and Henry's next tournament. Juliet gazed at the white sailboats and blue stretch of Mediterranean and couldn't remember why she had been anxious.

She studied Henry's wide shoulders and suddenly wanted to go back to their room and peel off her swimsuit. She wanted to climb under white cotton sheets and feel Henry's chest on her breasts. She wanted him to stroke her thighs and run his hands though her hair.

But the breeze picked up and Henry said he was starving. He kissed her on the mouth and told her he was going to change for dinner. Juliet felt a shiver run down her spine and thought making love could wait. First they would sit in a sumptuous dining room and eat wild turbot and chanterelle mushrooms.

Now she looked up and saw Henry walking toward her. He wore a white dinner jacket and beige slacks. His hair was freshly washed and his cheeks glistened with aftershave.

"You look gorgeous." He smiled. "I thought you were a model posing for a photo shoot."

"I stopped in the hotel gift shop." Juliet glanced down at her black Dior dress and gold sandals. "I feel like Audrey Hepburn in *Breakfast at Tiffany's.*"

"You'd look beautiful in a cotton T-shirt and blue jeans, but I'm glad you dressed up." He took her hand. "I asked the maître d' to sit us at the window. There's nothing like seeing the sun set behind the Rock of Gibraltar."

They sat at a round table and ate lobster and lamb cutlets with herb truffles. They sipped a pinot noir and talked about Marbella and the Costa del Sol.

"Marbella was a little fishing village after World War Two," Henry said. "Prince Alfonso of Hohenlohe-Lagenburg bought an estate and invited Frank Sinatra and Brigitte Bardot and Sophia Loren. Other celebrities heard about it and brought their yachts and sports cars. In the 1970s they expanded Málaga airport and the Costa del Sol became one of the most sought after holiday destinations.

"I played my first tournament at Los Monteros when I was seventeen. I glanced around the court at women in silver miniskirts and men wearing Gucci loafers and thought I'd never seen so many beautiful people. Then I won first place and they placed a wreath around my neck and popped a bottle of champagne and I thought I had the best job in the world."

Juliet nodded. "Stefan said you have the fastest serve on the circuit. He thinks you could win the Grand Slam."

"I used to love to feel my shins burn and my shoulders ache. I'd slam the ball over the net and know I was going to be the best player in the world," he mused. "Now I'd rather share a bottle of red wine and a plate of seafood paella.

"After the season ends I might open a tennis clinic in Santa Barbara. I've always liked California, the people are friendly and the scenery is spectacular and the fresh fruit is delicious." He touched her hand. "I can't stop thinking about you. I want to stroll on the beach in Santa Monica and visit wineries in Ojai."

"I only leave the office to pick up a chicken salad from Trader Joe's or a latte from Starbucks," Juliet replied. "On weekends I'm usually backstage at the Hollywood Bowl or at a nightclub listening to a new band."

"There's no hurry, but maybe in a few years you'll do something else," Henry suggested. "Work part-time and teach music at UCLA."

Juliet ate a bite of lamb and her stomach clenched. She reached for a glass of water and could barely swallow. She pushed back her chair and rushed to the bathroom.

Juliet stood in front of the beveled mirror and took deep breaths. Her hair had escaped its ceramic clip and her forehead had a light sheen.

It had been lovely sitting across from Henry, nibbling lobster salad. She gazed at his brown eyes and blond hair and couldn't wait to go back to their room. Then she ate the last bite of lamb and her stomach rose to her throat.

Maybe the lamb was bad or she was allergic to lobster. She remembered Henry talking about moving to Santa Barbara and shivered. That couldn't possibly have anything to do with it; she would love him to live in California.

She stood at the mirror and smoothed her hair behind her ears. She rubbed her lips with red lipstick and felt her knees buckle. She collapsed onto the velvet daybed and put her head in her hands.

"I don't know what happened. Maybe I drank too much wine and didn't have enough to eat," Juliet said. "I had so much fun at your match I forgot to have lunch."

They had left the restaurant and returned to their suite. Juliet unzipped her dress and slipped on a cotton robe. Now she sat on the four-poster bed, sipping a glass of water.

Henry nodded. "The Mediterranean sun is stronger than it looks. I should have insisted you have a burger and shake."

"I'm sorry, I spoiled our dinner." Juliet blushed. "I was look-ing forward to the caramel flan for dessert."

"There's a lot to look forward to, but we're not in a rush." Henry touched her chin. "I'll sleep in the living room so you get a full night's rest. I often slept on the sofa when I was touring. When I started doing tournaments, I'd share a suite with two other players."

"Are you sure?" Juliet asked. "You played a hard match, you should sleep in a bed."

"The sofa is handcrafted Italian leather." He grinned, grabbing a pillow. He leaned forward and pressed his thumb on her mouth. "I'll see you in the morning."

Juliet stood at the sliding glass doors and gazed at the lush gardens. She inhaled the scent of damp grass and tried to stop her head from spinning.

She had taken two aspirin but still couldn't sleep. She must have caught a summer flu and they'd laugh about it in the morning. She pictured eating muesli and pineapple and Henry teasing her that she'd do anything to have the bed to herself.

She climbed onto the four-poster bed and drew the crisp cotton sheets around her shoulders. What if she wasn't really sick, what if she wasn't ready? Maybe Lionel was right and she didn't know how to fall in love. She closed her eyes and let the tears stream down her cheeks.

chapter twenty

LIONEL LIT A CIGARETTE WITH a pearl lighter and inhaled slowly. He picked up the magazine and turned the page. He tossed it on the glass coffee table and ground the cigarette into a silver ashtray.

He had slept remarkably well and woke up with new energy. He swam twenty laps in the pool and did sit-ups on the terrace. Then he poured a cup of fresh coffee and carried Gloria's scrambled eggs and grilled tomatoes into the conservatory.

He picked up the copy of *Rolling Stone* and glanced at it warily. He had stopped reading it years ago, it usually had articles with terms he didn't understand and an undeserving artist on the cover. But now he couldn't help turning the page, like someone curious to see his own obituary.

He glanced at articles about Lady Gaga and John Legend. He saw the picture of Gideon and sucked in his breath. Gideon wore a pastel Ralph Lauren blazer and stood in front of an ivory Bentley.

He remembered when he and Samantha insisted they would never own a Bentley; it was like driving around in an overstuffed living room. But now he gazed at the creamy interior and walnut steering wheel and felt a pit in his stomach.

He heard a knock at the door and called: "Come in, I'm in the conservatory."

"It smells wonderful." Juliet stood at the door. She wore a turquoise dress and silver sandals.

"Gloria makes very good eggs," Lionel replied. "I taught her to cook with Tabasco sauce; my mother uses it on everything.

"Gideon is in *Rolling Stone*," he continued. "Gideon and Amber and I were on the cover once. The headline said 'Music's Golden Triumvirate.' It should have read 'Svengali and His Puppets.'

"He must have made a deal with the devil, he keeps getting younger. His salt-and-pepper hair is from Fred Segal and his eyes are done by Dr. Andrew Ordon. I remember the first time he tried Botox, I wondered how anyone could inject himself with pig collagen." He shuddered. "It's bad enough eating pork, I wouldn't want it living under my forehead.

"He always was an excellent dresser, he could walk into Fred Hayman's on Rodeo Drive and select which Calvin Klein blazer was the must-have piece of the season." He stopped and glanced at Juliet. "That's a pretty dress, is it new?"

"It's Nina Ricci." Juliet blushed. "I bought it at the hotel gift shop in Marbella."

"How was the getaway?" Lionel asked. "Did you sit on a chaise longue at La Cabane and watch sailboats glide across the Mediterranean?"

Juliet nodded. "Los Monteros was gorgeous. The gardens were full of birds of paradise and pink flamingos. The suite had a marble fireplace and a basket of mangos and papaya."

"Did you dance to Ella Fitzgerald in the moonlight?" Lionel mused. "Should I be expecting an announcement in *The Times*?"

"I got sick during dinner." Juliet fiddled with her necklace.

"You got sick?"

"I thought I was going to faint, so we went back to the suite." Juliet paused. "Henry slept in the living room."

Lionel sprinkled pepper on eggs and took a large bite. He blotted his mouth with a napkin and looked at Juliet.

"People think they can change but they remain as constant as the statistics on their birth announcements. Women try a dozen different hair colors but at the end of the day they're still a brunette or redhead." He paused. "I knew you didn't believe in love."

"Of course I believe in love, I forgot to have lunch and got too much sun," Juliet protested. "Henry was a perfect gentleman and put me to bed."

"If you are in love you'll get soaked in the rain and ruin the leather seats in your convertible. You'll scale an iron gate and get bitten by a German shepherd." He sat on a silk love seat and stretched his long legs in front of him. "And only when it's too late will you realize you would do it all again."

Lionel walked to the marble bar and poured a glass of scotch. He glanced at the platter of stone wheat crackers and soft cheeses and realized he wasn't hungry. He gazed out the window at the rain falling on the hotel swimming pool and felt a weight press on his shoulders.

———

Ever since they agreed he should go on tour, Lionel had felt a chill in the air. Samantha stayed on campus, claiming it was easier to read books in the library. Lionel ate cheeseburgers and steak fries alone and fell asleep watching old Gary Cooper movies. In the morning she was gone before he shaved and showered. He glanced at her porcelain coffee cup and inhaled the scent of nutmeg and cinnamon and thought he had made a terrible mistake.

He remembered when his parents left him on his first day at boarding school. He pictured watching their Range Rover roll down the driveway and being gripped by a terrible panic. He remembered telling the headmaster his Irish setter was having puppies, and he had to go home and be with her.

He tried to think of the reasons he should go on tour, but they evaporated like rain after a thunderstorm. He could always write songs and find artists to sing them. It didn't matter if he was a footnote in *Billboard*'s page for 1997 as long as they were together.

Now he drained his glass and knew he couldn't go through with it. He would tell Gideon he didn't care if the second album sunk faster than a torpedo. He couldn't possibly leave Samantha and he was crazy to think they could be apart.

He poured another glass of scotch and felt his shoulders relax. He had realized his error before it was too late, and everything was going to be all right. He picked up the phone and put it down. He would drive to Gideon's house in Beverly Hills and tell him in person. Then he would come home and he and Samantha would open a bottle of Möet & Chandon.

He drove down Gideon's long gravel driveway and buzzed the intercom. He gazed at the tall iron gates and sighed. Since

Gideon had a stalker a few months ago, his house was as impenetrable as a medieval fortress. He climbed into an oak tree and grabbed the top of the fence. He tumbled onto the grass and was met by a large German shepherd.

"Hans Solo, it's me, Lionel." He rubbed his shins. "I'm the guy who insisted Gideon feed you proper Alpo dog food instead of that spirulina crap Donovan recommended. I told him you're a dog, not bloody Popeye." He paused, watching the dog sniff his leg. "You're upset because you're wet, I hate this weather too. If I wanted rain, I would have moved to Oregon, though I don't know if I could live somewhere where they pillage Shakespeare. *Othello* wasn't meant to be performed in a redwood forest by a bunch of actors wearing hemp shirts and Birkenstocks.

"If you let me get up, I'll tell Gideon to bring you inside and get you a towel and a brandy." Lionel's teeth chattered. "There's nothing like a warm fluffy towel right out of the dryer."

He rang the doorbell and waited for the door to open.

"Inga is probably in the kitchen making strudel." Lionel glanced at the dog. "I don't know why Gideon needs a house with more rooms than Versailles."

He rang the doorbell again and felt the rain fall on his shoulders. His Paul Smith shirt was wet and his Santoni loafers were ruined. Suddenly he turned and saw a car in front of the garage. He looked more closely and saw it was Samantha's yellow Honda.

He stepped back as if he had been punched in the stomach. Samantha said she was studying and then had a late semantics class. What was she doing at Gideon's?

He pressed himself against the entry and wondered what to do. He could wait for someone to answer but he already felt feverish. He glanced at Hans Solo's sharp teeth and worried the dog might blame him for being left outside and take a bite out of his ankle.

He would drive back to the Beverly Hills Hotel and take a hot shower. Samantha must have a simple explanation; she was planning a surprise party for his birthday or hosting a going away dinner at Spago's. They would laugh and climb into bed. Lionel would drink heated brandy and try to stop shivering.

He gazed up at the stone turrets and slate roof and wanted to leap through the window. But he saw the iron bars and thought it would be as easy to storm the house as to infiltrate a terrorist cell in Iran. He ran down the driveway and climbed over the fence. He put the car into reverse and roared away.

Lionel sat at the glass dining table in the suite's living room and cracked a soft-boiled egg. He sprinkled it with salt and took a small bite.

He remembered when he was a child and came down with the flu. His mother promised him ice cream when he got better. When he was finally well enough to sit up and eat a bowl of chocolate ice cream it made his throat burn. He pushed it away and drank a cup of warm milk with honey.

Now he glanced at the table set with rashers and whole wheat toast and pots of strawberry jam, and his throat closed up.

He had come home from Gideon's and saw the light blinking on the answering machine. He glanced at the familiar red button and his breathing relaxed. Samantha had left a message saying her class was canceled, and she stopped by Gideon's to pick up

Lionel's new songs. She'd ask if he wanted anything from Safeway or Walmart and she'd be home in a minute.

But when he pressed PLAY he heard Gideon's voice on the machine.

"It's perfectly safe to come tonight. There's a baked chicken and roasted potatoes and a bottle of Rémy Martin. Lionel will never know."

He played it over and over like Sherlock Holmes deciphering a clue. But no matter how many times he listened to Gideon's clipped British accent, he said the same thing.

Lionel finally climbed into bed and drew the white cotton sheets over his shoulders. He woke in the middle of the night with a terrible chill and saw Samantha's side was still empty.

For two days he lay in bed and shivered. He waited for Samantha to appear but no one knocked on the door except the maid service with fresh sheets and fluffy white towels. He called Gideon's house but there was no answer. He tried his office but his secretary said he was away.

"I need to know where he is." Lionel gripped the phone. "I have something urgent to tell him."

"He left instructions that his location was confidential," Rosemary replied.

"I'm his best friend," Lionel protested. "I have the spare key to his Aston Martin."

"I'm sorry, I'm just following instructions," Rosemary said. "If he calls in, I'll tell him you are trying to find him."

Lionel put on his dressing gown and grabbed his keys. He would go to Gideon's office and insist Rosemary tell him where he was. He would camp out in the lobby like John and Yoko performing a sit-in.

But his eyes blurred and he felt his forehead. He climbed back into bed and poured a glass of water. He swallowed a couple of aspirin and prayed he could get rid of this fever.

Now he felt well enough to eat a soft-boiled egg. He glanced at Samantha's pile of textbooks and couldn't believe she hadn't come home. He called the police but they said statuesque blondes go missing in Los Angeles all the time. They were usually found ensconced in a movie producer's Malibu beach house.

He was supposed to leave on the first leg of the tour in the morning. He had called Donovan and said he was recovering from the flu. Donovan replied that unless he was in intensive care he better be in St. Louis or Yesterday Records would sue him for half a million dollars.

He pictured Samantha's car in Gideon's driveway and thought about the day John Lennon died. He remembered staring at the television and seeing the bouquets of flowers in front of The Dakota and thinking there must be a mistake. The greatest songwriter in history couldn't have been killed by a madman wanting to impress Jodie Foster. Just because he didn't want to believe something, that didn't mean it wasn't true. There was no explanation for the message on the answering machine and Samantha and Gideon's disappearance except that they were having an affair.

He entered the bedroom and pulled his suitcase out of the closet. He folded Ralph Lauren shirts and cashmere sweaters. He picked up his copy of Shelley's sonnets and put it down. Samantha was reading it for her Romantic lyricism class and might need it.

He walked back into the living room and sat at the table. If he was going to perform for thousands of screaming teenyboppers, he needed his strength. He ate a small bite of toast and marmalade and put it back on his plate. He glanced at the thick sausages and bowl of cut strawberries and wondered if he would ever be hungry again.

Lionel glanced at Juliet. "You look a little pale. I'll ask Gloria to make you some scrambled eggs, the Tabasco sauce will put color in your cheeks."

Juliet shook her head. "No thank you, I'm not hungry."

Lionel lit a cigarette and blew a thin smoke ring. He walked to the window and gazed at the turquoise swimming pool.

"If I could relive that day I would have driven to Gideon's office and demanded that Rosemary tell me where he was, I would have waited for Samantha to come home and begged her to tell me the truth." He paused. "If you don't love Henry, you have to tell him. It's like putting your beloved fifteen-year-old Irish setter down. It breaks your heart but it's the only kind thing to do."

"Thank you for the advice but we need to talk about your contract." Juliet stood up and smoothed her skirt. "Gideon called me this morning, he wants to know when you're going to deliver the new songs."

Lionel ground the cigarette into a glass ashtray and glanced at the copy of *Rolling Stone*. He looked at Juliet and his shoulders sagged.

"Tell him he'll get his new songs when hell bloody freezes over."

chapter twenty-one

JULIET STOOD ON THE BALCONY and gazed at the green valley filled with stone churches and citrus trees. She saw the sandy cliffs and the deep blue of the Mediterranean. She gazed at the harbor full of red fishing boats and remembered when she arrived in Majorca and thought she had never seen so much color.

She smoothed her hair and remembered thinking all she had to do for two weeks was listen to Lionel's story. She would have plenty of time to hike to Deia and eat tapas at cafés in Sóller. She would have time to meet someone who loved F. Scott Fitzgerald and outdoor markets.

After she left Casa Rosa, she strolled down the narrow path and gazed at the shimmering ocean. She bought an apple from a fruit stand and thought she had a wonderful career and a handsome guy who was in love with her.

She remembered all the times in the last few years when she'd come home from seeing one of her bands perform at a club to an empty apartment. She was on a rush from the throbbing music and sweaty crowd and the feeling she was part of something exciting.

But the minute she entered her tiny living room, the feeling of elation was replaced by silence. She wanted to text or call someone and tell them the band got a standing ovation. But her friends who worked at law firms or PR companies were all asleep. She finally poured a cup of chamomile tea and carried it into the bedroom.

If Lionel didn't fulfill his contract, she might be fired and have nothing. And when she closed her eyes and pictured Henry's wavy blond hair she felt a pit in her stomach.

She finally walked back to Hotel Salvia and climbed the stairs to her room. Now she stood on the balcony and gazed at the pink and orange sunset.

She was meeting Henry for dinner at Casa Isabella, and all day she tried to feel excited. But she remembered sitting across from Henry at Los Monteros and the air left her lungs. Lionel was right; she wasn't in love with him.

She would wait until after dinner and say she was leaving in less than a week; they should stop seeing each other. She had enjoyed his company and hoped they could stay friends.

She walked inside and saw an e-mail from Gideon. She read it quickly and picked up her phone.

"Juliet." Lydia's voice came over the line. "It's lovely to hear from you. I was just having a glass of rosé and a bowl of lobster paella. *Gigi* is on television; Leslie Caron is one of my favorite actresses. She is a wonderful dancer and sings like an angel."

"Gideon wrote that he's never heard a voice like Gabriella's," Juliet said quickly. "He wants her to come to Los Angeles and record an album. He'll get her a suite at the Beverly Hills Hotel and a driver." She paused and took a deep breath. "He thinks she'll be as big as Gwen Stefani or Beyoncé."

"That's wonderful news," Lydia exclaimed.

"I'm having dinner at Casa Isabella with Henry. I'll arrive early and tell her." Juliet bit her lip. "What if she is furious at me for sending Gideon the recording without asking her?"

"When I was young I dreamed of a handsome husband and wonderful children and a villa filled with elegant furniture and designer gowns," Lydia mused. "Instead I lived on a farm and sold oranges and olive oil. I raised one little boy by myself, and though I had a closet of Carolina Herrera dresses, I mostly wore them to watch the sun set. Gabriella is young, she doesn't know what will make her happy." She paused and her voice was light. "How can she possibly be angry when you tell her she is going to be a star?"

Juliet opened the gate of Casa Isabella and climbed the stone steps. She saw the garden filled with pink azaleas and tall birds of paradise.

"Juliet." Gabriella appeared at the entry.

She wore a navy dress and beige pumps and her hair was knotted in a low bun.

"You're early, your reservation is at seven P.M. The restaurant isn't open yet; I just returned from the flower market. I found the most beautiful peonies and lilacs."

"I wanted to talk to you," Juliet said.

"Come inside." Gabriella led her into the dining room. "We can talk while I fill the vases."

Juliet glanced at the teal silk curtains and mosaic ceiling and sighed with happiness. It was such a beautiful room; no wonder Gabriella loved working here.

"How was Marbella?" Gabriella asked, arranging lilacs in a crystal vase.

"The resort was gorgeous," Juliet replied. "Henry wore a white dinner jacket and we sat at a table overlooking the garden and ate lamb and grilled vegetables. He took my hand and said he couldn't stop thinking about me. He is going to retire and open a tennis clinic in Santa Barbara."

"What did you say?" Gabriella asked.

"When I was a child, my mother and I made oatmeal cookies for Santa Claus. Every Christmas Eve we placed them on a plate next to the fireplace, and every Christmas Day they were gone.

"One Christmas Eve I was terribly thirsty. I crept downstairs and saw my mother sliding the cookies into the garbage. The next morning my mother laughed, saying that if Santa Claus ate all the cookies he would be too heavy for his sleigh. I tried to believe her but I knew she wasn't telling the truth." Juliet paused. "I sat across from Henry and imagined sharing the Sunday *New York Times* and milky cappuccinos. I pictured romantic dinners and long walks and full days in bed.

"You can't make yourself believe in Santa Claus and you can't make yourself fall in love. I want to do those things, but I don't want to do them with Henry."

"What did Henry say?" Gabriella gasped.

"I'm going to tell him tonight," Juliet said miserably.

"He's a world-class tennis player, he'll find someone else." Gabriella placed the vase on the linen tablecloth. "You just need to be honest, he can't expect more than that."

"There's another reason I came early." Juliet took a deep

breath. "Your grandmother recorded you singing and asked me to send it to Gideon. He's going to fly you to Los Angeles and give you a hotel suite and a driver. He thinks you're going to be a huge star."

"How could you do that without telling me?" Gabriella demanded.

"Lydia saw Hugo with another woman at a café in Palma. They were sitting in the back and the girl was crying. She ran out of the restaurant, and Lydia saw that she was pregnant." Juliet paused. "She didn't want to hurt you but she didn't want you to miss out on a wonderful opportunity.

"Then you showed me the ruby earrings and I wondered how Hugo could afford them when he was saving for an engagement ring." She looked at Gabriella. "I thought you'd like to have an option in case . . ."

"In case Hugo left me?" Gabriella fumed. "The woman at the café is Hugo's cousin from Barcelona. Gia is in love with an artist who refuses to marry her. She was crying because her family will disown her if she has the baby, but she doesn't want to lose Antonio.

"Hugo did some work for a friend and he paid him with ruby earrings. Yesterday we went to Cartier and picked out a square-cut diamond on a platinum band. Hugo is going to pay it off, and then ask my parents for my hand in marriage.

"When he finds out I've been offered a recording contract, he'll be afraid to hold me back." She sunk onto a chair. "Who gives up jewels and limousines to live in a cramped apartment and work in a sweaty kitchen?"

"But Lydia called Hugo and another woman answered." Juliet frowned. "Lydia wanted to leave a message but she hung up."

"Gia left her cell phone at home so her family couldn't trace her," Gabriella explained. "She gave Hugo's number to Antonio and her doctor."

Juliet's eyes were huge. "I was trying to do the right thing. I didn't want you to get hurt."

Gabriella stood up and smoothed her hair. She walked to the hallway and turned around.

"I'm going upstairs, my mother will be in the dining room tonight," she paused. "The right thing is to tell the truth. I thought you understood that."

Juliet sat at a square table and gazed at waiters carrying platters of sautéed scallops and summer vegetables. She remembered what Gabriella said and shivered. She couldn't sit across from Henry and discuss his next exhibition match. She couldn't savor Mallorcan turbot and wonder when she should tell him how she felt.

She tossed her napkin on the table and ran down the steps. She opened the gate and saw Henry striding along the promenade.

Henry approached her. "I'm sorry I'm late."

He wore a tan-collared shirt and beige slacks. His hair was freshly washed and his cheeks glistened with aftershave.

He handed Juliet a bouquet of roses and orchids. "I wanted to get you flowers but the outdoor market was out of roses. I convinced the owner of a boutique to sell me the flowers in the window."

Juliet smiled. "They're gorgeous. It's such a beautiful night, I'd like to go for a walk."

Henry frowned. "But we'll miss our reservation."

"Let's just stroll along the promenade," Juliet suggested. "The fishing boats are coming in and I love the smell of fresh caught salmon."

They walked along the pavement and Juliet saw silver boats bobbing in the harbor. She saw couples holding hands and a young man playing the guitar. His guitar case was open and he was surrounded by a group of people.

"I attended my first concert when I was fifteen," Juliet said. "Destiny's Child played Madison Square Garden and I was so excited I changed my outfit three times. Beyoncé started singing and you could feel the electricity in the air. I gazed at the fans with their sweaty foreheads and glowing cheeks and knew what I wanted to do.

"It's not just music I love; it's the effect it has on people. Sometimes I feel like a babysitter or an errand girl on a constant loop between Starbucks and Whole Foods. But sometimes I stand backstage and feel like a magician.

"You were flat on your back and now you are poised to win a Grand Slam. You have plenty of time to buy a big house with a garden and golden retriever. Now you should be winning gold trophies and jetting between New York and Monaco.

"We both love what we do and we shouldn't give it up." She gazed at the lights twinkling on the water. "I've had a wonderful time, but I think we should stop seeing each other."

Henry stood quietly beside her. His forehead creased and his eyes flickered.

"But I'm in love with you and you must feel the same," he said. "I've never felt this way before, I don't want it to end."

"I do feel something but it's not enough." Juliet hesitated.

"We're in different places in our lives and that's not going to change."

"But we can make it change," Henry insisted. "We can fly and see each other a few times a month. I'm always in the air, I don't mind stopping in California."

"I'm sorry." Juliet shook her head. "I think it's better if we make a clean break."

"Are you sure there isn't someone else?" Henry asked softly.

Juliet inhaled his scent of aftershave and musk cologne. She looked at his wavy blond hair and blue eyes and took a deep breath.

"There isn't anyone," she replied. "I'm all by myself."

They walked along the promenade in silence. They reached the gate of Casa Isabella and Juliet smoothed her hair.

"I'm not really hungry," she said. "I'll take the tram back to Sóller."

"I'll see you back to Hotel Salvia," he offered.

"No thank you, I'll be fine." She held out her hand. "I hope we can stay friends."

Henry shrugged and stuffed his hands in his pockets.

"Perhaps after a little time apart." His face broke into a small smile. "How else would I get front row tickets to a Coldplay concert when they come to New Zealand?"

Juliet hurried to the tram stop and felt the cool breeze on her shoulders. She pictured Gabriella's flashing green eyes and hoped she could forgive her. She thought about Lionel and wondered if he would ever write a new song.

She stepped onto the tram and saw a familiar figure through the window. He had dark hair and wore a patterned shirt and silk slacks. She looked closer and realized it wasn't Lionel, it was a stranger. She closed her eyes and leaned against the hardwood bench.

chapter twenty-two

LIONEL STOOD AT THE MARBLE bar and stirred a Bloody Mary. He added pepper and Worcestershire sauce and took a small sip. He thought about Gideon's letter and his shoulders tightened.

What if Gideon was serious and really wanted his money? He could sell the flat in Chelsea but then he'd be living out of a suitcase. He pictured a succession of friends' Swiss ski chalets and New York penthouses. He imagined growing old and ending up in an efficiency in Euston.

He pictured his old Paris apartment in the first arrondissement with its Louis XIV furniture. He remembered thinking the French kept their rooms colder than the British and it was impossible to curl up with *Madame Bovary* on a spindly chair.

He sipped his drink and flashed on the day his bank manager froze his charge card. He rushed into the walnut offices on Bond Street and insisted there was a mistake. He remembered the manager pointing to the meticulous columns of debits and credits and flinched.

One of the greatest joys of his success was helping other

people. He happily wrote a childhood friend a check to open a taco store in Belgravia. He was thrilled to get in on the ground floor of a holiday resort in the Congo.

He pictured Gideon with his Patek Philippe watch and Louis Vuitton sunglasses. Gideon didn't need the money, all his investments turned to gold.

He heard a knock on the door and called: "Come in, I'm in the living room."

"Would you like a Bloody Mary?" He looked up at Juliet. "Gideon collects Bloody Mary recipes from St. Regises all over the world. The Misty Mary from the St. Regis Istanbul with turnip juice and the Chilli Padi Mary from the St. Regis Singapore with gingerroot.

"If it was up to me I'd just mix tomato juice with vodka. But he's always adding cumin or organic celery," he mused. "I don't understand the benefit of exotic spices or organic vegetables when vodka rots your stomach."

"It's a little early for a drink." Juliet hesitated.

"It's never too early when your best friend behaves like Tiberius." He sighed. "I remember when Gideon and I celebrated every gold record with an omelet at Spago's.

"Then he became consumed by power and status and started staying at the St. Regis in Moscow and New York. It's easy to feel like God when you look down on Fifth Avenue and the taxis resemble ants.

"But power can be dangerous, even God makes mistakes. Do you think He meant to bury Pompeii when Vesuvius erupted or wipe out an entire population with the Black Plague?

"If Gideon knew the damage he caused he may have acted differently." His eyes dimmed and he stretched his long legs in front of him. "Of course I'm to blame, I let him tell me what to do."

Lionel tossed his overnight bag on the thick ivory carpet and poured a glass of scotch. He gazed at the cream satin sofas and pink silk drapes and original Andy Warhols lining the walls. He saw the silver platter holding imported cheeses and designer chocolates and thought he'd never been so glad to be in Los Angeles.

He had spent three months at Best Westerns in Toledo and Chicago and Pittsburgh. He signed autographs at malls in Michigan and played at a stadium in the pouring rain in New Jersey. He felt the water seep through his shirt and ruin his leather loafers and wondered if he had been better off carrying Louis Vuitton luggage at Claridge's.

He didn't hear from Samantha or Gideon and drowned his pain in a diet of bourbon and cigarettes and minibar pretzels. He called Gideon's secretary from every city, but Rosemary said he was in Brazil or signing a new metal band in Finland. He rustled through his pockets and found the phone numbers girls shoved at him and almost picked up the phone. But he pictured someone seeing the misery in his eyes and tossed the notes in the garbage.

How could Samantha cheat on him with his best friend? They were like characters in a daytime soap opera. Then he pictured her smooth blond hair and long legs and felt the emptiness well up inside him. He stubbed out his cigarette and thought no matter what she did, he had to find a way to forgive her.

Now he carried his scotch into the bedroom and debated whether to take a nap or a shower. He gazed at the pink marble bathroom with its plush towels and silk robes and thought wealth and success had their virtues.

He walked into the closet and hung up his Hugo Boss blazer. He noticed the hangers were empty and Samantha's white Keds were missing. He pulled open the drawers and couldn't find her bras and cotton panties.

He walked into the bedroom and felt his heart pound. He saw an envelope propped on the bedside table and tore it open.

> *Dear Lionel,*
>
> *I have gone back to London, please don't follow me. I was relieved when Donovan replaced me in the video; I never wanted to be onstage. But I remember sitting across from you at the café in Stratford-Upon-Avon and knew I couldn't stand in your way. You were like an astronaut determined to land on the moon and nothing was going to stop you.*
>
> *You can be headstrong and stubborn so I think it's best we make a clean break. Please don't try to contact me, I have given Georgina strict instructions not to give out my number. And you don't want to knock on the door and cause a scene in front of Abigail.*
>
> *I called you at every tour stop in Rosemary's schedule, but you were always checked out. I finally had to give up and admit we weren't the invincible couple I imagined.*
>
> *You're not the first man to fall for a pretty face or large bust but I thought you were better than that. I can't say it didn't hurt to see you with Amber but I should have expected it. After all we are all human and you are more human than*

most. You can't write love songs if you are flawless, there would be nothing to write about.

Deep down I believed we were different but I guess all lovers do. We both read enough D. H. Lawrence to know anyone is capable of illicit lust and enough Tolstoy to realize every love story has a beginning and an end.

I can't say quite yet I wish you well because I am angry and hurt. But someday we will look back and remember eating spinach omelets at the Polo Lounge and seeing Casablanca *at the Roxie Cinema. I loved you very much and I will miss you.*

"What the bloody hell." Lionel crumpled the paper. Suddenly he saw a copy of *People* on the bedside table. He glanced at the glossy photo and bold headline and his stomach turned over.

The photo was of him and Amber standing under the Empire State Building. She wore a low-cut pink dress and her honey blond hair tumbled over her shoulders. His hand circled her waist and his lips brushed her cheek. The headline read: "IS AMERICA'S FAVORITE SINGING DUO NOW A ROMANTIC COUPLE?"

It was the photo for the cover of their new album and he wondered how *People* got hold of it. Now he knew why Samantha went back to England. She thought he was having an affair with Amber.

Surely she would have contacted him and demanded to know what was going on? He and Samantha were madly in love and she must realize gossip magazines made an innocent kiss seem like a trip down the aisle. And if she did call him every night, why did he never get the messages? Rosemary had a detailed itinerary of the tour dates and hotels in every city.

He thought about Gideon and knew there was only one way to

find out. He grabbed his keys and slipped on his leather loafers. He drove to Century City and took the elevator to Gideon's office. He strode past Rosemary at her sleek walnut desk and burst through the door.

Gideon looked up from his desk. He wore a blue silk Armani jacket and cream slacks. His hair was perfectly highlighted and he wore a gold Patek Philippe watch.

He nodded. "You look well, being on tour agrees with you. Donovan said the numbers were fantastic, you played sold-out shows in Tampa and Dallas."

"You ruined my life," Lionel stormed. "You are my best friend, how could you sleep with Samantha?"

"I haven't seen Samantha since the three of us had dinner at Mr. Chow."

"A few nights before I left on tour I went to your house and Samantha's car was in the driveway," Lionel continued. "I waited for Samantha for two days but she never came home. Rosemary said you were out of the office at a confidential location."

Gideon stood up and walked to the sideboard. He selected a mushroom quiche and took a small bite.

"I was in China having talks with the government about opening a recording studio."

"What was Samantha doing at your house?" Lionel asked.

Gideon shrugged. "Maybe she was asking Inga to borrow her potato pancake recipe."

"You left a message on the answering machine saying it was safe to come over. You said there was a roasted chicken and a bottle of Rémy Martin and Lionel would never know."

"You're suffering from overexhaustion from the tour." Gideon raised his eyebrow. "I can't stand bloody answering machines, I never use them. Perhaps she ordered a surprise going-away dinner from Wolfgang Puck's and the maître d' called to say she could pick it up."

Lionel clutched the *People* magazine and felt the sweat prickle on his forehead. Gideon was so calm and collected; he didn't know what to believe.

"I haven't talked to her in three months. I was too furious to call and she said she tried every hotel and I had always checked out. She left a letter that she went back to England." He tossed the magazine on the desk. "How did this photo end up in *People*?"

Gideon shrugged. "You know those tour schedules, they're always changing. I'm sure Rosemary sent her an updated one but we add venues at the last minute." He picked up the magazine.

"Amber looks wonderful in pink and your shirt brings out your eyes," he mused. "Donovan's research studies showed fans reacted favorably to your being a couple. Your popularity quotient rose ten percent after the photos were released in *US* and *People*."

"There are more photos?" Lionel gasped.

"*Seventeen* did a photo spread and you made the inside cover of *Hello!*" Gideon poured a glass of papaya juice. "Think about Mick Jagger and Jerry Hall or James Taylor and Carly Simon. Everybody likes a love story between stars, it makes them feel as if they are part of music royalty."

"But it's not true, Amber and I didn't even play Uno together," Lionel spluttered. "She has a blond boyfriend on the Olympic water polo team and she's never read Shakespeare."

"Do you think Rock Hudson romanced Doris Day on the set of *Pillow Talk*? He was too busy making eyes at the male grip,"

Gideon insisted. "Movie audiences lapped it up and they were one of the most successful duos in cinematic history."

"Samantha believed it and now she doesn't want to see me." Lionel walked to the door. "I have to go to London and explain. Tell Rosemary to book me on the first flight to Heathrow. I'll go back to the hotel and get the engagement ring out of the safe."

"You might want to wait." Gideon opened the desk drawer and took out a newspaper. He walked to the marble bar and filled a glass with vodka. "And you might want to drink this."

Lionel glanced down and saw a photo of Samantha wearing a white lace dress and clutching a bouquet of peonies. Her hair was covered by an ivory veil and she held hands with a man in a gray morning suit.

"Prominent London economist Brian Phillips marries socialite after a whirlwind romance."

Lionel took the vodka and swallowed it one gulp. He sat on the leather chair and read out loud:

"Brian Phillips and Miss Samantha Highbridge were married today at St. Matthew's Church followed by a lavish reception at the Connaught. Mr. Phillips is a renowned economist who lectures at London University and Cambridge. He and Miss Highbridge met a month ago at a Princess Diana fundraiser at the home of Georgina Towers. The previously confirmed bachelor remarked:

"'I never thought I'd get married; statistically love is a terrible investment. But the minute I saw Samantha I knew I had won the lottery.'

"The couple will reside in Chelsea and Cambridge."

———

Lionel threw the paper on the desk and ran his hands through his hair.

"Samantha isn't a socialite, she's the bloody nanny! How could she marry a mathematician?" Lionel demanded. "And she's only been back in London for two months, that's not enough time to get back her dry cleaning."

"Some women love whirlwind courtships, maybe he swept her off his feet," Gideon said. "And he's a world-famous economist; not a mathematician. His algorithms were used at the economic conference at Davos."

"He is at least ten years older and has a nose like a ski slope." Lionel slumped in his chair. "Everything's ruined, I can't show up and tell her she made a terrible mistake and needs a divorce. Samantha would never go back on her word. And she got everything she wanted, a terrace house in Chelsea and access to King's College library."

"I'm very sorry. I never meant for any of this to happen, but maybe you weren't meant to be together. Screaming fans and adoring women are part a musician's life, and you have to completely trust each other." Gideon dusted crumbs from his jacket. "Perhaps it's better it ended now before you become a huge star. You're going to have everything you dreamed of. The tour was so successful I'm in talks with booking agents in Australia and Asia."

Lionel gazed at the glaring sunshine streaming through the window. His shoulders sagged and his skin felt like sandpaper. He walked to the door and turned around.

"I may as well, I've always wanted to learn how to use chopsticks."

Lionel sighed, sipping a Bloody Mary. "Alcohol gets a bad rap but it can be a great comfort. I would never have survived the next few months without a glass of 1986 Château Lafite-Rothschild at dinner and a snifter of Rémy Martin before bed. Speaking of fine wines, how was your evening with Henry?" Lionel asked. "Did you patch up your differences and make up?"

Juliet sat stiffly on the sofa. "I'm going back to California in less than a week and Henry will be traveling all over the world. I told him we should stop seeing each other."

"I'm sorry to hear that," Lionel said slowly.

Juliet fiddled with her gold necklace. "Gideon sent me another e-mail this morning. He wants to know when he'll receive his songs."

"I haven't finished telling my story." Lionel refilled his glass. "Even if I did want to fulfill the bloody contract, I don't think I could write more love songs. Love is the biggest Ponzi scheme in the world, everyone believes it but it's a scam.

"How many millions are spent on pink roses and chocolate truffles on Valentine's Day, only to be tossed in the garbage when the husband comes home with lipstick on his collar or the girlfriend writes a Dear John letter? How many diamond rings are exchanged at the altar only to be used as the down payment on a condo post divorce?" Lionel stirred his drink. "You're almost thirty and have never been in love, and I thought Samantha and I were a modern-day Anthony and Cleopatra. All it took was one magazine photo to tear us apart, we were no better than teenagers playing spin the bottle."

"You've written the most popular love songs of the last twenty years," Juliet protested.

"It was the only thing I knew how to do." Lionel sighed. "I

would have rather been an accountant or a doctor. At least when you set a broken bone, you can tell if you've fixed it. You could spend your whole life figuring out love and not be any wiser."

"Do you mind if I get a glass of water?" Juliet stood up and walked to the kitchen.

Lionel sipped his drink and heard a loud crash. He raced into the kitchen and saw Juliet lying on the floor. One of her sandals had come off and her knee had a purple bruise.

"Are you all right? I should have warned you," he gasped. "Gloria just waxed the floors. It's like a bloody skating rink."

He knelt beside her and inhaled her lilac perfume. He gazed at her smooth hair and blue eyes and suddenly froze. He felt his heart pound and his throat was dry. He leaned forward and his hand brushed her cheek.

"I'm fine, it's just a bruise." Juliet stood up and walked to the entry. "I have some errands to run. I know I have to make up some hours, could I come back this evening?"

Lionel studied her red knit dress and gold bangle. He saw her slender neck and long legs.

"This evening will be perfect."

Lionel sat at the Regency desk in the living room and sifted through the bill from his London tailor and the tax notice for his flat in Chelsea. He gazed at the negative number on his charge account and the receipt for his order from Waterstones.

He sipped his Bloody Mary and wondered how he was going to pay Gideon back. Then he remembered Juliet's smooth cheeks and pink mouth. He groaned and thought he was in more trouble than he could imagine.

chapter twenty-three

JULIET STROLLED THROUGH THE outdoor market in Sóller
and gazed at the baskets of fresh peaches and apricots. She saw
rows of thick sausages and lamb cutlets. She felt the sun on her
cheeks and felt strangely light and happy.

She was going to Lydia's for lunch and she wanted to bring
her a jar of preserves or a bouquet of sunflowers.

Ever since she left Casa Rosa she felt something stirring inside her. At first she thought she was shaken by slipping on the
kitchen floor. Then she pictured Lionel leaning down to help her
up and a shiver ran down her spine.

She thought of all their previous sessions when he talked
about music and poetry. She pictured his hand brushing her
cheek and sucked in her breath.

She hadn't gotten ill with Henry because she didn't believe in
love. She was falling in love with Lionel. She sampled a plum and
felt almost dizzy. She was being ridiculous; he was older and famous and probably had a Rolodex full of women he could call if
he needed company. But she pictured him in his silk pajamas and

John Lobb slippers and knew that wasn't true. Lionel was too serious; he didn't do anything casually.

She filled her basket with dates and persimmons. She added a bunch of purple daisies and took ten euros out of her purse. First she would go see Lydia and then she would figure out what to do about Lionel.

"Juliet!" Lydia exclaimed. "This is a treat. When you called I thought there was nothing I'd rather do than sit in the garden and eat baguettes and Mallorcan cheeses."

"I have something to tell you, I didn't want to talk on the phone." Juliet entered the living room.

"That sounds ominous." Lydia frowned. "I found there's nothing that isn't made better by a delicious green salad and a bowl of gazpacho. Come onto the terrace, I poured two glasses of lemonade."

"I told Gabriella about the recording contract." Juliet sat at the wrought iron table. "She's furious, she won't speak to me."

"I was curious why she didn't return my call." Lydia smoothed her hair. She wore a cotton blouse and white capris and orange loafers. Her lips were coated with red lipstick and she wore emerald earrings.

"I told her you saw Hugo in the café and she said the woman was his cousin. Hugo and Gabriella picked out a diamond ring and as soon as he pays it off he's going to ask her parents for her hand in marriage," Juliet continued. "She said now Hugo will think she doesn't want to marry him."

"Why would he think that?" Lydia asked.

"She's afraid he will think he's holding her back," Juliet replied. "I don't know how to make her forgive me."

"When Felipe was seven I met a banker from Hong Kong." Lydia nibbled spinach leaves and round red tomatoes. "James was British with sandy blond hair and blue eyes and the softest English accent. He rented a villa in Palma for the summer and we went sailing and danced at Bar Ábaco.

"We drove all over the island in his red Aston Martin and visited the Castell d'Alaró and the Alfabia Gardens," Lydia continued. "He described his penthouse apartment in Hong Kong with its hundred-and-eighty-degree view of the harbor. I imagined wearing sleek black dresses and attending cocktail parties and elaborate dinners.

"One afternoon we strolled through the old section of Palma and stopped in front of my favorite jewelry store. James wanted to buy me a sapphire pendant but I protested we hardly knew each other and I couldn't accept a serious piece of jewelry.

"The next night we had dinner at Tristán's in Puerto Portals. It was the only Michelin star restaurant on the island, and James ordered salmon tartar and marinated scallops and a bottle of Möet & Chandon. He pulled out a black velvet box with a large emerald cut diamond and asked me to marry him.

"I was shocked and asked him to give me some time." Lydia paused. "Then I went home to Felipe and asked how he would feel about moving to a new city.

"We pulled out an atlas and studied Hong Kong on the map. He traced the distance from Hong Kong to Majorca and his eyes filled with tears. He loved his grandparents and the cows and sheep on the farm. He didn't want to live in a skyscraper and eat strange foods and go to a school where he didn't know anyone.

"I told James I couldn't marry him." Lydia dipped a baguette in olive oil. "He said we could wait until Felipe was older but he still wanted to be together.

"But I didn't want to spend my days waiting for James to return each summer. I told him it was best if we made a clean break." Lydia stopped and looked at Juliet. "Perhaps Hugo isn't the one who would hold Gabriella back."

"What do you mean?" Juliet asked.

"I sent James away because I was afraid I might weaken and make the wrong decision," Lydia mused. "Maybe Gabriella thinks if she is given the opportunity she couldn't say no."

"But she's always been certain she wants to marry Hugo and open the restaurant," Juliet replied.

Lydia placed her fork on her ceramic plate.

"She's never had another choice."

Lydia brought out a fruit salad with homemade vanilla ice cream.

"The peaches are delicious, I'm going to bake a pie with fresh whipped cream," Lydia said. "You should bring Henry for dinner."

Juliet's cheeks turned pale and she put down her spoon.

"Have I said something wrong?" Lydia asked.

"Henry is warm and handsome and everything I could ask for," Juliet began. "But I realized I wasn't in love with him and told him we should stop seeing each other. I was afraid I wasn't capable of love, and then I slipped on Lionel's kitchen floor. He knelt down to help me up and suddenly all I wanted was for him to kiss me.

"He said he doesn't believe in love anymore," Juliet continued.

"If I tell him I could ruin everything, but if I don't I'm afraid I'll never feel like this again."

"Everyone believes in love," Lydia mused. "It's completely unpredictable and magic."

Juliet imagined boarding the plane to Los Angeles. She saw long days in the recording studio and returning home to an empty apartment. She pictured curling up on the floral sofa with a tuna sandwich and a copy of *This Side of Paradise*.

Lydia looked at Juliet and smiled. "Love almost never happens to two people at the same time, but when it does it's like an Oscar de la Renta gown or Harry Winston diamond pendant. It takes your breath away and nothing can match it. There's only one thing you can do, you have to tell him."

Juliet gazed around the plaza and saw couples sitting at outdoor cafés, sharing hazelnut tiramisu. It was late afternoon and the sun settled over the cobblestones. She saw vendors selling bunches of tulips and baskets of cherries.

It seemed so easy to do what Lydia suggested. But now she pictured Lionel nursing a scotch glass and smoking endless cigarettes and her heart pounded. If he didn't feel the same, she would be too embarrassed to continue their meetings and he would never fulfill his contract.

She thought about returning to Casa Rosa tonight and her stomach rose to her throat. She would call Lionel and tell him she had to write some important e-mails and would come in the morning.

She entered a boutique and gazed at the rows of chiffon

dresses. She held one up in front of the mirror and admired the patterned fabric and pearl buttons.

The saleswoman approached her. "That would look wonderful with your hair. You should try it on with these silver sandals."

Juliet shrugged and stepped into the dressing room. She gazed at her reflection and saw her cheeks were flushed and her eyes sparkled.

She remembered sitting across from Henry at Los Monteros and trying to feel something special. She saw Lionel with his dark hair and green eyes and fine lines on his forehead. She remembered Lydia saying love was magic and unpredictable.

She unzipped the dress and slipped it on its hanger.

"What do you think?" the salesgirl asked.

Juliet handed her the dress and took a deep breath.

"I'll take it."

chapter twenty-four

LIONEL SPRINKLED BASIL INTO THE pot and added garlic and oregano. He inhaled the scent of tomato and onion and was glad he took the cooking class in Verona. He glanced at the bottle of Chianti and platter of duck pâté and wondered how he was going to explain to Juliet why he prepared an elegant dinner.

After Juliet left, he swam thirty laps in the swimming pool. He did twenty push-ups on the terrace and took a long shower. He pictured Juliet's blue eyes and slender cheekbones and thought he was being ridiculous. She was young and beautiful and he couldn't possibly tell her he was in love with her.

He remembered saying he couldn't write love songs because he didn't believe in love and frowned. Could he really try again after years of eating lobster with women who were only interested in whether he had flown in Bono's private jet?

He suddenly pictured climbing the steps of Georgina's white Georgian manor clutching a punch of purple daisies. He remembered seeing Samantha's blue eyes and alabaster skin. He remembered her leaning forward to smell the flowers and her hair escaping its bun and Lionel wanting desperately to tuck it behind her ears.

What if Juliet was the one and he would never know? What if he missed out on nights discussing the Beatles and F. Scott Fitzgerald? What if he never again felt like he could write an opera or conduct a symphony?

He heard the doorbell ring and untied his apron. He walked to the entry and opened the door.

"Are you expecting company?" Juliet entered the living room. She saw the table set with a white linen tablecloth and gleaming silverware. There was a crystal vase filled with tulips and bottles of vinegar and olive oil.

"I discovered a 2004 Castelli del Grevepesa in the cellar," Lionel replied. "One can't drink it without a bowl of spaghetti and a loaf of garlic bread. Then I tried a marinara recipe I learned in Tuscany. I couldn't eat it by myself so I thought you might join me."

"I haven't eaten since a green salad and fruit at lunch." Juliet smiled. "A plate of pasta sounds heavenly."

They sat at the table and ate butter lettuce and heirloom tomatoes and red onions. Lionel filled two bowls with spaghetti and added fresh Parmesan cheese and ground pepper.

"I took cooking courses in Provence and Italy," Lionel said. "It's easy to become a gourmet chef when you are only cooking for yourself. No one can tell you that you're using too much butter or the salt will kill you.

"I also took up racecar driving," Lionel continued. "But I hated being squeezed into a cockpit and there are better ways to die than explode in a fireball."

"Like drinking a bottle of scotch and smoking two packs of cigarettes a day?" Juliet asked.

"Sometimes you look ahead and see empty days filled with glaring sunshine. You try doing the things you love: sitting at the piano or reading Dickens or writing a new song. But you can't find the right key and you've already read *Oliver Twist* and you can't even think of a first line." He fiddled with his wineglass.

"The first few months after Samantha left I threw myself into music. I spent days in the recording studio and stayed up all night writing songs. Amber and I toured Asia and appeared on Jay Leno and David Letterman.

"We even recorded a third album using another singer, but it didn't sell as well and Amber got an offer to join a girl band.

"For the next fifteen years I wrote songs for other artists and crisscrossed the globe. I thought if I kept changing time zones, my loneliness couldn't catch up with me. But the thing about traveling is you always wake up somewhere. A beach in Fiji doesn't look that different than the sand in Tahiti and when it rains in Amsterdam you still get wet.

"Eventually I thought I should settle down, so I bought an apartment in the first arrondissement in Paris. I even married a French girl named Dominique, but she was quite bossy and deep down all French hate the British.

"She couldn't stand it when I left wet newspapers on the parquet floors and she hated fish and chips." He paused and sipped his wine. "I was almost relieved when she wanted a divorce except she took an original Monet when she walked out the door.

"About nine months ago I was in Los Angeles." Lionel's eyes were suddenly dark. "I hadn't seen Gideon for months but I sent him songs and he replenished my bank account. He had been married for fifteen years to a beautiful brunette named Rachel and they had a little girl named Sylvie.

"They lived in an even bigger house in Beverly Hills with English gardens and a ten-car garage." He paused and ran his fingers over the rim of his glass. "I remember approaching the double front doors and thinking with all the gardeners and mechanics he hired, he was good for the local economy."

"Inga." Lionel beamed. "It's wonderful to see you. How do you keep such a small waist? If I ate your strawberry crepes every morning I'd have to do a hundred sit-ups."

He walked into the marble entry and admired the gold plaster walls and mosaic ceiling. There was a framed Rembrandt on the wall and a marble statue of Aphrodite.

He whistled. "If Gideon is hanging Rembrandts in the entry, I can't wait to see the rest of the house. I just came back from George Clooney's villa in Lake Como. If all women were like Amal, no man would get married before fifty. She is fluent in four languages and makes a delicious pesto ravioli."

"Gideon isn't home," Inga said. "Sylvie is in bed with the chicken pox."

"I remember when my roommate had it at boarding school, they stuck him in the bathtub and filled it with porridge." Lionel shuddered. "I can't imagine ever wanting to take a bath again."

"I'm baking peanut butter cookies." She smoothed her apron. "Sylvie and her dolls are having a tea party."

"Poor Sylvie," he continued. "I'd read her a story but I never had chicken pox and I've heard it's terrible if you get it as an adult."

"She's covered in spots and keeps demanding ice cream and

lemonade." Inga smiled. "I remember when Samantha had chicken pox, all she wanted was warm milk and digestive biscuits."

"I don't remember Samantha having chicken pox." Lionel frowned.

"She didn't want you to get it so Gideon suggested she stay at his house," Inga replied. "The poor thing was in bed for days."

Lionel felt a chill run down his spine. He looked at Inga and his face was pale.

"When was that?" he asked.

"About eighteen years ago." Inga shrugged. "Samantha was a lovely patient, she taught me how to play checkers."

"I brought a bottle of amontillado and a packet of fresh linguini." Lionel pressed the bag in Inga's hands. "You take them, I have to go."

Lionel raced past Rosemary's sleek walnut desk and flung open Gideon's office door.

"How was Italy?" Gideon stood at the sideboard. He wore a pale blue Marc Jacobs blazer and gray slacks. His salt-and-pepper hair was brushed over his forehead and he wore soft Prada loafers. "Rachel and I want to take Sylvie on an Italian tour next summer. Rachel thinks she's not old enough, but I think you're never too young to appreciate Renaissance art and Italian shoes."

"I stopped by your house." Lionel poured a shot of Grey Goose. "Inga said Sylvie has the chicken pox."

Gideon nodded. "Poor thing. Rachel bought all the pink nighties at Bloomingdale's and I spent the morning coloring spots on Sylvie's American Girl doll."

"She said Samantha stayed at your house when she had it

years ago." Lionel's voice shook. "You told me you didn't know why Samantha's car was in your driveway."

Gideon selected a ripe peach and took a small bite.

"Samantha didn't come home for two days because she was confined to bed," Lionel continued. "I left on tour believing my two best friends were having an affair. By the time I returned she was gone."

"I knew you better than you knew yourself. You could as easily have gone on tour without Samantha as a fish could survive without water." Gideon threw the peach pit in the garbage.

"If you didn't go, you'd be a one-hit wonder like *CrissCross* or The Divinyls. Then Samantha called and said she had chicken pox and she was worried that you'd get it." Gideon looked at Lionel. "It was so simple to suggest she stay at my place. I was leaving for China but I said Inga would take care of her, and I would call and let you know.

"I thought if I put a little doubt in your mind you'd be angry enough to leave. It could all be patched up later after you performed sold-out shows in Miami and Philadelphia. I didn't know Donovan was going to leak those photos to the press." He sighed. "But you should thank me. 'Going to Catalina' is the third-most recorded love song of all time, behind 'Yesterday' by John Lennon. You're a legend and it's all because of me. I remember the scrawny kid with hair touching his collar who said he'd do anything to be a successful songwriter."

"What about the message on the answering machine?" Lionel demanded. "You said it was safe to come over and Lionel would never know."

"She was afraid if you knew, you'd come see her and get the chicken pox," Gideon replied. "I was trying to reassure her."

"I lost the woman I loved." Lionel slammed his shot glass on the desk. "I would rather shine shoes or wash dishes than be without Samantha. For eighteen years I've traipsed around the world when I could be living in a country house with two tow-headed children and a golden retriever. I would gaze at my wife with her fine blond hair and small pink mouth and think how did I get so lucky.

"We would drive into London to go to the ballet or opera and marvel that we still have something to talk about. And when we got home and she unzipped her black velvet gown I would gasp that her thighs were still smooth and her skin was creamy and all I ever wanted to do was to bury my head in her breasts."

Gideon looked at Lionel and there were new creases on his forehead.

"She's divorced, you know," he said quietly. "I ran into Brian Phillips at Per Se in New York a few months ago. He's a big shot now, head of some economic committee at the United Nations. He was with a brunette in a red dress and four-inch stilettos."

"Why didn't you tell me?" Lionel gasped.

"You were water skiing on Lake Como," Gideon replied. "And I didn't want—"

"You didn't want me to know that you betrayed me like Brutus and Julius Caesar." Lionel's eyes flickered.

"Samantha is living in London; she owns a bookshop on Portobello Road."

"That's a few blocks from my flat." Lionel jumped up. "I have to see her; I'll take the first flight to Heathrow."

"Lionel, wait," Gideon said. "They have a daughter, Brian showed me a photo. She's eight and her name is Annabel."

Lionel pictured a little girl with Samantha's blond hair and blue eyes and thought his heart would break. He raced out the door and pressed the button on the elevator.

Lionel gazed in the bookshop window and caught his breath. Samantha wore a navy dress and beige pumps. Her hair was a little paler and there were lines on her forehead but her eyes were bright blue and her skin was like alabaster. She wore small diamond earrings and pink lipstick.

He opened the door and heard the bell chime.

"Lionel!" Samantha gasped. "What are you doing here?"

"Gideon told me you owned a bookshop in Notting Hill," Lionel said. "I was surprised. I thought you'd be in Cambridge, swanning around St. John's College in a long black robe."

"I never made it to university, I was too busy being Mrs. Brian Phillips." Samantha arranged a pile of paperback books. "It's a shame because Brian quite liked students, he went to bed with at least six of them."

"I'm not good at choosing men," she continued. "But I do like owning a bookshop. I have a whole shelf devoted to Virginia Woolf and Vita Sackville-West."

"A few nights before I left on tour I realized I made a terrible mistake and couldn't be without you," Lionel began. "I drove to Gideon's to tell him and saw your car in the driveway. I knocked on the door and no one answered so I drove back to the Beverly Hills Hotel. There was a message on the answering machine from Gideon saying it was safe to come over. You didn't come home for two days and Gideon's secretary wouldn't tell me where he was. I was sure you were having an affair."

"I had the chicken pox and knew how stubborn you are,"

Samantha mused. "You would have insisted on taking care of me and got it yourself. I couldn't bear to see you itching and covered in spots."

"Donovan leaked those publicity photos to the press and by the time I returned to Los Angeles you were gone. I was going to fly to London and explain, but Gideon showed me the article in *The Observer* about your wedding."

"I tried not to believe the photos, but they were at the supermarket and the pharmacy and the hairdresser. I called you almost every night but the concierge said you checked out. I was sure you were avoiding me." Samantha sighed. "I had to leave, it hurt too much to stay."

"You didn't even wait. You went and married that capitalist wanker while the ink on your passport stamp was still wet," Lionel muttered. "If I saw him, I'd punch him in his very long nose."

"I was staying at Georgina's and he was so persuasive. We had champagne dinners and bright conversation. I can't say I'm sorry, I've got the most beautiful little girl. She's on holiday with her father in Crete but you have to meet her." Samantha smiled. "She's a wonderful artist and she's read all the Harry Potter books."

"We can start over, I have a flat in Chelsea with an extra bedroom. We'll furnish it with a pink bed and Hello Kitty sheets." Lionel ran his hands through his hair. "Annabel can take horseback riding lessons and we'll have afternoon tea at Harrods. I'll take her on the London Eye and to Buckingham Palace."

"She does all those things," Samantha said. "Her father spoils her every chance he gets."

"Then there'll be more time for us," Lionel urged. "We'll see *Othello* at the Royal Opera House and have picnics on the

Thames. We'll get someone to mind the bookshop and take holidays in Venice and Capri."

"I'm afraid it's too late," Samantha murmured.

Lionel heard the bell chime and turned around. He saw a man with blond hair wearing navy slacks and a cream shirt. He carried a sports coat in one hand and a bunch of daisies in the other.

"This is Antoine, he's from Paris and plays oboe in the London Philharmonic Orchestra." Samantha looked at Lionel and her eyes were soft. "We're engaged, we're getting married in Cannes next month."

"Why on earth did she marry a Frenchman?" Lionel moaned, wrapping spaghetti around his fork. "They're trained as teenagers to never keep it in their pants. How did French courtesans become famous if it wasn't for cheating husbands lavishing them with jewels?" He sipped his wine. "At least he's a musician, and he had quite good taste in clothes."

"I couldn't stay in London knowing she was close by, so I accepted the offer to stay at Casa Rosa," he continued. "It could be worse, the swimming pool is lovely and I'm getting used to Gloria's cooking."

"But you haven't written any songs," Juliet murmured.

Lionel finished his wine and took a deep breath. "There's something else I have to tell you."

He gazed at Juliet's smooth brown bob and slender cheekbones. He saw her blue eyes and pink mouth and knew he couldn't do it. He couldn't burden her with his drinking and cigarettes and his belief that everything in life was fleeting. She needed someone young and fresh who thought anything was possible.

He leaned back in his chair and said, "I forgot to put Gloria's strawberry pavolva in the fridge, we don't have any dessert."

They rustled up vanilla ice cream and chocolate syrup for dessert and sat under the trellis discussing Paul McCartney's farewell performance at Wembley Stadium. Lionel gazed at the stars shimmering on the swimming pool and felt consumed by an incredible sadness.

Lionel placed the last dish in the sink and folded his apron. He walked into the living room and poured a glass of sherry. He sat on the striped silk sofa and stretched his long legs in front of him.

He sipped his sherry and wondered whether Juliet would tell Gideon he shouldn't have to fulfill his contract. He walked to the piano and sat on the hardwood bench. He lit a cigarette and blew a thin smoke ring. He ground the cigarette into the ashtray and let the air leave his lungs.

chapter twenty-five

JULIET SAT UNDER THE TRELLIS and gazed at the lush birds of paradise and marble fountains. She saw the green hills and quaint villages of Banyalbufar and Sa Calobra. She glanced at the sun shimmering on the blue Mediterranean and cliffs covered with daisies and wished she could stop her heart from racing.

She woke early and swam twenty laps in the hotel pool. She wrapped herself in a fluffy white towel and lay on a chaise longue. Now she sat at a wrought iron table drinking fresh coffee and eating a warm croissant and wondered what to do about Lionel and Gideon.

She remembered eating ice cream on the terrace with Lionel and shivered. She wanted to tell him she was in love with him but she inhaled his scent of aftershave and cigarettes and suddenly felt like a schoolgirl.

She tore apart the croissant and wondered if she could really insist he fulfill his contract after what Gideon had done. And if she didn't, would she lose her job?

She heard footsteps and saw a familiar figure walk toward

her. She wore a yellow linen dress and her hair was twisted into a soft plait. Her cheeks were pale and she wore red lipstick.

"Gabriella," Juliet exclaimed. "What are you doing here?"

"The concierge said you were in the garden. I wanted to talk to you."

"Please sit down," Juliet said. "The croissants are delicious, and I can pour another cup of coffee."

"I'm not hungry." Gabriella shook her head. "I want to apologize."

"I'm the one who should apologize, I sent the recording without asking you."

Gabriella shrugged. "You did what my grandmother requested. Have you told Gideon I'm not interested?"

"I was going to e-mail him this afternoon." Juliet sipped her coffee.

"Hugo and I have a joint bank account to save up for the restaurant, we've been adding to it for years." Gabriella twisted her hands. "I happened to look at the statement yesterday and he withdrew two thousand euros. He has never touched it before."

"Maybe he wants to pay off your engagement ring," Juliet suggested.

"He would never use my money to pay for the ring." Gabriella frowned. "I looked through the check register, and a month ago he bought a plane ticket to Paris."

"Paris!" Juliet exclaimed.

"It must have been the weekend he said he was seeing his cousin, Gia, in Barcelona," Gabriella replied. "He was gone for three days; why wouldn't he tell me he was going to Paris unless he was hiding something?"

"There must be an explanation," Juliet insisted.

"I've changed my mind." She took a deep breath. "Tell Gideon I'm interested in coming to Los Angeles."

"You can't just leave," Juliet spluttered. "You have to ask him why he needed the money."

"If he had a good reason to go to Paris he could have told me, and if he needed the money he only had to ask," Gabriella said slowly. "You can't keep secrets in a marriage, then you are just separate people sharing an apartment." She stopped and her eyes filled with tears. "There was something else. I found a check written to a hotel in Paris. I called the hotel and they said they didn't have a record of Hugo." She paused. "They finally found it. The room was booked under the name Céline Gaspar."

"That's impossible," Juliet exclaimed. "Hugo wouldn't go to Paris with another woman."

"I thought I knew everything about him," Gabriella said. "Maybe I don't know anything at all."

"But what about Casa Isabella and your family?" Juliet asked. "You love everything about Majorca, why would you want to leave?"

"Lydia is right: just because I haven't traveled to New York or London doesn't mean I wouldn't enjoy it. And if I like singing in the kitchen with a sink full of soapsuds, maybe I'd love perform-ing onstage." She stopped and her lips trembled. "And when I discover why Hugo was in Paris, I might wish I was far away."

Juliet poured a fresh cup of coffee and added cream and sugar. She nibbled an almond croissant and they talked about Lydia and Casa Isabella.

"My grandmother can be overbearing but she loves me more than anything," Gabriella said. "When I was young I adored the Madeline books. I could recite every poem and wore a felt hat and Mary Janes. One Christmas all I wanted was a chocolate brown puppy like Madeline's dog, Genevieve. Lydia invited me to Christmas dinner and in the living room there was a plaid blanket that kept squirming. I lifted the blanket and discovered a soft brown puppy."

Juliet nodded. "She only wants you to be happy. I visited her yesterday and she made gazpacho and a green salad. We sat on the terrace and she asked when I was bringing Henry for dinner."

"What did you tell her?"

"I said I told Henry I was leaving soon, and we shouldn't see each other." Juliet stopped and looked at Gabriella. "And I told her I was falling in love with Lionel."

"What did you say?" Gabriella gasped.

"I slipped in his kitchen and he helped me up, and suddenly I felt like I was shot with an electric current. I realized I couldn't fall in love with Henry because I'm in love with Lionel. He's witty and intelligent and loves music and books. Last night we ate spaghetti marinara and fresh bread and all I wanted was for him to kiss me."

"You have to tell him," Gabriella urged.

"He's older and sophisticated and he's been terribly hurt," Juliet hesitated.

"Being in love can be the worst feeling in the world. You can't sleep and in the morning your cheeks are pale and your skin feels like sandpaper. You drink a cup of coffee and eat a piece of toast, but the coffee scalds your tongue and the toast gets stuck in your throat." Gabriella's eyes glistened. "But not being in love is worse, then you feel nothing."

Juliet stood on the balcony and gazed at the turquoise swimming pool. After Gabriella left she took a bath and slipped on a cotton dress. She smoothed her hair and rubbed her lips with pink lip-gloss. Now she leaned on the railing and inhaled the scent of lilacs and bougainvillea.

Suddenly she felt her heart pound. If she told Gideon that Gabriella wanted to record a song he would be so thrilled he might let Lionel out of his contract. She glanced at her watch and saw it was 5 A.M. in California.

She would go and tell Lionel the good news and then she would call Gideon. She gazed at the green inlets and wooden fishing boats and sleek white yachts. She saw the cobblestoned plaza with its quaint boutiques and elegant galleries. She saw window boxes filled with purple and yellow pansies and thought she never loved anywhere as much as Majorca.

chapter twenty-six

LIONEL GLANCED AT THE NOTEPAD and tapped his pencil on the piano. He crumpled up the paper and tossed it in the garbage. He walked to the bar and poured a glass of scotch. He sat on the wood bench and stared at the empty page.

After Juliet left he heated a snifter of brandy and climbed into bed. He tossed and turned for hours but couldn't sleep. Finally he slipped on his silk robe and padded downstairs to the library.

He devoured Baudelaire and Rimbaud and Descartes. He read Plato and Socrates and *The Odyssey*. Suddenly he saw the leather binding and raised gold letters. He drew Sir Walter Scott's *Ivanhoe* off the shelf and curled up in the leather armchair.

He flipped through the pages and remembered when he discovered the book in boarding school. He remembered being so consumed by the knights and battles and impossible love he forgot to take a Latin test. He remembered knowing he wanted to write words that would make someone stop everything they we were doing and that would last six hundred years.

Now he tossed the book on the walnut desk and walked to the living room. He emptied the ashtrays and collected the newspapers. Then he sat at the piano and took out his notebook.

If he couldn't tell Juliet he loved her, at least he could make sure she didn't lose her job. He would write the songs and fulfill his contract. But he watched the sun rise over the hills and sighed. The words were drivel and he couldn't write two lines without wanting a scotch or a cigarette.

He remembered the years that lyrics came as easily as breathing. There were enough women with glossy hair and pink lips to make him think love was possible. He would come home from eating chateaubriand and drinking a full-bodied cabernet and think this was the one.

He would scribble all night and sleep past noon. But the next night when he took the woman to Tour d'Argent or The French Laundry, he realized she laughed too loud and had never read Somerset Maugham.

He heard a knock on the door and called, "Come in."

"I'm disturbing you," Juliet said. She wore a floral dress and white sandals. Her hair was held back by a beaded headband and her eyes sparkled. "I should have called."

"I was doing a little cleaning." Lionel hastily arranged magazines on the coffee table. "I gave Gloria the morning off to visit her sister."

"I have some wonderful news." Juliet sat on the striped silk love seat. "I have a friend named Gabriella. Her family owns Casa Isabella in Puerto de Sóller. The first time I heard her singing in the kitchen I couldn't catch my breath. Her voice is high and clear and I knew she could be a star.

"But she's been dating her boyfriend, Hugo, for five years and didn't want a recording contract. They were going to get married and open a restaurant.

"Her grandmother asked me to send Gideon the recording anyway so I did." Juliet fiddled with her necklace. "I felt terrible going behind Gabriella's back and she was furious. But yesterday she discovered Hugo might not be telling the truth so she wants to accept Gideon's offer and go to Los Angeles.

"When I tell Gideon he'll be so thrilled, he'll let you out of your contract." Juliet's cheeks flushed. "You won't have to write any songs."

"What did Hugo do?"

"He bought a ticket to Paris and took out half the money from their bank account without telling her," Juliet replied.

"Are you sure you want do that?" Lionel asked. "If I don't fulfill my contract, you might lose your job."

"When you hear Gabriella's voice, you'll understand." Juliet smoothed her hair. "It's like discovering Diana Ross or Barbra Streisand."

Lionel placed his shot glass on the marble bar and straightened the cushions on the sofa.

"I have to run an errand, will you join me?"

"Where are we going?" Juliet asked.

He slipped on his blazer and grabbed the car keys.

"Somewhere magic."

They drove into the Tramuntana Mountains past Selva and Camairi. They passed lemon orchids and churches with tall spires. Lionel turned down a gravel road and saw the huge iron gates and sandstone buildings.

"The first time I came here I wanted to turn around and go back." He opened Juliet's car door. "I've always been afraid of heights and the air is so thin I felt like I couldn't breathe. But I looked up and I'd never seen such a blue sky or white clouds."

"Where are we?" Juliet followed Lionel down an arched pathway lined with gold crosses.

"The Lluc monastery is the oldest monastery in Majorca," Lionel explained. "In 1242 a boy name Lluc found a black statue of the Virgin Mary in the forest. He took it to the priest in Esconca, but the next morning it was gone. He went back to the forest and discovered it in the same place. This went on for days; every time he moved the statue it found its way back to the forest.

"In 1260 the monks built the Lluc monastery in the spot where he found the statue. It has been a monastery ever since, and people come from all over to walk in the gardens. The chapel of the Black Virgin is one of the most beautiful chapels I've ever seen."

Lionel drew her into the chapel and gazed at the domed ceiling and stained glass windows. He saw the polished mosaic floor and gold altar. He gazed at gilt candelabras and huge paintings lining the walls.

"The statue of the Black Virgin is hidden behind the altar." Lionel stopped in front of the statue. "Legend has it if you ask her for something she will answer."

Lionel led Juliet back into the hallway. They crossed the courtyard and stopped in front of a whitewashed building. He tapped on the door and waited for someone to answer.

The door opened and he saw a man wearing a long robe and leather sandals. Lionel clapped him on the shoulder and handed him a brown parcel. He took Juliet's hand and they walked quickly across the cobblestones.

They emerged in an interior garden with rose bushes and a wide oak tree. Green trellises were covered with pink bougainvillea, and there was a sundial and a marble fountain.

"Father Jorge was a serious smoker before he became a monk." Lionel sat on a stone bench. "Once a month I bring him a carton of Marlboros and he allows me into his private garden. I love the chapel of the Black Virgin, but it's hard to talk to God when you're jostling tourists carrying cameras and backpacks."

"I didn't know you were religious," Juliet murmured.

"How can anyone not believe in God? It's like not believing in Leonardo da Vinci. Do you think the flowers and trees got here by themselves? Somebody had to have a grand vision," Lionel asked.

"I've always thought confession is ridiculous, why on earth would I tell my failings to a stranger in a black box who never gives advice? I'd much rather visit a psychiatrist. But there is nothing more humbling than sitting on this bench and contemplating the blue sky and green mountains."

"I just thought . . ." Juliet hesitated.

"Thought what?"

"That if you didn't believe in love anymore, you didn't believe in anything."

Lionel leaned forward and kissed Juliet softly on the lips.

He felt her kiss him back and suddenly the earth was spinning. He felt the sun on his shoulders and a light breeze on his back. He kissed her harder and tasted honey and cinnamon.

He tucked a hair behind her ear and took her hand.

"Where are we going?" Juliet asked.

"Somewhere a little more private." Lionel looked up at the blue sky. "I have the odd feeling someone is watching."

They drove silently back to Casa Rosa, and Lionel opened the car door. They raced up the stone steps of the villa and entered the living room. Lionel walked to the closet and pulled out a basket of CDs. He put on *Some Girls* by the Rolling Stones and sat next to Juliet on the striped silk love seat.

They listened to the Beatles and Foreigner and Boston. He introduced her to The Darkness and she pulled out Imagine Dragons. Lionel rustled up a carton of orange juice and two turkey sandwiches and they played John Butler and Mumford & Sons. He watched Juliet wipe mustard from her mouth with a napkin and talk about Jack Johnson and thought his heart would explode.

Finally they moved to the library and searched through the shelves. He read verses from *The Waste Land,* and *Absalom, Absalom!* and *The Raven and Other Poems.* She recited the first paragraph of *Lolita* and read the last page of *The Great Gatsby* out loud. He saw the evening sun filter through the window and the smooth curve of her neck and kissed her softly on the mouth.

"I think I have to take you home," he murmured.

"But we haven't read *Ethan Frome* or *The Old Man and the Sea*," Juliet protested.

"If I didn't have a conscience I would take you upstairs into the bedroom." Lionel loosened his collar. "I would unzip that lovely floral dress and fold it carefully on the chair. I would unsnap your bra and marvel at the creamy texture of your breasts. Then I would pull you down on the bed and kiss you as if the night would last forever." He paused and ran his hands through his hair. "But even God took six days to make the world; we can't expect to accomplish everything in one night."

Lionel walked to the marble bar and poured a glass of brandy. He twirled the snifter in his hand and inhaled deeply. He walked to the piano and sat on the wood bench.

He pictured Juliet's glossy brown hair and blue eyes and pink mouth. He remembered the way her mouth turned up at the edges when she laughed. He opened his notebook and began to write.

chapter twenty-seven

JULIET SAT AT AN OUTDOOR table in the plaza and sipped a glass of lemonade. She sprinkled pepper on a spinach salad and took a small bite. She gazed at the boutiques filled with brightly colored scarves and fruit stalls crammed with oranges and plums and felt her shoulders tighten.

She called Gideon when she woke up but Rosemary said he was out of the office with an emergency root canal. She paced around her suite and thought even if Gideon released Lionel from his contract, how would Lionel feel if she kept working for him? And would Gideon really keep her on if she didn't return with the new songs or a check for one hundred and sixty-six thousand dollars?

The music industry was full of bright young people eager to devote themselves to demanding artists and impossible hours. What if she quit and couldn't find another job?

She remembered sitting in the living room in Casa Rosa eating homemade ice cream and listening to Muse and never wanting the night to end. But now it was early afternoon and Lionel hadn't called. Maybe he had been swept up by the beauty of the monastery and reconsidered in the morning. He didn't make love to her because she was too young and they lived in different countries and it was impossible to be together.

She stood on the balcony and gazed at the green valleys and shimmering Mediterranean and suddenly needed fresh air. She slipped on a cotton dress and leather sandals and hurried to the plaza.

Now she nibbled round red tomatoes and tried to stop her heart from racing. Maybe Lionel had slept in and would call soon. She pictured him in his silk robe and John Lobb slippers and felt like an awkward schoolgirl.

"Juliet," a female voice said. "I was going to the Hotel Salvia to see you, but now I've discovered you in the plaza. It's such a gorgeous day I thought I would treat myself to a plate of tapas and a sparkling cider."

"Lydia, you look beautiful." Juliet admired her yellow crepe dress. "You are more stylish than any tourist in Sóller."

"There's a boutique on Aveneido Via Gran that receives designs straight from Paris. Maria put aside this Céline dress and silver sandals." She paused and patted her hair. "I find there's nothing better for working up an appetite than a little shopping.

"You are positively glowing." Lydia sat opposite Juliet. "Have you discovered a new spa?"

"Lionel and I visited the Lluc monastery yesterday," Juliet began. "We sat in a private garden and he kissed me. Then we went to Casa Rosa and ate turkey sandwiches and pistachio ice cream. We listened to music and read books and it was the most wonderful night of my life. But he hasn't called and I'm afraid he thinks it's a mistake. I work for a man he despises and we live on different continents."

"I remember the first flush of romance when you spend hours interpreting a smile or the way someone squeezes your hand. The best thing is to distract yourself with a long walk or a good book." She fiddled with her earrings. "I'm worried about Gabriella, she told me about Hugo."

"I thought you would be pleased; I can't wait to call Gideon and tell him she accepted his offer."

"Last night I watched *Sabrina* with Audrey Hepburn and William Holden and Humphrey Bogart," Lydia began. "It's one of my favorite movies. Audrey Hepburn is the daughter of the chauffeur and has been in love with William Holden since she was a little girl. She goes to cooking school in Paris and returns with glamorous clothes and a European haircut and impossibly long eyelashes." Lydia sighed. "Suddenly William Holden is madly in love with her.

"I sat on the sofa with a box of tissues and realized I always wanted to be Sabrina. I wanted to arrive in America and be surrounded by men in silk tuxedos and women wearing black cocktail dresses and mink stoles. I wanted to hold parties with a ten-piece orchestra and waiters in white dinner jackets serving platters of fresh oysters and French champagne.

"The problem with getting old is one confuses age with wisdom and there are fewer people who tell you when you make a mistake." She twisted her hands. "I came so close to going to America and then it was taken away. I wanted Gabriella to fulfill my dream, not hers."

"But she said you were right; just because she hasn't traveled doesn't mean she won't enjoy it." Juliet frowned. "And she thinks she might love singing in front of an audience."

"What if she comes down with the flu in Brazil or is terrified by the bright lights of the stage?" Lydia paused. "I don't want her to become a singer because she's angry at Hugo, I want her to do it because she can't imagine doing anything else."

"What should I do?" Juliet asked.

"First you can help me eat aubergine with sautéed mushrooms and tell me about Lionel." Lydia glanced at the menu and her eyes sparkled. "Then you can go to Casa Isabella and talk to Gabriella."

Juliet felt the late afternoon breeze on her shoulders and wrapped her arms around her chest. She had done what Lydia suggested and spent hours gazing at the Miros and Picassos at Ca'n Prunera. She bought postcards at the gift shop and tried on pastel sweaters in a boutique.

But she didn't feel like buying new clothes and couldn't think of anyone to write to. Finally she walked back to Hotel Salvia and entered the stone lobby.

"Miss Lyman, it is lovely to see you," the concierge called. "I have done something I'm not proud of, I let a gentleman into your room. He insisted you were friends and he had to make a personal delivery. I said it was out of the question but . . ."

"But what?" Juliet prompted him.

"He claimed he was friends with Bono and could get me tickets to the concert in Málaga," the concierge admitted. "He was only in your suite for a few minutes and U2 is my wife's favorite band."

"How long ago was that?" Juliet asked, hurrying up the staircase.

"About an hour ago," the concierge replied. "I feel terrible, please forgive me."

Juliet felt her cheeks flush and her heart expand. She turned to the concierge and her face lit up in a smile. "Don't worry, it's perfectly all right."

She entered the suite and gazed at the four-poster bed and mahogany desk and high-backed velvet chair. She glanced at the oak end table and saw a black velvet box and ivory envelope.

She slit open the envelope and read out loud:

> *Dear Juliet,*
> *When I said jewelry always came with an agenda, I was wrong. Sometimes it as simple as trying to match the beauty of creamy skin and bright blue eyes.*
> *I searched all day and finally found what I was looking for. I hope you will wear them tonight and join me at Cap Rocat for dinner. I will pick you up at 8 p.m. I suppose you will have to wear a dress to go with my gift, as we will be eating in public. Please don't wear anything with complicated buttons or zippers.*
>
> *Lionel*

Juliet opened the box and saw diamond teardrop earrings. She held them up to the mirror and gasped. She stood at the balcony and watched the sky turn pink and orange and the sun melt into the Mediterranean and had never been so happy.

chapter twenty-eight

LIONEL STOOD IN FRONT of the closet and selected a white dinner jacket. He paired it with a silk bow tie and black slacks. He slipped on gold cuff links and padded down the staircase.

He entered the living room and grabbed his car keys. He slid his gold cigarette case in his pocket and smoothed his hair. He pictured Juliet with her dark hair and blue eyes and felt like a schoolboy attending his first cotillion.

He walked to the bar and poured a shot of scotch. He remembered the way Juliet's eyes lit up when he recited Emily Dickinson and how her cheeks glowed when she listened to Cat Stevens and put the glass on the marble counter. They were going to sit at a table overlooking the Bay of Palma eating grilled octopus and sipping a Merlot, and he didn't want to miss anything.

"Cap Rocat used to be a medieval fortress," Lionel said. "Antonio Obrador turned it into a hotel and restaurant ten years ago, and now it's a secret hideaway for the jet set. Michael Douglas and Catherine Zeta-Jones introduced me to it. People think Catherine is reserved because she has that clipped British accent. Give her a few gin and tonics and she lets her hair down and dances on the tables."

They sat in a courtyard surrounded by high stone walls. The tables were covered with crisp linen tablecloths and flanked by tall fir trees. Plush white sofas were scattered over the cobblestones and twinkling lights were strung between lush palm trees.

"I've never seen anything like it," Juliet said, eating artichoke hearts drizzled with olive oil. She wore a red chiffon dress and gold sandals. Her cheeks were brushed with powder and her lips were coated with red lipstick.

"The fortress was built on the Bay of Palma so the inhabitants could ward off pirates." Lionel gazed at the black velvet sky and dark ocean. "Now all you see is twenty-foot yachts and giant catamarans. But the architecture is magnificent and the food is delicious. Victor makes a lamb cutlet with herb truffles and pear confit that is superb."

"The earrings are breathtaking and this place is stunning." Juliet hesitated. "But I thought you were worried about your bank account."

"I convinced Geraldo to let me buy the earrings on credit." Lionel sipped a glass of Montenegrin. "I'll pay him back when I sell my flat."

"You're going to sell your flat?" Juliet asked.

"Even if I don't have to pay Gideon back, I won't have an income for a while," Lionel replied. "I'm tired of wearing Shetland sweaters in July and always needing a raincoat. I thought I might live in Beverly Hills. Posh Beckham and I played Madison Square Garden once, and every year they send me a Christmas card. Perhaps they'll let me stay in their guest cottage."

"I thought you didn't want to go back to Los Angeles," Juliet said.

"It suddenly sounds more attractive. I spent the last eighteen years wandering around the globe like Don Quixote. Eventually I have to stop chasing windmills and make peace with Gideon." Lionel's brow furrowed. "Though if I see him trying on Zegna silk blazers at Fred Hayman or eating sirloin tips at Cut, I may have to restrain myself."

They ate quail with baby yams and talked about OutsideLands and Coachella. Lionel gazed at Juliet's creamy skin and pink mouth and couldn't believe he was sitting across from her.

"I stayed here during the grand opening," he said, nibbling a slice of chocolate torte. "The rooms look like an illustration from *The Canterbury Tales*. They have canopied beds and thick brocade curtains and handwoven tapestries."

"It sounds wonderful," Juliet murmured.

"I don't want to be presumptuous, but I thought we could reserve a suite and sip Armagnac and read *Troilus and Cressida* and *Beowulf.* I studied Middle English at Cambridge and have a soft spot for Chaucer."

Juliet scooped up raspberries and hazelnut ice cream. She looked at Lionel and her eyes were huge. "I'd love to."

Lionel stood on the terrace and gazed at the half moon and dark ocean. He turned around and saw Juliet through the gauze curtains. Her eyes were like a young doe, and she rubbed her lips with red lipstick.

He walked inside and folded his dinner jacket over a leather armchair. He loosened his tie and dropped his cuff links in the silver ashtray. He walked over to Juliet and ran his hands over her dress.

"The thing about sex is when you climax you may as well be Einstein or Socrates, you have the whole world figured out. But the minute it's over it's like waking from a dream, you know it was good but you can't quite put your finger on it. But when you are in love you feel like that all the time, it's like walking around in a state of exquisite rapture."

He pulled her close and kissed her softly on the lips. He took the ceramic clip out of her hair and tossed it on the desk. He felt the creamy satin of her cheeks and tasted the sweet chocolate of her mouth and moaned.

He led her to the bed and unbuttoned his shirt. She unzipped her dress and let it slip to the floor. He studied her full breasts and the alabaster stretch of thigh. He touched the wet spot between her legs and felt like an explorer discovering a sacred temple.

He gently slipped his finger inside her and saw her look of surprise. He saw her lips tremble and the sudden intake of breath. He felt the warm wetness and her body shudder and pulled her tightly against his chest.

She lay on the bed and drew him on top of her. She wrapped her arms around his back and urged him to go faster. Lionel paused for a moment, filled with the terrifying sensation that he would come and all this would end. Then he let himself go until his skin was slick and his body shattered and he collapsed on her breasts.

———

Lionel slipped on a silk robe and padded into the suite's living room. He walked onto the terrace and leaned over the railing.

He gazed at the sky full of stars and the moon glinting on the bay and felt an incredible stillness. He wanted to thank someone for something but he wasn't sure what.

He walked back inside and entered the bedroom. He lay down on the high white bed and fell asleep.

chapter twenty-nine

JULIET STOOD IN FRONT OF the closet and selected a green linen dress. She paired it with a pair of beige slingbacks and slipped on a gold bangle. She brushed her hair behind her ears and coated her lips with pink lip-gloss.

The night with Lionel was magical. After they made love they slept in the high four-poster bed. She woke in the morning and gazed at the dark wood floors and thick plaster walls and felt like a princess in a storybook.

They ate Spanish omelets and grilled tomatoes on the terrace and talked about history and art. They drove leisurely back to Sóller, stopping to buy figs and plums and olives. Lionel dropped off her at Hotel Salvia and kissed her slowly on the mouth.

Now her phone rang and she picked it up.

"Rosemary said you called." Gideon's voice came over the line.

"Yes, I have some news," Juliet replied.

"Gabriella's voice is superb, it's like winning the lottery," Gideon said. "She's going to be bigger than Mariah Carey or Beyoncé."

Juliet thought about what Lydia said and wavered. But then she remembered Gabriella's eyes flashing when she talked about Hugo and took a deep breath.

"She's very excited, I think she wants to accept your offer."

"That's fantastic news, tell her I'll get her a suite at the Beverly Hills Hotel and a driver."

"She'll be delighted." Juliet clutched the phone. "There is something else. Lionel shouldn't be required to fulfill his contract, he has suffered a personal trauma."

"What kind of trauma?" Gideon asked.

"It doesn't matter," Juliet said. "But you must let him out of his contract. I don't want Gabriella to reconsider."

The phone was silent and Juliet thought she went too far. She was about to say something when Gideon's voice came down the line.

"If you say so. God, he was always emotional, like a girl before her period." Gideon paused. "But that's what made him a brilliant songwriter. He could turn simple words into poetry."

Juliet hopped off the tram and strode down the promenade. She saw fishermen pulling in wooden fishing boats and couples eating ice cream cones.

She climbed the stone steps of Casa Isabella and wondered if she should have waited and talked to Gabriella first. She would ask Gabriella if she was certain this is what she wanted, and if it wasn't, she would tell Gideon she had changed her mind.

She entered the dining room and saw tables set with white china and gleaming silverware. Crystal vases were filled with yellow tulips and a fire glowed in the marble fireplace.

"Juliet," Gabriella exclaimed. She wore a navy dress and beige pumps. Her hair was wound into a chignon and she carried a stack of ivory menus.

"It's the first time I've lit the fire this season," she mused. "I love it when the weather grows cool. You should be here in the fall, the fog settles on the harbor and one can wear boots and sweaters. My father makes a delicious potato soup with fresh Parmesan cheese."

"I can't believe I'm leaving soon," Juliet said. "Lionel and I had dinner at Cap Rocat last night."

"What happened?" Gabriella gasped.

"We spent the night in a room decorated like a medieval castle. It had a four-poster bed and beamed ceiling and terrace overlooking the bay. We sipped Armagnac and talked about books and music, and it was the best night of my life."

Gabriella beamed. "I'm so happy. What will you do when you return to California?"

"We haven't figured it out exactly," Juliet replied.

"I'm going to tell my parents I'm going to America tonight. My mother will be thrilled; she adored her months in Paris. My father will complain he can't find anyone to oversee the dining room, but he'll be proud."

"What about Hugo?" Juliet asked. "Are you sure this is what you want?"

"I've barely seen him; he's been working late at the hotel." Her eyes suddenly filled with tears. "When I think about what he did, I get so angry I can barely breathe."

"I had lunch with Lydia," Juliet began. "She wanted me to talk to you."

"Excuse me." Gabriella said. "I have to tell the pastry chef what is on the menu for dessert."

Juliet walked over to the fireplace and gazed at the signed menus lining the walls. She saw Antonio Banderas's scrawled signature and Leonardo Di Caprio's broad cursive. She suddenly saw Lionel's name scribbled in black ink and frowned.

"Juliet, it's nice to see you." Gabriella's father entered the dining room. He wore a white apron and carried a bottle of olive oil. "I hope you stay for dinner, I'm preparing roasted chicken breast with Mallorcan artichoke hummus."

"I didn't know Lionel ate here." She pointed to the ivory menu.

Felipe nodded. "He came in recently. My wife was so excited, 'Going to Catalina' is one of her favorite songs.

"The whole dining room was abuzz," he continued. "He was with the tennis player, Henry Adler."

"He was with Henry?" Juliet asked. Suddenly she felt cold and a shiver ran down her spine.

"They ate grilled salmon in a citrus glaze and chocolate panacotta for dessert."

"When were they here?" Juliet whispered.

"July fourteenth." Felipe pointed to the menu. "I always write the date on the top corner."

Juliet ran to the door and turned around. "Please tell Gabriella I had to leave, I had a previous appointment."

Juliet sat on the tram and tried to stop her heart from racing. Why had Lionel never mentioned he knew Henry, and why did they have dinner together?

Suddenly she remembered when she and Lionel first met and he asked if she had a serious boyfriend in California. She remembered him saying she was young and single and should go dancing at Barracuda or Nikki Beach. She remembered him musing that Gideon had sent someone to make him write love songs who had never been in love.

She pictured Henry approaching her at the guest reception at Hotel Salvia. She saw his curly blond hair and blue shirt and tan slacks.

She remembered eating lamb skewers and talking about New Zealand and tennis and music. She pictured standing on her balcony, her cheeks flushed from the wine and her heart beating a little faster and thinking she met someone special.

She scrolled through the calendar on her phone and tried to remember the date of the guest reception. She gazed out the window at the green hills dotted with stone churches and the shimmering ocean filled with white sailboats and felt the air leave her lungs. She met Henry the day after Lionel and Henry had dinner at Casa Isabella.

chapter thirty

LIONEL JUMPED UP FROM THE piano and paced around the living room. He scooped up a handful of macadamia nuts and washed them down with a glass of orange juice. He stood at the French doors and gazed at the turquoise swimming pool and marble statues and felt like a million dollars.

He had dropped Juliet off at Hotel Salvia and come home and changed into a polo shirt and slacks. He grabbed a carton of orange juice and a green apple and sat down at the piano. He wrote all day, only getting up to refill his glass or toss the apple core in the garbage.

Now he glanced at the untouched turkey sandwich Gloria left on the glass coffee table and his unopened packet of cigarettes and couldn't remember when he had so much energy. He wanted to swim fifty laps or hike up to Valldemossa. He wanted to do a hundred sit-ups and take a cold shower.

He walked back to the piano and scanned the verses in his notebook. He had worked all day on one song, scribbling and erasing the same words. He remembered when he read *Cat's Cra-*

dle and thought Kurt Vonnegut couldn't have arranged the sentences any other way. He let out his breath and knew the lyrics were perfect.

He entered the kitchen and inhaled the scent of garlic and butter and basil. Juliet was coming over for dinner and Gloria had made warm spinach and goat cheese salad and lobster paella.

He gazed at his reflection in the steel fridge and thought he should go upstairs and shave. He pictured the way Juliet's face lit up when she smiled and felt he had been entrusted with a priceless piece of art. God, she was beautiful and young and bright. He could spend hours nibbling sliced pineapple and discussing Frank Zappa and Henry Miller.

Then he remembered the silky smoothness of her skin and felt he didn't have a right. He should have given up such perfection years ago; it belonged to young men with business degrees and a closet full of pinstriped suits. She should marry a man who could offer her a house with a garden and a Range Rover.

He thought about Gideon and his new song and sighed. Even if Gideon let him out of his contract he would have to find a new record company. He would have to write a whole album of songs and hope someone would buy them.

He heard a knock at the door and called, "Come in."

"You are early. I was going to go upstairs to change," Lionel said. "Gloria left a delicious salad and I discovered a 1982 Château Lafite-Rothschild in the cellar. I thought we could eat on the balcony and go for a swim after dessert."

"How could you lie to me?" Juliet exclaimed. She wore a green linen dress and beige slingbacks. Her hair was held back with a ceramic clip and she wore a gold bangle. "I went to see Gabriella at Casa Isabella and your autographed menu was on the wall. Felipe said you ate dinner there with Henry."

"I should have told you, I've known Henry for years," Lionel admitted. "The first time I saw him at the French Open it was like watching a kid in a candy store. He cleaned up the court without breaking a sweat. I knew he'd go on to great things, he had an amazing serve and a smile that lit up the stadium."

"You set the whole thing up. You felt sorry for me because I never had a boyfriend so you asked him to go out with me." Her eyes filled with tears. "Henry told me he was falling in love with me and I believed him."

"I ran into him a few weeks ago. I forgot how young he was; tennis players start the circuit when they are practically in diapers. You told me you hadn't had a serious boyfriend since college. I couldn't imagine what it was like to be twenty-eight and never been in love." He paused. "I didn't want you to miss out."

"Maybe I was happy with my career and my apartment in Santa Monica," Juliet replied. "If I wanted to fall in love I could find someone myself."

"It's not what you think." Lionel clutched the shot glass.

"He took me to dinner and dancing and Los Monteros. He bought me a pearl necklace and told me he always wanted us to be together." She paused and her eyes were huge. "What would have happened if I fell in love with him? How would I feel if I found out he never loved me at all?"

Lionel gazed at her flushed cheeks and flickering eyes and felt a heavy weight crush his shoulders.

"I had the best intentions," he murmured.

"I could never be with someone who lies," Juliet said. "I'm leaving in two days and I think it's best we don't see each other."

She walked to the entry and opened the door. She turned around and her eyes glistened.

"It's such a shame, because I had a lovely time."

Lionel stood at the bar in the living room and poured a glass of scotch. He lit a cigarette and blew a thin smoke ring. How could he be so stupid? He was like Cary Grant in the movie *Charade*.

He sat at the piano and opened his notebook. He put his head in his hands and moaned. He could as easily write another song as climb Mt. Kilimanjaro.

He gazed at his reflection in the gilt mirror and felt like Dorian Gray when he discovered his portrait in the attic. His forehead was lined and his cheeks sagged and he was only going to get older.

He had been a fool and Juliet had every right to be furious. He could tell her the real reason he set them up but knew it didn't matter. He had broken her trust and she would never forgive him.

He refilled his scotch glass and swallowed it one gulp. He sat on the striped silk love seat and poured another.

chapter thirty-one

JULIET SAT AT AN OUTDOOR table and gazed at the elegant boutiques and bright art galleries. She saw men in silk blazers and women in chiffon cocktail dresses. She inhaled the scent of cigars and perfume and felt a tightness in her chest.

After she had left Lionel, she called Henry and asked him to meet her in the plaza. She thought about her conversation with Lionel and shivered. How could he lie to her about everything?

She remembered the suite at Cap Rocat with its thick plaster walls and beamed ceiling. She pictured the high white bed and Lionel stroking her thighs. She remembered his warm mouth and slick chest and knowing what they had was perfect.

"Juliet." Henry approached her. He wore a blue polo shirt and khakis. His hair was brushed across his forehead and his cheeks glistened with aftershave. "This is a pleasant surprise, I thought you left for California."

"Thank you for meeting me." She looked up from her coffee. "I don't know how to begin, but I had to see you.

"I went to Casa Isabella to see Gabriella and Lionel's auto-graph was on the wall. Felipe said you and Lionel ate dinner together." She stopped and fiddled with her bangle. "Lionel admitted you've known each other for years and he asked you to go out with me. You were never in love with me; the whole thing was a sham."

"I met Lionel when I played my first Wimbledon." Henry nodded. "My manager messed up my hotel reservation and there wasn't an available room in London. Lionel discovered me in a pub in Belgravia. I had a tennis bag with four tennis racquets and a vinyl suitcase.

"He said he admired the way I thrashed Sampras at the French Open and offered me his flat." He ran his hands through his hair. "He slept on the sofa and let me have the master bedroom.

"We ran into each other a month ago, and he told me he was spending the summer in Majorca. Last week he called and asked me a favor. He said Gideon sent a young female executive to make him fulfill his contract," Henry explained. "You were here for two weeks and he asked me to take you to dinner and dancing and sailing."

"I don't understand how you could both lie to me," Juliet whispered.

"The first night we met in the garden I thought you were the most beautiful girl I'd ever seen," Henry replied. "Then we visited the monastery in Valldemossa and explored the old town of Palma and all I wanted was to be together.

"You are bright and warm and generous," he continued. "I asked you to go to Los Monteros because I wanted to, not because of Lionel.

"Lionel asked me to go out with you and keep you busy, but I fell in love with you by myself." He paused and touched her hand. "I never would have said 'I love you' if it wasn't true."

"How am I supposed to believe you?" Juliet demanded. "Lionel said I was twenty-eight and had never been in love. He didn't want me to miss out."

"Is that what he told you?" Henry asked.

"Is there something else?"

"He told me he was forty-two with a two-bedroom flat in Chelsea and creditors on three continents. He had no idea how he'd pay Gideon back, and he'd probably never write another song. He smoked too many cigarettes and drank too much scotch and woke up in the middle of the night." Henry paused. "And he was madly in love with you and didn't know what else to do."

"He said that," Juliet whispered.

"He was afraid if you were unattached, you would start falling for each other," Henry continued.

"But he couldn't have been in love with me," Juliet protested. "He had only known me for a few days."

"He said he knew you were special the minute you entered the Casa Rosa," Henry said. "He tried to stop his feelings but they grew. He thought if you fell in love with me, there was no chance you and Lionel could be together."

"How dare he?" Juliet's eyes flashed. "I'm old enough to make my own decisions about love. He could have said he had a girlfriend in Paris or a fiancée in London."

"He didn't trust himself," Henry replied. "He wanted to make it impossible."

Juliet pictured Lydia saying she sent James away because she was afraid she'd make the wrong decision. She remembered Lydia saying maybe Gabriella didn't want to send Gideon a tape because she didn't want to have a choice. Would she have fallen in love with Lionel sooner if she hadn't spent time with Henry?

She twisted her hands and thought it didn't matter. She could never trust Lionel now; he ruined everything.

"I have to go." She stood up. "Thank you for meeting me."

"You can't blame Lionel," Henry said slowly. "Sometimes there's nothing worse than being in love."

"He's a grown man," Juliet snapped, picturing his cocky smile. "He acted like a melodramatic teenager."

Juliet hung her dress in the closet and slipped on a cotton robe. She poured a cup of English Breakfast tea and added lemon and honey. She pictured Henry's wavy blond hair and thick chest and thought it could all have been so easy. If only he had been in love with her and she loved him back.

She put the cup on the ceramic saucer and wrapped her arms around her chest. Her head throbbed and her throat burned and her skin felt like sandpaper. She remembered Gabriella saying being in love made your stomach turn but not being in love was worse.

She climbed into bed and lay against the turquoise silk pillows. She pictured Lionel's green eyes and smooth cheeks and knew Gabriella was wrong. She pulled the soft cool sheets around her shoulders and closed her eyes.

chapter thirty-two

JULIET STOOD IN THE BOUTIQUE and admired the silk blouses and soft leather purses. She remembered when she arrived in Majorca and thought she would spend her afternoons eating tapas and exploring galleries. She remembered gazing at the window boxes full of yellow tulips and the fruit stand filled with ripe peaches and thought she had landed in the most beautiful place in the world.

Now she flashed on her long flight tomorrow and shuddered. She tried to think of the things she had to look forward to: showing Gabriella the Venice boardwalk and the Getty Museum. Taking her shopping at Neiman Marcus and eating frozen yogurt in Santa Monica.

She fingered a gold belt and thought she had to find a present for Lydia. She turned and saw a familiar figure approach her.

"Juliet, I've been looking for you everywhere," Gabriella called. She wore a floral dress and white sandals.

"I want to get your grandmother a gift, but she has so many beautiful clothes," Juliet explained. "I was going to come to Casa Isabella this afternoon and say good-bye."

"I have to talk to you," Gabriella said.

They sat at an outdoor table and ordered fruit salad and iced coffee.

"Yesterday Hugo asked me to dinner and said he had something to tell me," Gabriella began. "He made reservations at Es Raco d'es Teix in Deia, it is nestled in the mountains and the food is superb.

"Hugo ordered octopus with Mallorcan vegetables and olive oil. I gazed at his curly dark hair and blue eyes and couldn't eat a thing.

"He took my hand and said he did something terrible and hoped I could forgive him. He said he always dreamed of being a Cordon Bleu chef and preparing lamb noissettes and the lightest vanilla mascarpone. He didn't want to own a restaurant that served tapas to tourists; he wanted to create a menu that attracted diners from all over the world.

"A friend told him about a Cordon Bleu cooking course in Paris taught by a former chef at the Crillon. It was a six-month course and you needed a recommendation just to apply.

"He flew to Paris for the interview and said the kitchen was full of young men and women wearing starched white aprons." Gabriella sipped her coffee. "They beat eggs into a soufflé and whipped Chantilly cream as if they learned to cook in preschool. He didn't mention it because he thought he had no chance of being accepted.

"Then last week they called and offered him a place. He had to send the two-thousand-euro fee immediately or they would choose someone else." Gabriella paused. "He asked his uncle for an advance and he's already put the money back in our account. He said he never meant to do anything without asking me but it all just happened.

"After he finishes the course we can open a restaurant in Majorca that serves coq au vin and chocolate crepes. We'll get reviewed by *Bon Appétit* and maybe one day get a Michelin star.

"I wanted to be angry but he was like a child who received a shiny new bicycle. He couldn't believe this wonderful thing was his." Gabriella stopped and ate a slice of pineapple. "He asked me to go to Paris and I said yes."

"What about the hotel room in Paris?" Juliet asked. "You said it was booked under a woman's name."

"The owner of the Cordon Bleu course made hotel reservations for all the applicants," Gabriella replied. "Her name was Céline Gaspar."

"But you can't go to Paris." Juliet gasped. "Gideon offered you a recording contract."

"I feel terrible, Gideon's offer is so generous and it would be lovely to be with you in California. But I have to go with Hugo, I can't breathe when we're not together." She smiled. "And if I'm going to run a French restaurant, I have to speak perfect French. I'll browse in the boulangeries and sit at outdoor cafés eating croissants and drinking espresso."

"You could still accept Gideon's offer," Juliet suggested. "You'd earn enough money to open a restaurant and you could commute between Los Angeles and Paris and Majorca."

"Hugo and I talked about it, but he's wanted this for so long, he has to take the Cordon Bleu course," Gabriella replied. "And I don't want to be a singer. It sounds glamorous, but I have no desire to spend my time in concert halls or on international flights. I don't want to Skype Hugo at night or live in different time zones. Since I was twenty, I've known I wanted to open a restaurant with Hugo and start a family. Why would I do anything to get in the way, when everything I hoped for is right in front of me?"

"It sounds wonderful," Juliet murmured. "If that's how you feel I wouldn't want you to do anything else."

"There's one more thing." Gabriella reached into her purse and took out a black velvet box. She opened it and displayed an emerald cut diamond flanked by two sapphires.

"Hugo gave it to me last night." She slipped the ring on her finger. "He asked my parents for my hand in marriage."

"But I thought he had to put the ring on layaway." Juliet frowned.

"He visited Lydia. Apparently years ago she fell in love with a British banker who lived in Hong Kong. He asked her to marry him but she said no because it wasn't the right time." Gabriella gazed at the sparkling diamond. "She gave Hugo the ring and said she didn't want that to happen to us."

"I can't wait for the wedding." Juliet smiled. "You'll be the most beautiful bride."

"Lydia insists on coming to Paris to pick out a Yves Saint Laurent wedding dress." Gabriella paused. "I'd rather get married in a small church followed by a simple lunch of lobster ravioli. But if she wants the wedding to be at the Cathedral de Seu with a twelve-tier chocolate fondant cake and bouquets of pink roses, I'll do anything to make her happy.

"I've been talking so much." Gabriella sighed. "I want to hear all about Lionel."

Juliet suddenly remembered watching Gabriella and Hugo dance and how they moved like one person. She pictured the way Gabriella's eyes lit up when Hugo entered the kitchen.

Gabriella believed in love, there was nothing more important.

She couldn't tell her Lionel set her up with Henry, and Henry was never in love with her. She couldn't tell her Lionel lied and she wasn't going to see him again. She dabbed her mouth with a napkin and smiled.

"There's nothing to tell, everything is perfect."

chapter thirty-three

JULIET STROLLED ALONG THE cobblestones and inhaled the scent of oranges and honey. She climbed the steps to Lydia's house and knocked on the lacquered front door.

"Juliet," Lydia exclaimed. Her silvery hair was pulled into a bun and she wore a yellow cotton shirt and white slacks.

"I was having afternoon tea, it's a lovely British tradition." She ushered Juliet into the living room. "The Spanish take a nap and miss half the day. I'd rather have a cup of black tea and a fresh scone and spend the afternoon in the garden."

Juliet glanced at the ivory plaster walls and mosaic ceiling. She saw the tile floor and ceramic vases filled with sunflowers and thought how much she would miss Lydia.

"I brought you a present." She handed her a small package.

Lydia unwrapped the paper and discovered *The House of Mirth* and *The Age of Innocence*.

"Edith Wharton is one of my favorite authors," Juliet explained. "The concierge said I could take them from the hotel library if I promised to send him more books."

"Gabriella told me you're leaving tomorrow." Lydia put a

salmon and watercress sandwich on a plate and handed it to Juliet. "She also told me she's moving to Paris with Hugo.

"There's nothing better than being in love and she'll return with an appreciation of Versailles and the Louvre. I'll visit and we'll browse in Chanel and Dior and stock up on books at Shakespeare & Company." She stopped and looked at Juliet. "I didn't judge Hugo fairly, he loves Gabriella and will take good care of her."

"I've never seen her so happy," Juliet agreed.

"What will you do now that she declined Gideon's offer?" Lydia asked. "Will Lionel have to fulfill his contract?"

Juliet felt the bread get stuck in her throat. She put the plate on the coffee table and took a deep breath.

"I couldn't make him do that after what Gideon did to him." She hesitated. "Even if he lied to me."

"What happened?" Lydia raised her eyebrow. "The last time I saw you, you were madly in love. You were sitting at an outdoor café waiting for Lionel to call."

"He took me to Cap Rocat and we ate berries and ice cream and spent a night in a suite." Juliet bit her lip. "It was the best night of my life and I didn't want it to end.

"The next evening I went to Casa Isabella to see Gabriella and discovered Lionel and Henry were old friends. Lionel had asked Henry to take me to dinner and dancing and pretend to fall in love with me. Lionel said I was twenty-eight and never had been in love, and he didn't want me to miss out."

"I see," Lydia murmured.

"But then I saw Henry and he said that wasn't the real reason," Juliet continued. "Lionel was in love with me from the beginning, but he thought he was too old and had too many bad habits.

"He decided if I fell in love with Henry, there was no chance we could be together." She looked at Lydia. "He lied to me and I told him I couldn't see him again."

Lydia stood up and walked to the French doors. She smoothed her hair and turned around.

"You and I went behind Gabriella's back and sent Gideon the tape," Lydia said. "Sometimes it's necessary to bend the truth."

"But we never did anything to hurt her," Juliet insisted. "You just wanted to give her a choice. If I had fallen in love with Henry and he wasn't really in love with me, I would have had my heart broken."

"You were so in love with Lionel, are you sure that's what you want?"

"I want everything to be the way it was after our night at Cap Rocat," Juliet exclaimed. "I want to wake up and think the sun is brighter and the sky is bluer and the platter of fresh fruit couldn't be sweeter. I want to climb the stone steps of Casa Rosa and know Lionel is waiting for me. I went to spend all day reading Shakespeare and listening to the Beatles." She twisted her hands. "But relationships are based on trust and I can't be with someone who lies."

"People think the hardest part about being a priest is teaching people the scriptures. But anyone can read the Bible and they teach John and Matthew in Sunday school," Lydia began. "The one thing people don't understand is forgiveness. Being able to forgive is as important as knowing how to love; it's impossible to have one without the other.

"It would be so easy if we could spend all our time in church, but sometimes we have to learn to forgive each other. Lionel did a terrible thing, but he did it because he loved you."

"What if he lies to me about other things?" Juliet asked. "Nothing is more important in a relationship than honesty."

"Everyone makes mistakes, but being in love means you are completely selfless," Lydia mused. "If you both put each other first, how can you not be happy?"

"Maybe life is easier without love." Juliet frowned. "You said you love living alone. You eat whatever you like and watch old movies without being disturbed."

"When I was young I spent all my time with Felipe, there's nothing better than the love of a child," Lydia continued. "All you have to do is give them a bowl of ice cream and they think you are the greatest mother in the world.

"Then Gabriella was born, and I showered her with pretty clothes and shoes and books. All week I looked forward to taking her to the library in Palma." She paused. "You need someone to love or life can be empty. And if you find someone who loves you more than he loves himself, how could you possibly let him go?"

Juliet ate the last bite of sandwich and brushed the crumbs from her skirt. She pictured Lionel's wavy hair and green eyes and wondered the same thing.

Juliet stood on the balcony and gazed at the ragged cliffs and pink and purple Mediterranean. It was early evening and she could see fishermen pulling their boats to shore. She watched the mist drift down from the Tramuntana Mountains and felt her shoulders tighten.

She had spent the afternoon buying a silk scarf for her mother and leather slippers for her father. She debated buying a linen shirt for Gideon; then she remembered Gabriella declining his offer and her stomach turned over.

She folded cotton dresses into her suitcase and sighed. If Lionel didn't fulfill his contract, she might be fired. And could she really work for Gideon when she knew what he was capable of? But then she thought of how hard she had worked to get her position. If she quit without a reference she might not find another job.

She remembered her conversation with Lydia and thought she made it sound so easy to forgive Lionel. But she had been raised to tell the truth, it was the basis of everything.

Without trust a relationship couldn't survive, there were too many things waiting to tear it apart. You had to have complete faith in the other person or you didn't have anything at all.

She pictured Lionel standing in his kitchen, slicing turkey onto whole wheat bread. She saw him pacing around the living room, flicking ashes into the silver ashtray. She picked up her phone and felt like everything was ending. She dialed Gideon's number and pressed SEND.

chapter thirty-four

LIONEL SELECTED A WEDGE OF soft cheese and added a sausage. He rummaged through his pockets and found a ten-euro note. He handed it to the woman behind the counter and strolled through the plaza.

He had walked down to the newsagent because he was out of cigarettes. He bought a carton of Marlboros and a copy of *The Observer* and a packet of Mentos. He inhaled the scent of fresh fish and roasting chicken and thought he would explore the outdoor market. But the stalls were crowded and the pavement was strewn with fruit and he kept bumping into tourists.

Now he glanced up and saw a woman looking at him. She had dark hair and wore a floral dress and white sandals.

"I didn't mean to stare," she said. "You must be Lionel Harding, I recognize you from the cover of my mother's CDs. I'm Gabriella, a friend of Juliet's."

"The girl with the amazing voice." Lionel nodded. "It's nice to meet you."

"She told me all about you." Gabriella blushed. "I shouldn't say anything, but it's wonderful to see her so happy.

"I felt terrible when I turned down Gideon's offer," she continued. "But Juliet said she couldn't imagine me doing anything else."

"You turned it down?" Lionel asked.

"I'm going to Paris with my fiancé, Hugo," Gabriella explained. "I never wanted to be a singer, it must be difficult living in hotel rooms and performing in front of thousands of people."

"It has its moments," Lionel hesitated. "Did Juliet tell you anything else?"

Gabriella picked out a purple eggplant and put it in her basket. "Was there anything else to tell me?"

Lionel shook his head and slipped his hands in his pockets. "I can't think of a thing."

Lionel entered Casa Rosa and tossed his shopping bag on the kitchen counter. He walked into the living room and poured a glass of scotch. He tapped a cigarette from his gold cigarette case and lit it with a pearl lighter.

Ever since he met Gabriella his thoughts were spinning. Why hadn't Juliet told Gabriella he lied to her? And what would Juliet do if she lost her job?

He drained his scotch and stared at the piano. A Cadbury Fruit & Nut bar and a packet of peanuts and an apple littered the glass coffee table. His collar was loose and he sat on the hardwood bench. He opened his notebook and wrote as if his life depended on it.

All night he wrote; crumpling pages into the garbage. He discovered a bottle of Hennessy in the cellar and pulled out Keats sonnets from the library. He paced around the living room, watching the stars glimmer on the swimming pool. He made a midnight snack of white bread and marmite and wrote some more.

Finally he saw the sun stream though the French doors and heard the bells chime in the plaza. He stumbled to the kitchen and poured a cup of black coffee. He took it back to the piano and read through his notebook. He felt the hot liquid scald his throat and knew he had succeeded.

He pulled out his computer and opened his e-mails. He transcribed his verses for an hour, cursing that he never learned to type at boarding school. He pressed SEND and leaned against the striped silk cushions. He ate the last wedge of Cadbury chocolate and wondered what he had done.

Now he stood in the kitchen, frying eggs in a pan. He wiped his hands on his apron and heard his phone buzz.

"How is Majorca?" Gideon's voice came over the line. "Are you lounging around the swimming pool with a bevy of Spanish girls wearing string bikinis and toe rings?"

"It's fine, thank you," Lionel snapped.

"I got your songs," Gideon said. "You bloody bastard, you had the whole office in tears. Rosemary had to go out and buy boxes of Kleenex."

"You liked them?" Lionel clutched the spatula.

"They are the best thing you've written, you can take two years if you produce songs like that," Gideon continued. "The title track had me weeping more than when the Red Hot Chili Peppers signed with Warner Brothers."

"I'm glad." Lionel felt the air leave his lungs. "I wasn't sure I could still do it."

"I'm going to double your advance on your next contract," Gideon said. "Did I tell you Sylvie is getting married? You have to come to the wedding; Rachel rented out the Getty Museum. Cirque du Soleil is going to perform and JayZ will sing."

"I don't think so, I'm going to go back to London," Lionel murmured. "I'm running out of marmite, and Harrods has increased their shipping rates."

"I know you were very angry about Samantha. My rabbi said it was never too late to apologize." Gideon's voice softened. "I'm sorry for what I did, I didn't mean to hurt either of you."

"I have to go, I'm about to burn a Spanish omelet." Lionel paused. "Tell Sylvie I'll send her a wedding present. And tell Rachel to wear Oscar de la Renta, every mother should look like a film star at her daughter's wedding."

Lionel hung up the phone and brushed his eyes with his apron. He put sausages and whole wheat toast on a plate and sat at the dining room table. He poured ketchup on eggs and chuckled. When did Gideon become Jewish?

Lionel strode through the plaza and approached the Hotel Salvia. He glanced at the three-story building with its black shutters and wrought iron balconies and peaked slate roof. He saw the lush gardens filled with green trellises and beds of pink azaleas. He opened the gate and wiped the sweat from his forehead.

He had hung up with Gideon and put his plate in the sink. He remembered Gideon saying "I'm sorry," and suddenly his heart pounded in his chest.

How could Juliet forgive him if he never said he was sorry? He ran upstairs and put on a Paul Smith patterned shirt and tan slacks. He slipped on Gucci loafers and grabbed a blue blazer. He raced out the door and walked all the way to Hotel Salvia.

Now he entered the lobby and approached the concierge desk.

"I am looking for Juliet Lyman," he said. "Could you tell her someone is here to see her?"

"You're Lionel Harding," the man replied. "I let you into her room, I was afraid she would be furious but she seemed pleased. Thank you for the U2 tickets, my wife is thrilled."

"I'm glad she likes them," Lionel said impatiently. "Could you please tell Juliet I'm here?"

"She checked out an hour ago," the concierge replied.

"Checked out?" Lionel repeated.

"She's on her way to the airport." The concierge nodded. "I'll miss her, she was a delightful guest."

Lionel raced up the path to Casa Rosa and took a deep breath. He would drive to Palma airport and tell her he made a mistake. She had to forgive him; he had been a fool and he was terribly sorry.

The front door was open and he saw a red leather purse on the marble end table. Juliet stood in the living room, gazing out the window at the turquoise swimming pool.

He studied her glossy brown hair and slender neck and felt a pain deep inside him. He had never thought he would feel like this again and now he had thrown it all away. He treated her like a child when she was the most beautiful woman he'd ever seen.

"The door was open," Juliet stammered. She wore a red linen dress and beige slingbacks. Her cheeks were dusted with powder and she wore a gold necklace.

"I'm leaving and I wanted to return the earrings. You said you won't have an income for a while, and I thought you might be able to sell them."

"Actually I sold an album of new songs." Lionel poured a glass of scotch. "And I've been promised double my last advance on my next contract."

"Whom did you sell the songs to?" Juliet asked.

"I met Gabriella at the outdoor market yesterday," Lionel began. "She mentioned she's going to Paris and not accepting Gideon's offer. I couldn't let you lose your job, so I sat down and wrote a dozen new songs.

"People wonder why artists drink but something has to help you stay up all night staring at an empty notebook. But when you finally hit the groove and the words come faster than you can write, you feel like Harrison Ford or David Beckham.

"And when it's five o'clock in the morning and your mouth tastes like cigarettes and you can't keep you eyes open, you read what you've written and realize you're a bloody genius.

"I sent the songs to Gideon, and he loved them." Lionel sipped his scotch. "He even invited me to Sylvie's wedding, JayZ is going to perform."

"That was very kind of you." Juliet walked to the door. "I have to go, I'll miss my flight."

"I ran all the way back from Hotel Salvia." Lionel stopped her. "I shouldn't have asked Henry to go out with you, but I didn't tell you the real reason. The minute you walked through the door the first day, I knew you were special. You are intelligent and beautiful and passionate about what you do, I couldn't help falling in love with you.

"But I drink too much and smoke too many cigarettes and

leave chocolate wrappers all over the living room." He smiled. "Even Dominique couldn't put up with me and I was earning a paycheck. I couldn't risk you falling in love with me and ruining your life. You deserve someone with a bright future who expects life to give them a family and a lovely home and three weeks vacation in the Maldives." He paused. "Not someone who keeps his scotch glass next to his toothpaste."

"Like Henry," Juliet murmured.

"I thought you'd make the perfect couple. He's a star athlete and a genuinely nice guy." Lionel stopped. "I wanted you to be happy.

"But I realize what I did was wrong, you are a mature woman and can make your own decisions," he continued. "If you want to throw your life away on an aging British songwriter who reads dead poets and can't go to bed without a cup of Ovaltine that's up to you." He paused and touched her arm. "But what's worse is I didn't apologize. I would give my signed *White Album* to hear you forgive me and I didn't even say I was sorry.

"I broke your trust and I'll never do it again," Lionel finished. "I need a chance to show you how much I love you."

Juliet walked to the French doors and gazed at the turquoise swimming pool. She turned around and Lionel saw her cheeks were flushed and her eyes glistened.

"I love you too," Juliet whispered.

He crossed the room and kissed her softly on the lips. He put his arms around her waist and drew her toward him. She kissed him back and he inhaled her scent of jasmine and vanilla.

"You have a signed *White Album*?" She smiled, pulling away.

"I bought it at an auction at Elton John's Princess Diana fundraiser," Lionel said. "George and Ringo and Paul all signed it, and John wrote in purple pen." He tucked a stray hair behind her ear. "I can't wait to show it to you, it hangs on my bedroom wall in Chelsea."

"I really have to go." Juliet fiddled with her gold necklace. "I'll miss my flight."

"I'll call Gideon and tell him to book you on a flight tomorrow," he continued. "He owes me, the new songs are going to make him bloody millions. You can help me log onto a computer and find a place to rent in Los Angeles. Maybe I'll get a house in the Hollywood Hills, the lush foliage and ocean views remind me of Majorca."

He took her hand and led her to the piano. He gazed at her blue eyes and small pink mouth and felt like he had been given an incredible gift.

"First I want to play you my new song. It's called 'Juliet.'"

chapter thirty-five

JULIET STROLLED THROUGH THE PLAZA and gazed at the narrow buildings with their green shutters and lacquered window boxes. She saw elegant boutiques filled with brightly colored dresses and fruit stands selling baskets of figs and melons.

She had spent the night at Lionel's, and they ate eggs Benedict and waffles on the terrace. She drank Gloria's milky coffee and listened to his new songs.

Now she bought a magazine and a packet of Life Savers for the plane. Her flight left in a few hours and Lionel was going to drive her to the airport.

She walked back to Casa Rosa and admired the beds of pink azaleas and white hibiscus. She saw the bright citrus trees and tall birds of paradise. She turned and gazed at the sparkling Mediterranean and thought she didn't know one could feel so happy

She pictured Lydia and thought she would invite her to Los Angeles. They would go shopping at Hermès and eat California burgers at the Beverly Hills Hotel. She thought about Gabriella's high, clear voice and sighed.

She remembered what Gabriella said about love and finally understood how she felt. She opened the door of Lionel's green Mini and waited for him to join her.

Lionel ran down the front steps carrying a black leather Tumi overnight bag. He wore a Ralph Lauren shirt and beige slacks. His sunglasses were propped on his forehead and his cheeks glistened with aftershave.

"Why do you have a suitcase?" she asked. "You're dropping me off at the airport."

"I just got a call from the Beverly Hills Hotel." Lionel backed the car out of the driveway. "They named a drink after me to celebrate the twenty-third anniversary of 'Going to Catalina''s release. It's going to be called THE LIONEL, black cherry vodka with lime juice and agave syrup. They offered me five free nights in the Paul Williams Suite if I came and signed the first glass."

"It sounds delicious." Juliet grinned. "I've had artists stay at the Beverly Hills Hotel. They renovated the bungalows and the spa does deep tissue massage."

"I've never liked massages." Lionel bristled. "Why would I want a stranger prodding my naked flesh while I listen to Yanni over the loudspeakers? I do remember the beds have the finest down comforters and their spinach egg-white omelet is delicious." He leaned over and kissed her gently on the mouth. "Maybe I can convince you to join me."

The car swerved and narrowly missed a white Fiat. Juliet straightened her skirt and laughed.

"Keep your eyes on the road, so we get to the airport in one piece."

"You didn't answer my question." Lionel clutched the steering wheel.

Juliet gazed out the window at the quaint farmhouses and green valley and clear blue Mediterranean. She saw the stone monastery in Valldemossa and the orange wood tram. She turned to Lionel and smiled.

"It sounds wonderful. I can't think of anything I'd like better."

Acknowledgments

Thank you to my fantastic agent, Melissa Flashman, and my wonderful editor, Lauren Jablonski, for being such a joy to work with. I am so fortunate to have a tremendous team at St. Martin's Press: Staci Burt, Karen Masnica, and Laura Clark in publicity and marketing, Elsyie Lyons for her wonderful covers, and Jennifer Enderlin, and Jennifer Weis.

Thank you to new and old friends for always being there: Traci Whitney, Pat Hazelton Hull, Laura Narbutas, Andrea Katz, and Christina Adams.

And thank you to my family: my husband, Thomas; and my children, Alex, Andrew, Heather, Madeleine, Thomas; and my daughter-in-law, Lisa, for giving me everything I could wish for.

1. Working in the music industry has meant that Juliet never had the time or opportunity to fall in love. If you were Juliet, would you have chosen a career more amenable to getting married and starting a family?

2. Gabriella has no interest in being a big star—all she wants is to own a restaurant and start a family with Hugo. Can you understand her choices? What would you do in her position?

3. Do you think Henry really falls in love with Juliet? Give examples of his words or actions that support your position.

4. Lionel finds reading poetry and classic literature to be soothing when he is depressed. What do you do when you are feeling down?

5. What are your feelings about Gabriella's grandmother, Lydia? Do you approve of the choices she has made in her life? How do you feel about her relationship with Gabriella?

6. Juliet and Gabriella are great friends, but Juliet still goes behind Gabriella's back. How does Juliet defend her actions? Do you agree with her?

7. Do you think Juliet is right in giving Lionel a second chance? What would you do if the person you loved lied to you, even if it was for the right reasons?

8. The setting of Majorca plays an important part in the book. Is it somewhere you would like to visit? If so, what attracts you most?

9. What are your feelings about Samantha? Do you think she really loved Lionel, and did she act too hastily?

10. When an author writes a book, often characters evolve and take on traits the author never imagined. *Island in the Sea* has some strong characters. Who is your favorite and why?

St. Martin's Griffin